The Boom Economy

The Boom Economy

Or,
Scenes from Clerical Life

Brian Bouldrey

THE UNIVERSITY OF WISCONSIN PRESS
TERRACE BOOKS

The University of Wisconsin Press
1930 Monroe Street
Madison, Wisconsin 53711

www.wisc.edu/wisconsinpress/

3 Henrietta Street
London WC2E 8LU, England

1   3   5   4   2

Printed in the United States of America

Library of Congress Cataloging-in-Publication Data
Bouldrey, Brian.
The boom economy, or, Scenes from clerical life / Brian Bouldrey.
        p.   cm.
ISBN 0-299-18900-7 (alk. paper)
I. Title: Boom economy.   II. Title: Scenes from clerical life.   III. Title.
PS3552.O8314 B66   2003
813′.54—dc21   2003006266

Terrace Books, a division of the University of Wisconsin Press,
takes its name from the Memorial Union Terrace, located
at the University of Wisconsin–Madison. Since its inception in 1907,
the Wisconsin Union has provided a venue for students, faculty, staff,
and alumni to debate art, music, politics, and the issues of the day.
It is a place where theater, music, drama, dance, outdoor activities,
and major speakers are made available to the campus and the community.
To learn more about the Union, visit www.union.wisc.edu.

For
Lewis and Mary
friends and parents

I did not know the ample Bread—
'Twas so unlike the Crumb
The birds and I had often shared
In Nature's Dining Room—

The Plenty hurt me—'twas so new—
Myself felt ill—and odd—
As Berry—of a Mountain Bush
Transplanted—to the Road—
                              —Emily Dickinson

Acknowledgments

Earlier versions of four of the chapters in this book appeared in *Genre,* the *San Francisco Bay Guardian, Beyond Definition,* and *Speak.* Sincere thanks to Peter Weltner, Michael Lowenthal, Greg Satorie, Gretchen Mazur, Miriam Wolf, Hugh Rowland, Boris Pokrovsky, Janet Kauffman, Paul Reidinger, Reginald Gibbons, and Mary Kinzie.

The Boom Economy

Vicar, Victoria

Vancouver, September 1999

Other than the waitresses, big surprise, Isabelle was the only woman in the entire restaurant. Here in green, islandlike Vancouver, the three of them—Isabelle, Jimmy, and Dennis—had been fierce tourists with a strict itinerary: the anthropology museum and University of British Columbia (hosting an international Sasquatch conference!), a long walk through Stanley Park, an examination of the new library. What had revitalized them so? The rain? This was the last evening of their three-day stay, and they'd exhausted outdoor activities, so they'd been in buildings all afternoon: they shopped, drank coffee, and went five pin bowling at the Commodore. It took them three games before clever Isabelle figured the right way to tally (and when he discovered that he was losing, Jimmy no longer wanted to play).

Now the three of them had come to Robson Street to eat dinner in a Hooters restaurant. They were squabbling over which of them was responsible for their being there, nursing weak beer among a sorry assortment of Sasquatch conference attendees, Winnipeg ad men, investors fleeing Hong Kong, and the odd loner taking up a whole booth.

Certainly not Jimmy, for he opposed all objectification of women. Certainly not Isabelle, for she was not remotely lesbian. Certainly not Dennis, oh no—for he was almost a Jesuit priest.

"Well, I think it was you, Brother Bacchus," said Jimmy, and he drank absently from his mug. "God, Budweiser!" he scoffed.

"Thee king of beers," said Isabelle. Dennis wondered whether she found Vancouver disappointing, because it was a city in a country that was supposed to be bilingual, and there was only a passing whisper, even a mocking, of French. But she was only twenty-six years old, almost half his and Jimmy's age, and she had been resilient on this whole journey through the Pacific Northwest. Only today, for the first time in two weeks, did any of them show real signs of weariness.

"She sure loves the exchange rate," Jimmy said when Dennis suggested they pull out of Vancouver a day early, for her sake.

They'd all splurged on the strength of their currency, hauling back to their ivied old bayfront hotel some tony, full, and damp-to-the-point-of-breaking shopping bags from Banana Republic, Eaton's, and HMV. Dennis liked Roots and Marks & Spencer, because he

4

could buy lots of nice things (he'd sworn poverty along with chastity and obedience, but still liked nice things. Sure, to buy designer clothes was as forbidden as breaking chastity, but it didn't seem as bad to him, because policing his consumerism wasn't nearly as difficult as policing his libido) with obscure designer tags, and the other, far less worldly Jesuit colleagues would never know.

At a big record store, Dennis went to the listening stations and found out what kids these days were listening to, but couldn't discern the difference among trance, techno, and electronic. And when he pulled the headphones off, he noticed that a very fancy cologne, worn by some hip boy who'd worn the phones just before him, had rubbed off on him, and now he felt absolutely a poseur.

"Ooh, *Frère Denis,*" Isabelle had sniffed behind his ear, "You are defeeneetly down with le Oh-Pee-Pee!"

"O.P.P.?"

"Ozair people's poocey?" she tried it out.

They ate and drank, too, and Dennis got into the spirit of it because he wasn't really spending any money. Every restaurant had a full bar, and since the wine was not famous, Dennis drank martinis, and was therefore two or three steps ahead of the beer-swilling Jimmy. Isabelle drank Cokes.

Canada was just America, only much nicer. The differences seemed to be more unsettling to Dennis, though, than they were in, say, France. It wasn't just the one- and two-dollar coins but the wholesomeness and the "oh gee's," of the friendly lawn bowlers in Stanley Park, along with the public ordinances for dog owners that included the rule "Be Courteous," as if courtesy were quantifiable and enforceable.

"Courtesy is more efficient than the law," said Isabelle, after Dennis had pointed out the rule and she had thought about it. "You Americans make me laugh with your signs in every street, 'Eet ees forbeedden to park here, except between the ow-airs oav two and seeks.'"

In America, he told Isabelle, as in Catholicism, they depended on the precise measure of the law.

"In America," Isabelle said, "This Coca-Cola, which is called 'a large' in Canada, would be called 'a medium.'"

Dennis was mildly alarmed that Isabelle had already and swiftly been corrupted by the United States: she'd let Jehovah's Witnesses into his home, loved the action movie they saw in Portland, insisted on the all-male production of *Mourning Becomes Electra* in Seattle. And now this—this!—a Hooters restaurant.

What would she be like if she were an American girl? Would she be a courteous Canadian, or a chickie-woo with a little black sticker on her RAV4 that read "Mean People Suck"? In the record store, he presented Isabelle with the problem of differentiating among trance, techno, and electronic, and she blew out her pretty cheeks in exasperation, as if Dennis were not clear on the difference between the colors yellow and blue. Jimmy said that she was very attentive to the club scene in Paris and London, and fancied herself a "handbag house" type—she was one of the girls who threw their purses into a pile on the dance floor and shimmied around them in a circle so that they wouldn't get stolen. Dennis imagined penguins protecting their young, rubbing together to keep warm.

In any event, Isabelle was still through-and-through French. This fact was revealed in the puzzling occurrence at lunchtime. They'd gone into a tatty little diner near the library, and Dennis remarked only to himself how many Canadian boys he'd seen with black eyes. Was it some badge of courage? Away from home, he was hyper-aware of patterns; in Spain, he'd seen dozens of abandoned shoulder pads in the street. In Rome, dead birds.

After they placed their orders, the three of them fell silent, a rare thing, but they were tired from their sightseeing itinerary. Dennis put his hands in a prim position on the table, set them like the children's hand game—"Here is the church, here is the steeple"—and there they stayed. Jimmy was scribbling away with such an enthusiasm that his beer washed over the edge of his mug. He looked slightly crazy, with a wiry-wired intensity that often made Dennis uncomfortable.

Dennis monitored over the years as Jimmy was whittled down to bones and sinew, a stretched-out jockey. His friend's face did not so much wrinkle as crease. Dennis was aging in a different direction, a burly middle age. Though he didn't have a gut, there was a thickening going on somewhere between his chest and his belly. In the full-length mirror, he allowed himself a moment of vanity but found he looked like a wedge doorstop on end. He'd worried his face into lines over his brows, around his eyes. The parentheses around the corners of his mouth were so mournful and, he feared, judgmental, that he'd grown a beard, as blond as the hair on his head.

Jimmy was filling out a little questionnaire he'd picked up in a Starbucks coffee shop, one that sat kitty-corner—kitty-corner!—to another Starbucks. Jimmy had been outraged. "They're taking over the world!" he cried.

"It's good coffee," shrugged Isabelle, and Dennis found it easy to side with an apolitical French girl.

"I'm going to protest," Jimmy had said, and ducked into one of the two cafes to get a folded brochure: "How Are We Doing?" it read on the cover. Now, in Hooters, Jimmy scrawled, "Just terribly. Why would I need two Starbucks in the same block?" Next to the question "Which store are you referring to?" he'd written in bold capital letters, "ALL OF THEM!"

"Perhaps we shall go to the shopping island?" asked Isabelle.

"Let's find out when the ferries run." Dennis saw an American couple in the next booth with two travel guides. He got up and went to them. "May we borrow this for a moment? We'd like to check a schedule."

They barely murmured an assent, buried as they were in the local newspaper. He carried it back to their table and found, to his surprise, that Isabelle was mortified.

"What's wrong?" asked Jimmy, finished with his questionnaire.

"I can not believe it," said Isabelle, shaking her head gravely.

"What?" asked Dennis.

"That you would do such a thing. That you would just walk up to a stranger and ask for their guidebook."

Dennis laughed, the freest laugh he'd belted out during the entire trip. "I borrowed their guidebook?"

"A person must never do such a thing."

Jimmy looked as puzzled as Dennis, but Dennis did not want to share anything with Jimmy now, and so he said, "Why is this a wrong thing?"

Isabelle shrugged her shoulders with a furrowed brow, as if it were as obvious as the difference between trance and techno. "You put the person in a position in which they have no choice but to say yes."

"But I'll give it right back! They weren't using it!"

When Isabelle fell silent, Dennis immediately returned the guidebook to the couple. They never found out the ferry schedule and did not go to the island.

Isabelle was genuinely hurt—about the guidebook or maybe something else. Dennis pondered the terrors of foreignness. Perhaps Canada was not a Nice America, after all. Must going to a faraway land always undo a traveler? For the rest of the afternoon, they didn't speak much to each other. Dennis felt punished by Isabelle for that inscrutable crime. And Jimmy—oh, Jimmy.

Only now, in Hooters, was she beginning to return to her gregarious self. They studied the menus, full of too many choices that tried to span the cuisines: chop suey, burritos, spaghetti, hamburgers. Dennis felt queasy around such icky heterodoxies, common along the Pacific Rim. In San Francisco there were at least four shops called "Chinese Food and Donuts," and other stores sold "Indian Food and Pizza," "Deli, Ice, Bait, Liquor." Was there nothing pure left in the world? Sex and food, both nice ideas, but not together. Even if he were his old self, unvested.

The waitress moseyed to their table. Her name tag read "Cheryl," and she seemed rather dumpy to be considered a sex star. Her hair was pulled back in a severe manner, perhaps to show some sort of toughness. Indeed, there wasn't much soft on her. Her breasts were not so huge, either. She was indifferent, sullen.

He studied her, looking for sensuality. The longer he stayed away from sex, and other people's bodies, the more strange, artificial, and puppetlike sex and bodies seemed to be. Long expanses of skin draped and stretched over a framework of bones, the T of neck and spine crossing shoulders, seemingly tied off like balloon animals at the lips and sphincter, and perpetually shriveling like an applehead doll. And the way that skin darkened in crevices—obscene!

In youth, the gracefulness of the body was unconscious, unintended. As one became more aware of its mutability, one became more aware, more sentient, more egotistical—unlovely qualities. And the body became more unlovely in the same way—not ugly because of age, but because of vanity.

She caught him studying her, and she stopped her pen on her pad long enough to make an "oh brother" sort of face. He wanted to explain to her, no, I'm not drooling over you, no, don't you see, I'm a homosexual and a priest! Almost. But she went to scribbling Jimmy's club sandwich and Isabelle's tomato salad. "More beer?" she asked Jimmy, and then went to the kitchen.

"I hate the name Cheryl," Dennis confided, thinking they'd both surely agree.

"Why?" asked Isabelle.

How could he explain? How could he convey to a French girl the loathsome sound of the name Cheryl, given to girls to make them sound soft when they were in fact hard and vulgar. Even Jimmy wouldn't understand. He once told Jimmy that Kevin was a name for dullards, every Kevin he'd ever known was a dunderhead, and Jimmy disagreed, bewildered. The world was made up only of foreigners, and a man, thought Dennis, is existentially quite alone with his prejudices.

He excused himself—the martinis were going straight through him. In the hallway leading to the bathroom, there were fake street signs on the wall that said "Bumps" with two schematic ta-ta-like hills;

another read, "This sign is in French when you aren't reading it." Which seemed an obscure anti-Montrealism. One of the other waitresses, Hooterettes, whatever, was talking into a pay phone, her serving tray and towel tucked under one arm, her free hand plugging her free ear. She was saying, "No, no. If she's sound asleep, just let her stay."

In the bathroom, the graffiti was as nice as it had been in the born-again Christian diner, where the cowboy butt spanker had left his mark. "Life is a universally fatal sexually transmitted disease." Highly deep. Still, this was a Hooters, and the evidence of what men did when left, unmothered, to their own yahoo devices was everywhere: the toilet seats of all three stalls were splashed with urine, toilet paper clogged two of them. The urinals were glazed at pectoral level with the blue word "Adamant," the same shade and quality of blue used in plates with the Anglo-Oriental willow pattern, which, in hopes of becoming a self-styled village vicar, Dennis had begun to collect as his china pattern, perfect for those imagined teas that this parson would have one day with aging ladies of the diocese. So far, however, he had had only a six-month tour of duty as an assistant pastor for a small church in Minneapolis. After, he'd gone running back to the Bay Area, realizing that he was better off planning to be a teaching Jesuit, not a preaching one.

Just as he was zipping up, two Quebecois men came in in cheap suits with blue fleur-de-lis lapel pins, growling and mooing and braying and bleating about some

Hooter-related outrage. Perhaps having overheard the single mother Hooterette on the hall phone advising her babysitter had spoiled their fantasy. Not that the fantasy was precariously complicated.

Dennis came out and said, "I'm sorry I took so long, but I had to have a heavy discussion about poetry with two gentlemen from Table Nine."

"Oh, they are not so different from us," Isabelle said. The chill between the two of them was not quite gone. She was not ready to collaborate with Dennis. They all looked over to Table Nine, for trouble was apparently brewing.

"I hope you don't think we're as big a buncha morons as the rest of the guys in this place," said Jimmy, not at all joking.

She picked his camera off the table in front of him, its neckstrap tangling around his beer mug. "I have seen what you do with this camera all day."

On their day-long walk through Stanley Park, Jimmy snapped surreptitious shots of stripped-down boys on park benches, sweaty in-line skaters, tennis players, lifeguards. Dennis and Isabelle would hang back while Jimmy, pretending to take pictures of ships in English Bay, slipped up behind these men, and took their photos. Dennis noted that almost every time, after Jimmy snapped the shutter, the bathing beauty would turn around, wake up, somehow sense that perhaps, as the natives believed of intrepid *National Geographic* photographers, Jimmy had stolen his soul.

"That's different," said Jimmy.

"Why is it different?" asked Isabelle.

"Men like to be looked at." Jimmy said it as if it was only half thought out.

"Men like to be looked at when they are kicking a soccer ball or wrestling with an octopus," said Isabelle. Wrestling with an octopus? "I like to be looked at," she added, "I like to be told that I am pretty."

Before anybody could respond to or qualify her, six of the unshaven Quebecois men at Table Nine suddenly burst into some sort of discontent at Cheryl the waitress, all at once. What was the problem? Weren't her boobs big enough?

"Uh-oh, trouble," said Jimmy. "I think they just asked her to take off her T-shirt and she said no."

Isabelle shook her head. "The waitress cannot speak French and they are outraged," she explained, putting the accent on *rage* and not *out,* as if she were outraged herself.

"Doesn't every Canadian speak French?" asked Dennis. "Don't they learn it in school?"

"You learned French in school," said Jimmy. "Can you speak it?"

Isabelle leaned over and tugged on the passing waitress's apron. "Perhaps I can help you?"

Cheryl shook her tightly restrained ponytail. "I'm going to get the manager."

The three of them sat back and watched the pantomime as a pasty man with a too-short and too-wide tie came from behind the swinging kitchen doors and asked the gentlemen how he could help them. When it became clear that he also could not speak French, the Quebecois shouted. One pushed Cheryl in the shoulder.

"Back off, Jack!" she shouted.

Jimmy snickered but Isabelle quelled it with a face she made. "They might hurt her," she murmured. How odd her concern. Why was Isabelle worried about the plight of a rather unfriendly waitress with so many witnesses around and when she had been fearless around all the other strangers she'd encountered, with their ominous black eyes? "How will she solve this problem?" Isabelle asked, and returned her attention to Table Nine. That was the only way Dennis could get Isabelle to respond to anything: pose it as a problem to be solved.

Now the Quebecois were shaking their heads and snapping, "*Non. Non.* No-no." Meaning, apparently, that they would not be leaving until they were properly served and entertained and spoken to in their native language. For a moment, there was silence.

Cheryl and her boss fell back. They began to whisper to one another, and sidled away to a place near the door.

Isabelle stood up. Untucking her serpentine-colored T-shirt, she bunched it in front of herself and knotted it, accentuating her curves marvelously. She was far prettier—no, Dennis thought, sexier—than any of the waitresses. She went up to Cheryl and, without asking, took the order pad from her hands.

15

The men from Quebec had watched all this, too, and when they realized what was happening, they broke simultaneously into a lascivious cheer.

"Bon jour," said Isabelle, her face as open as the sky, an unlocked house ready for a thief.

"Bon jour, mademoiselle," said a man in an outer seat, mustachioed like a ringleader. She had their attention; the looks on their faces said that they had not expected real sex in Hooters, but perhaps God in his heaven was going to give it to them as a small miracle. The room was suddenly full of heat, and curves, and odors.

And she proceeded to take their order, fearlessly. Jimmy gave a single heave of a laugh. Dennis slapped his own forehead and shook his skull, pivoting it on the heel of his hand. But they didn't move, and when Isabelle was finished, she handed the pad back to Cheryl.

Cheryl, however, was not amused, nor did she thank Isabelle. Unfazed, Isabelle unknotted her shirt and returned to her companions, offering the same smile she gave the men. "I am sure," she said, "that there is some law against what I have done. But courtesy is more efficient, isn't it?"

Jimmy touched her shoulder but it was a gesture of the mildest disapproval.

Isabelle recoiled. "You think that I am a slut, don't you?"

"No, no! I've always approved of sexual activity, haven't I, Dennis? I even approve of Dennis's sexual activity."

Isabelle pouted before and after saying, "Dennis does not have sexual activity."

"Well, he used to. He even knows about big tits."

Oh no, Dennis thought, he wouldn't dare.

"You know, Brother Bacchus used to work for pornography."

"Pornography?" Isabelle looked as if she'd mistranslated something.

"I'm not a brother," Dennis said. "I'm a seminarian. I don't know why you keep calling me that."

"Sure, magazines called *Horny Girls, Shenanigans, Bodacious Ta-Tas.*"

The Quebecois ringleader was calling for Isabelle. She turned her head to see if they had a real need, like pepper or butter, but he said something and she scowled and waved him off and said, "Quebecois French is as ugly as the name Cheryl," and returned her attention to Jimmy's story.

Did Dennis have to regret everything to do with his relationship with Jimmy? Why had he told him about this secret period in his distant past? It lasted half a year. He'd spent that much time at the church in Minneapolis. He never willfully embraced the role of pornographer. To tell a secret was forever, he thought; he oddly recalled at that moment that he still got junk mail addressed to Jimmy Bacchus. In a giddy moment, the two of them had conjoined their names as a way to see where junk mail came from, entering it on a mailing list, and the marriage of their two names was indeed passed from catalogue to crummy catalogue, the name splitting and proliferating. Dennis rued the day. It seemed now an unthoughtful thing to have done, as uncaring of the future as having unprotected sex—yes, he regretted it in exactly the same way.

"Tell her about it, Brother Bacchus," Jimmy took a long drink of beer.

Well, perhaps he should. He felt he was losing Isabelle's affection, a warmth they once had. Maybe he could sully himself with a little confession in order to win her back. He said, "I was just out of school and in lust with a performance artist." He would tell her this story and that would patch the rift created earlier that day. He looked at her to see if she was listening. Indeed, Isabelle was aghast, again, but this time in a merry way. "He had a temporary job doing paste-up for *Gallery*. 'Big Busts of the Big Ten,' stuff like that. They lost an editor, those things happen every day in that business, and they needed somebody. The performance artist gave me the job."

"What did you do for them?"

Dennis shrugged. "Wrote dirty stories. Filled in Letters to the Editor when there weren't enough."

Isabelle giggled. "Homosexual stories."

"No, just kinky stories. Not really even kinky. Just kinky locations. In a tree house. On a plane. In Bombay."

"In a church," Jimmy said. His beer mug was up, as if the real thing he said was as charming as *"À votre santé!"*

Isabelle sat back, shaking her head. "Gay homosexuals writing pornography for the straight people."

"It's not that difficult. It's not like describing brain surgery. We can't see God, but many have written about him."

"Oh, but there is a difference," she scolded, tapping her down-tipped left eye with a fingernail painted black (a new thing she found in Seattle). "It's in the eye. You gay homosexuals will only talk about the penis and the thrust and the sword fight and the high-five-dude—"

Jimmy wanted to exchange a look of surprise with Dennis, but Dennis would have none of it.

"—and never to the soft and the nape of the neck and the little tiny star in your belly that gets warm and—and the breasts!" She pointed around the room.

"Breasts," Dennis waved her away. "All those letters would come in, and the breast lovers, they were the stupid ones." As if to emphasize, the group of shaggy Quebecois laughed heartily. Dennis thought of trappers on a beaver hunt. "The fetishists, they were the brains of the outfit. They had style. Imagination. And they could spell."

Over at Table Nine, Cheryl was slamming down six hamburgers and six orders of fries. How did they get their food first? Monsieur Ringleader was making a request and pointing at Isabelle. Cheryl looked in the direction of the finger and then shook her head, no. More mooing and braying. "Taber*nac*!" one of them swore, and Dennis thrilled at the antique notion that cursing might still be a profanity against the sacred.

Cheryl stomped over to Isabelle. "Thanks a lot. You're a big help." Then she stomped to the kitchen.

Isabelle got up and went to the men. More cheering. But this time, Isabelle would not smile. She asked them what they wanted but they just made noises. The manager with the unfashionable tie came out, followed by his harem of three waitresses.

"Please, miss," he said to Isabelle, "we'll take care of this. Sit down."

The Quebecois made threatening noises.

The manager put his hands up the way a teacher who couldn't control his class might. Isabelle did not sit down. Now the waitresses were telling her to go away. That made them look dowdier, stupider. Their jealousy of her simple beauty, Dennis felt, made them ugly.

"Will you please take off," said Cheryl.

This angered Isabelle. Her own face crumbled into defiance. She crossed her arms. "It is a free country," she said.

"No," said Cheryl, "that would be the States."

Oddly, the men grew quiet. They saw a cat fight brewing, and perhaps that was the fun they were looking for this evening. The waitresses were smoothing themselves, primping, the way people who are about to dive in and make a mess of themselves do.

That's when Jimmy tried to calm the mob. "Ma'am, can I get another beer over here?" He waved at all three waitresses. "Ma'am? Ma'am? We're getting pretty hungry."

Cheryl glanced their way, but would not be deterred. She tried to get hold of Isabelle's wrists, soldered to her own bosom. "Take a hike."

"Non!" Isabelle screeched. "You ungrateful Cheryl!"

"God damn it, Isabelle," Jimmy said. He slumped in his chair.

Dennis thought, all the stupid people are mad at her, and that means I must find a way to not be mad at her. This will be a pivotal moment in making a pact with her. What could he do? The Quebecois were making noise again, and three buxom girls were trying to get a piece of Isabelle, pushing, pulling, poking. Perhaps Isabelle would be leaving Vancouver with her own souvenir black eye.

Dennis stood. He hiked up his own T-shirt and tied it off. For some reason, Jimmy wasn't watching, or wasn't noticing Dennis. Dennis went to the cart in the corner of the restaurant and grabbed handfuls of paper napkins and began to stuff his shirt.

When he felt he was stacked enough, he sashayed to the Quebecois table. *"Bon jour, comment allez-vous?"* he squealed, not quite falsetto. Everybody stood still.

Then the laughter: the burly unshaven men whooped and clapped. Three of them grabbed Dennis and forced him to lay across their table, and Dennis didn't fight them. Memories came up, but this was a parody of them. Sex was far away from this place. Any sensuality Isabelle had created with her sweet kindness had evaporated. Where only sweat and curves and lips and breasts had been, there were now ketchup bottles and menus and a big drag queen sprawled before them.

The waitresses were laughing, too, and despite the mock molestation, Dennis could see Isabelle had slipped back to Jimmy, pointing to the action. Jimmy sat up straight. When he saw Dennis, the rescuer, he began to yell, "He's almost a priest! Hey, that guy's almost a priest! Get your hands off him or you'll all go to hell! He's almost a priest!"

But they didn't stop. Either they didn't understand any English or they didn't understand the irony that they were making sexual advances on somebody who was nearly a priest. And Dennis Bacchus, earnest seminarian, made a minor discovery laid out there on Table Nine, his head in a little mustard, pelted with French fries: perhaps they did understand irony, but they just didn't care for it.

He let the men have their fun, and when they all sat down again, the room settled into its quiet mockery of sex, the way it always had been.

Back at their table, Cheryl brought them their bad food with a smile. She did not meet Isabelle's eye, but she winked at Dennis. "Are you really a priest?" she asked him.

Jimmy leaned forward. "Almost a priest. Do you know what I'm going to give him as a present when he's ordained?"

Cheryl put his plate in front of him. "What?"

"Knee pads."

Cheryl laughed. "You guys."

In the corner of the booth, Isabelle glowered at Dennis and ate nearly nothing.

Breathing

San Francisco, January 1991

It was a week after New Year's, and city workers had taken down the holiday decorations. The city was under scaffolding, under repair. Even though the earthquake had done its damage a year and a half before, the insides had to be trussed up, and all the money in San Francisco was thrown at mending its backbone. Every building was surrounded by a jerry-rigged jungle of fitted metal pipes and warping two-by-eights, and the entire town seemed Closed for Repairs, See You Next Year!

On the train ride in, Dennis noted where the money was being taken from: on the Muni bus, huge tarry smears of inscrutable gang names were jagged onto the windows. Old newspapers blew around pedestrian ankles. It would be years before the snazzy French self-cleaning toilets were installed, so the homeless, their infrastructure devastated as well, found a jungle gym wonderland of nooks and crannies. Dennis still followed his drought-era water-conservation habits by showering with a bucket at his feet and using the run-off to flush the toilet, and even then, observing the rhyme, "If it's yellow, let it mellow; if it's brown, flush it down." It was a habit for life, despite the nonstop rains this winter had brought.

Dennis saw Rigo first, when he walked into the clinic, framed at the receptionist desk, already hard at work. Dennis thought he had the loveliest, most girlish eyelashes in the history of beautiful men, but Rigo was into leather, and he wore chaps to work every day. Mostly he sat behind his desk, so you would never know it. But chaps were not what he was remembered for.

"Two nuns are traveling around Europe," he told Dennis as he signed in. "And after they visit the Vatican, they head for the Balkans, and in Transylvania, a vampire jumps on the hood of their rental car! The driving nun asks, 'What'll I do?' And the passenger nun says, 'Turn your headlights on!' And she does, and the vampire curses the light, but holds tight. 'Now what should I do?' asks the driving nun and the shotgun nun says, 'I just filled our windshield washer fluid with holy water from the Pope, to bless our journey, so squirt that on him!' So she squirts holy water on the vampire and his skin is burning and he's shrieking, but he still hangs on. 'Now what will I do?' asks the driving nun, and her nun friend says, 'Show him your cross!' And the driver says, 'Perfect!' And she rolls down her window and leans out and yells at the vampire, 'Darn it, I'm very frigging angry!'"

Say fuck, thought Dennis, or even damn. But Rigo never swore. Dennis believed certain good and beautiful things in the world coexisted with—required—obscenity. Behind him, Sue the nurse breezed in. Her hello to Rigo and Dennis was sunny but vacant, a pretty, rentable apartment.

This was the second time in his life Dennis had seen her. The first time was when he came in to have his blood drawn for the test. He felt as if they were intimate friends, similar to the feeling he got after telling a total stranger some terrible secret. Rigo, positive and proud, had cajoled Dennis to come in. "Knowing is better than not knowing," he told him. "At first it hurts like h-e-double-toothpicks, but then it makes you stronger."

Sue went through the office door and the next thing they knew, she was standing next to Rigo with the clipboard. "James Thornton," she said through the window of the reception area. Dennis looked over. How had he missed this only other, weeping guy in the room? Sue didn't bother to usher James through the door. Dennis felt the press of time all around Sue—got to save lives here, got to get this man healthy again, got to make a grown man stop crying. She didn't even put her purse away.

Dennis watched Rigo weigh James Thornton like a flyweight, his lean body slouched over the little beaded weights. From the way Rigo stood close, Dennis could tell that the two men knew each other, were friends or something, a similar suitor-to-sister relationship Dennis shared with him. Probably, Rigo had talked Jimmy Thornton into the test, too, and here it was, hurting like h-e-double-toothpicks.

Rigo escorted the man to an exam room. Sue followed. The door clicked shut.

Dennis asked Rigo, "Bad news, huh?"

Rigo said, "Yes, but he doesn't know it yet."

"Then why was he crying already?"

"Because he's not stupid. Like I know you're not stupid."

"You get to know the results of my test?"

Rigo looked at him from a corner of his wan face. He'd been losing weight like crazy, sinking into his own frame. His dark eyes looked permanently surprised. He said, "I'm having a party tonight, will you come?"

"A party? Is it your birthday? Did I forget your birthday?"

"No, you didn't forget. This is just a party I'm throwing."

Dennis had been to a lot of these no-occasion hoedowns recently. They'd ranged from modest—dinner for eight with strings of pearls for party favors found at the bottoms of goblets full of Chateau d'Yquem sauternes from the turn of the century—to the decadent—a warehouse recreational drug blowout with go-go boys. "Of course I'll come. What should I bring?"

"No, sweetie, this party is to help *you* cheer up, too."

When Dennis joined Sue in her little room, he passed James Thornton, lingering, reading a copy of *Time:* "Countdown to War." He looked as if he was reading a prayer there. "I'm sorry I've kept you waiting," she said. "The whole city is torn up. My commute is twice as long."

"Everything is broken, isn't it?" said Dennis. "I walked down the street and those guys who trim the branches around the trees so they don't hang on the electrical lines had just been through. I saw a crazy homeless guy putting Band-Aids on the cut parts."

Sue seemed both pleased and alarmed with that—she told him that she recognized the impulse in herself, as a nurse. Then she said to Dennis, "You know Rigo."

"We go back," Dennis said, and he hoped his curt reply might be interpreted in only two ways: embarrassment by the association and the fact that his mouth was wrapped around a thermometer.

"You into leather?" she smiled. She checked the thermometer so he no longer had an excuse. Ninety-eight-point-six, perfectly fine.

"Oh no, too expensive. And pain? Not into it."

"I promise I'll never inflict any pain."

"You're really good at drawing blood," Dennis said. She was. "I love your technique. Rigo says you're better than any doctor. Rigo loves you."

"Now see, how am I supposed to read that? A guy who's into pain says he loves me." The Velcro rip of the blood pressure band, the wheeze of the pumping bulb. Everything to investigate bodily filth and corruption must be spick-and-span.

"Rigo says you're going to become a nurse practitioner." From the way she used the tool and penciled checkmarks on a sheet, he knew: ears, normal, eyes, normal.

"God, doesn't anybody get a private life?" she said, but she seemed pleased to have been talked about.

⁓

And outside the clinic, Dennis sat in a garden created by a green between two office buildings. The tulips surrounding the benches were pretty, but he couldn't allow himself to enjoy them. He knew the connectivity of things, the roots of things. These corporate gardens were diabolical, a thousand daffodils landscaped into an artificial meadow, only to be ripped out two months later for a completely landscaped makeover. The tulips, still in ragged bloom, were already half-ripped-up in one corner, left to dry and die in the sun on the sidewalk.

Rage's flush distracted him, but that only contributed to this terrible shortness of breath, which could be psychosomatic, but felt real. As if his lung sacs could not fill up, as if he had the terrible pneumocystis, the first of the full-blown symptoms.

"Conversion," Dennis let himself say the word out loud, on the bench; let passersby think he was a nut, he

29

didn't care. At the moment. He needed to say the word aloud because he was Catholic, and things didn't exist until they'd been named.

A little girl's mother let her toddle up to the up-rooted flowers piled in a sheath. What more harm could she do? Grabbing a stalk, the girl held it to her mother. "Pretty?"

Her mother nodded. "Pretty." Although Dennis could think of a hundred and one arguments against this confirmation.

The little girl touched her nose with her tongue and decided for herself—for the world must be reinvented every day by the thousands of people born into it—"Pretty."

Then she did a shocking but, Dennis thought later, inevitable thing: she pulled the blossom from the stalk.

Delighted at first, she held the daffodil head to her mother. "No, Sage, put it down now."

But Sage immediately set herself to the task of reassembling blossom and stem, chanting, or inquiring incessantly (for it had become a question again), "Pretty? Pretty? Pretty? Pretty?" But she could not get the flower to stay on its stalk. The planet: full of hard lessons. She began to cry desperately.

Dennis began to breathe again, deep gobbets of breath, the air palpable and nourishing: bread. He didn't in the least feel as if he had pneumocystis. This fact made him giddy, then laugh—now he had too much oxygen. Sage's mother, deeply conciliatory toward her heartbroken child, glared at Dennis, but then looked down. They were near a clinic, after all; maybe he was waiting for his lithium.

He'd stopped laughing, for Sage's sake, when Rigo and the guy named James came out into the corporate garden in a classical grouping, like *The Annunciation* or *Job and a Comforter,* only with leather chaps. They took over the bench among the daffodils, and scared Sage and her mother away.

"Dennis, Jimmy was just like you, he completely foresaw his results, so he was ready."

The fact was, however, Dennis had not anticipated the positive test. Or rather, believed that he was just naturally immune, he'd been let off the hook by some fabulous escape clause, as the angel of death took only the first-born. Without the word, the virus was invisible — "not being positive" meant "being negative."

⁓

Rigo's party was held in the penthouse apartment of a grand old building, part of the edifice parade along Van Ness Avenue. It belonged to yet another Rigo lover Dennis had met years ago, a southern lawyer who'd had it since the early 1970s and paid '70s rental prices for an entire labyrinthine floor, with rooftop access. Since nature abhorred a vacuum, Rigo had invited every acquaintance, ex, and friend in town, or at least the interesting ones. Dennis took part in a conversation with a man named Art DeBris, shared cheese and crackers with a guy employed to compose an opera commissioned by and about the life of a rich, ailing opera lover, and discussed the challenges of painting with mascara and blush tones with a painfully skinny artist clad only in women's lingerie. Dennis would remember the garters, nagged up the unwilling legs of that beauty.

Because this was not carnival enough, the southern lawyer requested every guest to wear a wig from his vast drag wardrobe kept in a walk-in vault.

Wigs were not Dennis's thing. Drag didn't make him look feminine, it just made him look older. But in order to blend in in San Francisco, Dennis held, it was necessary to wear outlandish outfits, wigs, Easter bonnets.

"You look beautiful!" said somebody in a tall bouffant wig, somebody Dennis was supposed to know, but didn't.

"No, I don't," Dennis said, more annoyed at being called out than being called beautiful.

"You don't take compliments well, do you?"

"I'm spooked by generosity," said Dennis. "Do I know you?"

"You don't know?" The wigged guy was in an incredulous snit for a moment, but then Dennis could see his face rearrange itself into confidence—he was going to take advantage of the disadvantage. He said, "You seem perfectly comfortable with the generosity of our host—" and clinked the base of his champagne flute against Dennis's own—full, a third refill, in fact.

"And the lawyer has been very free with his outfits," Dennis agreed, and took a long sip, in honor. On cue, Rigo stepped forward, wearing his chaps, boots, and a fright afro. On his arm, he explained, was Billy, he of the penthouse view.

"Billy, this is Dennis and Jimmy," he pushed the two of them together. "And God Bless America, they're too dense to know that they ought to be lovers!" Jimmy didn't look the same without tears rolling down his cheeks.

Dennis said, "And I'm too drunk to be embarrassed when you say things like that—aren't we, Jimmy?"

"And Rigo, just think what the babies would look like," Billy drawled. Dennis thought Billy was extremely sexy, but Dennis felt supremely unsexy, what with his not going to the gym much lately, what with his wig, what with this nasty virus. He felt the shortness of breath again. This penthouse, so high up, stratospheric.

"May I have your attention!" It was Sue the nurse, transformed—a spiky-haired toughie standing on a footstool, clanging her own champagne glass. How did she get her hair to do that? Why didn't she have to wear a wig? "As you know, tomorrow Rigo checks in for surgery."

Dennis was aghast. "You are?" he hissed, knocking Rigo in the upper arm.

Rigo nodded. "Lymphoma," he said, and the way he said it was so very typical; you couldn't tell if a man

33

was being serious or if it was gallows humor or a little bit of both. He walked casually away from Dennis as if he'd just unloaded the hot potato at a children's birthday party.

Stranded. Oh no, oh no, oh no, Dennis thought. He had entered the kingdom of the sick and surrendered all. Yet relinquishing it all, he felt more like a terrorist. Terrorism was a kind of freedom, at least for this moment, especially when one let the champagne go to one's head, and felt the easy fact: well, this is new, I must eat rich fatty foods, I must throw my own party, I must kiss everybody good-bye, I must *leave a good impression*.

Dennis reached out and held Jimmy close. Scrutinizing Jimmy under this wig made him work harder to evaluate afresh, without the first eye, say, of the tracker, the lover; this time, he noticed how wolfish were Jimmy's features, as Richard III was said by Shakespeare to have his teeth before his eyes; there was that upturned nose, too, and his eyes bright and big: the better to see you with, my dear. He made restless, deliberate lupine movements too, as if he wished to roam alone, but knew himself a pack animal with grudging social ties to family and food. And then Dennis saw the wig for what it was: the fleece of a sheep.

"Leave something on me," Jimmy said, recognizing Dennis's undressing eye, "or I'll catch cold."

Caught, Dennis hugged him a second time, though he was a stranger, and he had trouble taking in a gulp of air and thought again, it's pneumocystis. The panic for oxygen made his eyes bulge, and he pulled away, so that Dennis saw the look as a question: "How are you doing now?"

Jimmy calmed Dennis by explaining how he could quickly purchase a life insurance policy and sell it off at an advantageous moment, when Rigo returned to see how his bad news had sunk in. Dennis studied those chaps, and big black boots, too, spit-shined ones. "Counting your phages before they're hatched?" he asked, somehow managing to tap a shit-kicking toe in a motherly way. "You two are not keeping up with the champagne." He topped them off.

Up on the footstool, Sue, still wigless, was saying, "I'm Zoe—" (Zoe?) "—and as you also know, Rigo has been one of the biggest boosters of the men's health crisis clinic. We'll miss him down there." Some clapping, some champagne tipping. People who'd been out on the balcony and up on the roof had straggled in to see what all the noncommotion was about.

"So tonight we have a big surprise! Rigo—" and here Sue-Zoe pulled a trophy up with her, an acrylic arm flexed to show a biceps, mounted on a golden standard, some sort of magic scepter. "We would like to announce the winner of the First Annual Rodrigo Dominguez Booster Award—Rodrigo Dominguez!" Huzzahs all around. Sue-Zoe handed the statuette to Rigo, whose fright wig was suddenly appropriate, the stopped clock, telling the right time for the second time that day. "Oh, fudge," he shouted at them all.

"Given each year," Sue-Zoe shouted, "to the person who does the most to help infected men in our community through new drug studies!"

Rigo returned to Dennis's side a tearful blur. Dennis was feeling his own insides open up, becoming soft, like a sea anemone, something nourished by making itself vulnerable.

Rigo used the muscle-arm scepter to knight Dennis, then kissed him wetly on the cheek. "It's hard to believe today," he said, "but when you just decide that all your life is gone, every extra minute feels like a Crackerjack surprise."

"Oh, shut up," said Jimmy, and Dennis couldn't have said it better.

But: dizzy. Dennis could suddenly breathe. As if he'd been too worried that his lungs could not take in any oxygen, and he'd suddenly realized that he'd been hoarding it and keeping it from other people. Not deprivation, but surfeit had caused the head to swim.

"Next year," Rigo said, turning to Jimmy, "I want you to be the winner of the Rigo Dominguez Award."

Jimmy wept. "I won't take it," he vowed, "unless you present it to me." These days, vows were made all the time: to-the-end, til-it's-gone, not-without-you: these vows were easy. Dennis thought of tougher ones, even then.

And then Rigo began to cry, and all three of them, so newly close to the grave, exalted, refreshed themselves in tears.

Dennis said, "I think I'm having a revelation."

Jimmy said, "It's the champagne." He looked even more sarcastic when saying this in a wig. A fire-eater and a snake charmer, hired for the party, were about to perform up on the roof. Everybody was going up.

"No, it's more than drug induced," said Dennis. "It's poverty induced." It felt absurd to say it, what with having a roof over his head, money in the bank, champagne in his hand. He pointed at the champagne for Jimmy. "Why be stingy with what's left? Just look at Rigo."

"Or," said Jimmy, "or you could do what I plan to do, and indulge yourself for the rest of your life." He also pointed to the champagne glass in his hand.

"I'm rich! I'm poor!" shouted Dennis. In ten days, President Bush would declare war in the Gulf, and the whole world would feel a little of Dennis's zeal. Somebody would steal his car that night, the '84 Honda Civic that he'd driven down here, and crash it into a bunch of bushes two neighborhoods away, and Dennis would never report the business to the police, and never buy another car again.

The windows were open and the doorway to the rooftop was left open, and oxygen came through, a whole wind tunnel of it. And Sue-Zoe, the spiky-haired nurse-practitioner-to-be, shouted from the bathroom, "People, hello! Drought's over! It's okay to flush the damn toilet!"

Moss

France, May 1993

Europe sacked!

That's what Dennis thought when he looked out onto the platform and saw another American with two bags loaded down with ceramics, cheeses, bolts of fabric, religious figurines.

Dennis, on the other hand, felt himself paring down: his body, physically, and his possessions, specifically. It felt great. He saw himself as a sleek weasel, or one of those animals that lay in brush on a riverside and, at the least hint of trouble, could slip into the water like another kind of liquid.

However, this train trundled—first through Spain, then French countryside—like an overdressed matron with too many suitcases. He'd been on a bicycle for over a month, beginning in mid-France, crossed a pass in the Pyrenees, and peddled through Spain to the pilgrim cathedral of Santiago de Compostela. Now, even the bicycle was gone, sold to a vagabond German boy for a song. Disabused of it, all that was left for Dennis to do was carry his single pannier to Paris for a flight back to the States. Sitting in the compartment of six seats, shared only with a taciturn yet smiling Dutch couple, he was watching the Basque-French country-side roll by.

The train stopped again—could it have been only twenty or so meters from the last village? More obscure places that existed only because of the train tracks. Dennis reminded himself to like these open expanses. Out on the platform, he saw a girl get on, maybe twenty years old at most, in a short skirt that was pink with white polka dots. She had no hat, but she should have had one, to match her little brown suitcase. She was not sacking Europe.

Just as the train chuffed twice, four lanky soldier boys, all with big flattened French noses that their faces might grow into the way dogs did their paws, raced to the doors—wait! Wait! They piled in. Dennis could just take in the action from his window. If he craned his neck too much, it might look like desire to the Dutch couple. Longing, Dennis maintained, has a uniform look that transcends cultures, as did any uncontrollable urge of the senses: pleasure, frustration, fear.

Down the narrow passage, examining compartment after compartment, the girl with the small suitcase came. She looked in on Dennis and the Dutch, smiled, and entered.

Why? Couldn't she find another seat? Dennis wondered. The train was nearly empty. Perhaps she could smell the clean air in here, and surmised that the three of them didn't smoke, or would mostly be quiet. She pushed her luggage in the rack up next to Dennis's lone pannier and said, in French, "But you have been to see Saint Jacques?!"

She'd figured this from a patch he'd sewn on the small pack, one of a gold scallop shell on a red field, the emblem of the pilgrim, and an easy way to get cheap accommodations in *gîtes* and *refugios*. "Yes," he said, in English. Not *oui*. If he made it clear he couldn't (well, wouldn't) speak French, maybe she'd leave him alone.

"And you are English?!" she said in English.

"American," he said, which made the Dutch couple frown; evidently this was bad news to them.

She plopped down in the seat beside him, and Dennis thought momentarily of a black-and-white era child star, the way her dress spread and settled like a dropped handkerchief. She could have chosen the seat by the door. That's okay, he assured himself, personal space is an unnecessary possession too, one eschewed by right-thinking Europeans.

One army boy pushed a second down the aisle. They were surpassingly handsome, in a skinny way. Everything they needed was in one big duffel bag. He had that in common with them. But Dennis was thirty-five. He consoled himself thinking they were probably terrible in the sack. Not that he was interested in that, either. A forty-day pilgrimage on bicycle had been mostly one of moving and sleeping. No privacy, no chance for nooky, although he'd bought a porno magazine at the Gare du Nord with cheesy photos of too-skinny underaged French boys, eyes straight ahead, the look of those who can recognize destiny, or a trick. He'd picked it up all those weeks ago and pawed it so many times in various bathrooms throughout the journey that he'd come to memorize every crevice of the boys on the pages, and it became pointless to carry smut. But this he had hung onto, while he had jettisoned various items of clothing instead. Even now, the magazine was folded up like historical parchment in the bottom of the pannier.

She leaned close to him and grasped his leg. "Do you feel feet?" she asked.

"No, I went by bicycle, I didn't walk, so my feet are all right."

"No—do you feel feet?" she repeated, squeezing the leg muscle, which was indeed fit. Feet.

"I do," Dennis said, and didn't see himself as bragging when he added, "I lost twenty pounds, too."

For years he'd been terrified by weight loss, watched friends fall ill and shrivel, which reminded him of the way his forlorn grandmother had caught "the dwindlies" after her husband had died, and evaporated over years until she was a tiny brittle thing in her coffin. But he felt well, strong, feet; he was actually proud of his new lithe self.

"Incroyable," she said, "I must make this pilgrimage too, so I may lose such weight." Oh sure, like she was fat! She was a slip of a thing, very pretty if you liked

girls, Dennis thought, and noted that her hand was still on his leg. "But first I will shop in Paris," she smiled.

The Nederlanders had closed their eyes in tandem, and rested their heads against each other, Tweedledee and Tweedledutch. Probably faking it, to escape the conversation. Dennis wished he had a book. He'd brought with him a copy of *The Portable Dante,* but left it in a hostel early on, for it was definitely not portable enough. Here, all the papers were in French, and he was better with Spanish.

She let the hand slip off when another of the soldiers sauntered by. Probably she wanted to look available. "My name is Isabelle. Will you let me practice the English so that I may come to your country for adventure?" Isabelle was looking for adventure.

Was Dennis? Was adventure a kind of personal possession, sacked from Europe like tapestries or antique books? Did experience accrete on the soul literally, like mother-of-pearl, or lime, or moss? Well, longing did, he thought, as a French soldier passed once more, this time a little unbuttoned. Yes, Dennis wanted, of course he wanted, but he was older and poisonous and even if the soldier liked men, he wouldn't like this man. Traveling so light, unwilling to encumber himself with even an assignation with a soldier, he felt free. There'd be nothing to leave in his will, he thought—but then, there was nobody to leave a will for. No, if Isabelle was looking for adventure, Dennis was hoping to melt away.

"What do you want to talk about?" he asked her.

"I will tell you about me and then you will tell me about you. I am first." And so she did, so she was: just twenty years old, her mother rented guest rooms in their home, which was blue and too big and old. The patron saint of their town was Saint Roque, a pilgrim himself, one who cared for plague victims along the road and caught the illness too, and when he went into the forest to die alone, the Lord sent him a little dog with bread in his mouth, isn't that a pretty story? Some time ago her mother lost interest in this sort of inn-keeping, and Isabelle would have to cook dinner for the guests, but she knew how to impress foreigners with simple, expensive things like smoked salmon from the grocer and white asparagus from a jar. If she put out enough wine, she told Dennis, the guests hardly no-ticed she'd served them boeuf bourguignon and store-bought sorbets.

Truth was, her English wasn't shabby, in a thick French accent sort of way. She got all the words, now and then an adjective leaped a noun, but she got her-self across, and Dennis even laughed about the boeuf bourguignon.

That pleased her, making him laugh. "Now it is your time," she said, and promptly opened her little purse and began applying makeup.

He must have looked abashed, because she had to say, "I am listening."

What was there to say? He tried to tell her what

there was of it simply, and without contractions; he cleared off the bracken of language that Nothing is often hidden in. "I have a room that I rent in San Francisco. There has been only a jar of mayonnaise and two Coca-Colas in my refrigerator for two months. I am an editor and it is easy for me to get different kinds of work, but I do not have a job that I go to every day. I usually travel with a man named Jimmy, but he had lots of work and hates bicycles. I once wanted to be a train conductor, but now I want to be a monk. I have never been in love."

He knew she'd say, "Neh-vair?" and he might've gambled that she'd click her compact mirror shut and snake the mascara wand up into its snug tube. "But I have been in love at least ten times and I am only half your age."

"I know," he smiled.

She took his hand and looked into his eyes. He couldn't tell where she had applied that makeup. And anyway, she didn't need it. That was the thing about makeup. "Then you must fall in love with me," she said, earnestly. All that work in the bed and breakfast business had made her gregarious!

For a moment, he did not answer. He wondered whether she too noted that the train—that trains in general—waltzed: *one*-two-three, *one*-two-three, *one*-two-three, with the bumptiousness of a friendly peasant girl, all dressed up and happy to be on the dance floor.

"Well, you see," Dennis smiled, "I don't fall in love with girls."

She kept staring at him and he thought, she doesn't understand, she thinks I mean I prefer women, and she's only a girl. But more words, he didn't extend. Then she smiled without showing her teeth, and patted his hands, letting them go. "Now I understand."

She got up and went to the bathroom, or somewhere like that. When Dennis leaned forward, he could see that one of the soldiers had pulled down a seat in the aisle so that he could smoke. He spotted Dennis and gave him a wink.

Dennis was aghast. Was that cruising? Should he act on it? How?

When Isabelle came back in she threw her purse up into the luggage rack and plopped down next to him. Her presence was a vague distraction, irritating, like not being able to find the teaspoon to stir the coffee when he'd just put that teaspoon down a second ago. The Dutch woman stirred against her husband. Somewhere in the effort to fake sleep, they really did fall asleep.

Isabelle looked at Dennis. "I'm sleepy too," she said, and, snuggling up next to him, she closed her eyes.

He shifted a little, looked out the window at pretty much nothing. He cleared his throat, but throat-clearing did not translate for Isabelle.

The position wasn't uncomfortable. Her head was light and since the car was just a little chilly, he liked her warmth. It must have pleased Isabelle, too, for a few minutes later, she put her feet up onto the third seat and crossed her arms, using Dennis's as a pillow. She said, without opening her eyes, "Tell me a story, in English. For sleeping."

Dennis looked down and giggled. He'd tell her a story in soft low tones that would be drowned out by the waltz of the train. He'd use fancy words so she'd never understand the secret of his story.

He said, "There once was a man who loved to eat delicious food and experience the other pleasures of life too, and he wanted to talk to God—"

"He should pray," she said without opening her eyes. She startled him.

"Well, he talked about praying a lot, but he did not pray on his knees with his head lowered and his hands together."

"Sometimes when I am cooking, I pray."

"How are you going to sleep when you keep talking?"

"I pray when I put on my lipstick, so the words will be red and pretty. What did the man look like?"

"He was not pretty."

"So it is not a story about you."

"Shh. No, the man had fruit punch mouth. His mouth was red, blood red, because he was always enjoying something good to eat or drink. Every Christmas, all of his friends would give him bottles of wine or perfect cuts of meat, because he loved these fine things and they loved to watch him enjoy such pleasure. Anyway, the man decided to go to a place where God was easier to reach, to one of those places where people go. Like a special phone booth. He bought a bicycle and two panniers, one for each side of his bicycle, to hold his things. Forks and knives, the good ham and cheese he might find along the way. He knew that in Spain, where he was going, the people did not like to put spices in their food. So he brought for himself a small bottle of cayenne pepper, which he could use on all of his food."

"In English. Panniers in English."

"Shh. In English, they are called panniers."

"What a silly language."

"He put the bicycle and the panniers in a big brown box to carry them to Paris and Le Puy."

"Why didn't he simply buy a bicycle in Paris?"

"Because he wanted to break the bicycle in, and he wanted to get to know it, how to fix it if it broke," he said, hoping the idiom would confound her; she needed confounding. "Besides, it was cheaper to buy a bicycle in his own country. His country was the land of nice things of all kinds."

She opened her eyes. "What a wonderful country."

The waltzing peasant lady suddenly hit a rough patch of iron, and began to teeter and sway. Dennis grabbed Isabelle by the shoulder to keep her from slipping to the floor. He let go of her soon enough and said, "If you do not remain silent, I won't continue the story."

He looked across to the Dutch couple. They hadn't stirred. Perhaps they could sleep through bombs, or perhaps they'd had something to drink at the station in Bayonne. He looked out at the cropped head of the handsome smoking soldier. He was standing now, fumbling with his luggage for something, but looked over at Dennis as if he too were listening to the story, waiting for it to continue. And Isabelle had her head in Dennis's lap now, eyes shut tight. She made the sign of somebody zipping up their lip.

"Along with his cayenne pepper and his clothes, the man had a book of Italian poetry, a camera, a journal, special gloves for his bicycle, fancy shoes, a coat made from the skin of a fabulous animal, super vitamins to make him strong."

He pulled his own hands off of her. Where his fingertips had touched her skin, he felt a burning sensation, the kind of burning he felt when his hands had been cold for a long time.

"But the train for Le Puy was a train that was just like this one, only going south, only more disorganized, only with not so many handsome soldiers roaming the aisle. And the man was afraid for his self and his things, that somebody would pick his pocket or that one of the big green floor polishers in the Gare du Nord would run over his feet and injure him. He was glad that his bicycle and panniers were sealed in a big box and locked in the storage car of the train."

Out in the aisle, the soldier was still fumbling with

his luggage. When Dennis looked directly at him, he noted that the cheekbones turned away but betrayed a tiny smile. What should Dennis do? Nothing. He didn't need this kind of trouble.

"But when the train arrived and the train men unloaded the bicycle box, somebody . . . somebody had taken a knife and slit a square and stolen one of his panniers, so that there was only one left. The pannier that was stolen contained his pants and the coat of a fabulous animal, and other nice things. So there were not enough of his things that he thought he needed. The man looked at the train conductor who had unloaded the box. 'Look at this,' the man said in his own language. 'Who did this?' But it was clear that the two people didn't speak the same language."

That's when Dennis saw it—the military guy's hard-on! An erection pressing out in his pants, raging, large, as clear a gesture of desire as his own neck-craning earlier. Up to now, Dennis had a little bit of fear of the French soldier. He had suspected there might be foul play in the guy's handsome head, or at least a practical joke, some humiliating scenario in which the other military boys lay in wait to burst out of a hiding place to see Dennis down on his knees, worshipping at the fount.

But no longer did he fear. Desire like that was vulnerable and unfakeable. He was embarrassed by it, look!, Dennis thought to himself, now he's trying to conceal it.

It was the sexiest thing Dennis had seen in months. In years. He took one of his hands and pressed it to his own groin, to awaken himself, a pump-priming gesture. He had forgotten, momentarily, Isabelle's head so close by, and he suddenly felt terrible, to have her lips so close to his penis, raging for the attention of François or Michel or whatever the hell the soldier's name was. Desire was for men, Dennis thought, and caught his own sexism in action—girls were ornamental, and ought to be protected from carnal acts. He tried to get the attention of the soldier, but now he wouldn't look.

Look at me!, he thought, but what he did was resume his story, in the superstitious belief that it was the tale-telling that had woven his erotic spell, a reverse Scheherazade, and if the story went on, the soldier would want Dennis more.

"The man could say a few words to the train conductor, because he knew how to say, 'I have' and 'I want,' in practically every language. They were the words he knew the most, said the most.

"But still the train man shrugged and walked away, leaving the pilgrim with his ransacked box. There were no shops in the town to sell more panniers. How would he enjoy the beautiful food without his fine utensils? And he thought in that moment: despair."

But the soldier did not turn around. Perhaps he was too nervous that Isabelle might awaken amid the semi-public seductions. Damn this French girl. How could

50

Dennis ditch her? How? He cleared his throat again. He jiggled his knee as if he were dandling an infant— ugh: which he was.

She did not awaken, but her short little skirt fell away so that Dennis could see what the soldier had seen all along. Isabelle was not wearing any underwear.

The movement of the pretty flowered material caught the soldier's attention again, for bulls see red and charge. He turned to get the new, improved view, and Dennis was looking right along with him. The soldier winked at Dennis again. It was the same wink, but Dennis thundered at the mistranslation. But still, the ricochet of ardor benefited Dennis, too, for he also got a full frontal view. The now un-shy soldier had unbuttoned his fly.

What did the guy think? wondered Dennis. That Isabelle and he were into some kind of weird scene? But now that the soldier was in on the imaginary scenario, he was getting bolder and bolder. Isabelle stirred, as if her lullaby had been cut short.

"But just as he despaired," Dennis blurted—and continued in a murmur that perhaps the soldier mistook for something sexy—"a man appeared on the platform with a dog eating old bread. The man had a sore on his leg, which he exposed to let the air breathe over it. In a situation like this, the pilgrim usually avoided such people, the city's lowlifes, the semicrazed. But the man with the dog was clean and kind and spoke the pilgrim's language. He said, 'Somebody has taken things from you.'"

Should he cover Isabelle? God, does he think I'm her boyfriend? And with that thought came the strangest sense of possessiveness: how odd, to consider his that which he did not want.

"'I don't think I can go,' said the pilgrim, 'not with just one pannier.' 'That's nonsense,' said the man, and he showed how, with a small backpack, the pilgrim could bring just the bare essentials, two shirts, two pairs of socks. He said this all with gentle authority, and then he said good-bye."

The soldier appeared selfishly handsome, now. His wanting Isabelle, his unfazed gaze at her cho-cho, it made him fearless, reckless. The hand twiddled with a third button on his pants. Dennis wanted, and did not want.

"And the pilgrim decided to go with just one pannier. He gave up his corkscrew and cheese knife and all of the accoutrements of pleasure. He did not take his little journal, but carried only maps, which, when he had passed over the described land, he discarded. For a few days, it's true, he took photographs of beautiful places, but because he was alone, the photos were always of unpeopled landscapes, shabby versions of postcards he found in any shop along the way, and because he would not appear in any of his own photos, what kind of record was he trying to keep? So he left the camera one day in a little hostel, half of the role shot."

Dennis now decided to look at her naked flesh. The complicated folds of women were something he'd rarely—no, never—seen in his life. Look at the mystery of her, he marveled, look at her difference! How could she be so different? Who could be sexually excited when there was so much enigma to puzzle over?

The soldier was now looking at her as if he might take her from Dennis, as if that were the secret goal he had hiding in his unbuttoned trousers. But Dennis wondered, Would he take something else out of the pants, too?

"The pilgrim made the journey. As he went along, he lost weight and became something like a machine that functioned only to move a bicycle across mountains and plains. With only a pannier, there was a little imbalance and so one arm grew stronger than the other. And see how the sun tanned his hands only where it shone through the air holes in his gloves? It is as if he had received the stigmata."

That's when Dennis took one of the hands he tried to show a sleeping Isabelle and pulled up part of her skirt and tucked it gently between her legs, hiding the girl's vagina and bit of perfect ass. She frowned a little—probably the cool breeze from the window had felt good on that unleashed place.

The soldier frowned, too. He had also misinterpreted somebody else's desire and pleasure. And Dennis put a single proprietary arm around Isabelle's shoulder, as if to say, "Hands off, she's mine."

The soldier made a menacing French word with his mouth, and slunk off to the compartment, probably to trump up the story as he told it to his friends. At least he had a story to distort. That was usually enough to have of such stuff, the better part. Someday, Dennis thought, the boy would discover that pleasure was nothing more than a momentary denial of tribulation, like deciding which hand to treat to a pocket while walking in a biting winter wind and holding a dog's leash, or a cigarette.

Dennis waited a minute, listening to the chug and shift of train wheels, and went on. "When the pilgrim got to the shrine, the big phone booth to God, he was asked to fill out a questionnaire. The questionnaire was available in every language and multiple choice in nature. Why do you pray? One, to ask for something, two, to ask for something for somebody else, three, to improve yourself, like that. The pilgrim didn't fill out the form, and he did not go into the shrine, though he marveled at its grand exterior. Why? Because to want like this—to speak of desire is not a conversation, but solely a piercing one-way ray: I have, I want. A thousand voices in this same place, constantly proclaiming those two things. How could God ever get a word in edgewise? We want, but the curse of wanting is that it deafens us. Does God speak?" Dennis shrugged, trying to answer his own question. "I cannot hear him."

And did Isabelle hear him? He shifted a little. "But he left his little vial of cayenne pepper on the steps of the big shrine, because he had become accustomed to the blandness of things."

As if she could hear the ending of the story by the sounds of his finality, Sleeping Beauty woke up. Dennis smiled at her but found it more comfortable to study the landscape out the window. He thought, no, experience doesn't accrete like mother of pearl, for look at this French girl, who remains unchanged by the adventure she had just had. "No person in Spain would ever take such a thing, for it would give no one any pleasure. It did not fulfill anybody's desire, not for miles. The pilgrim imagined it would sit on the steps for all eternity, like an unwished-for miracle."

Conversion

San Francisco, May 1994

The city sparkled, unveiled like a new statue, cleaned up for the United Nations rededication. Some of the scuzziest streets in town were tidy and bright for the ceremonies. The homeless were, for the moment, maybe squirreled away somewhere like the czar's peasants during European state visits. Ground had been broken for the grand edifice of the new public library, and stately rows of full-grown palm trees had been planted in the greens dividing Market Street.

"Conversion," Dennis said out loud, because he wanted to simplify it, or isolate it, or God, even *convert* it into something new or else.

But really, he conversed with himself as he tromped toward Muni, he was thinking about that flat in his house, which was being converted into a condo, and did he want to buy his own place?

But when somebody converts, or something converts, to condos, or Christianity, or compost, there's that *going to* place, but a *coming from* place as well, and just last month, his sister had left her husband of seven years for an Austrian medical student and moved abruptly to some Tyrolean ski town to serve *après ski* hot toddies while her new boyfriend spent his off-hours giving ski instructions to rich girls (which was how they met, his sister and the ski instructor med student, for she said he looked sexy in lederhosen but who could look sexy in that stuff? But that wasn't the point, though, was it?—the point was that she was happy and in love).

The point, actually, was that his sister had converted, passed up her admittedly frumpy and way-sexist husband Matt, that pig, and she was having a ball while Matt was feeling betrayed. He'd called Dennis and said his sister was a "fucking renegade, and while it might be okay for you gays to act that way, it was different with straight people." What one person might call conversion, another could call betrayal.

After Rigo dressed Jimmy and Dennis in shirts and trousers far too big for their bodies, Jimmy did Dennis's face. Jimmy was doing a good job. Jimmy had already done his own face, and maybe it was his sharp rosy complexion that made him a shape-shifter. But where had he learned to make Dennis look real, too? He caked a pale, waxy makeup to simulate huge cartilage deposits, and had ready a case full of little inserts for the nostrils, made of gray splayed hairs that looked like fly-fishing lures. He used some kind of thin syrup that puckered his skin when it dried. Rigo had found toupees that made them all look like they were balding and unkempt, and while Rigo finished with Dennis, Jimmy practiced hobbling around with a cane.

"This is all so very freaking Fall of Rome," said Rigo.

Dennis agreed. The difference between them was that Rigo liked the idea of decadence. Dennis waited for Jimmy to weigh in, but if there was one thing Dennis had learned about the crusading journalist, it was that he kept things to himself. Like maybe a career in theater?, he thought, marveling in the hand-held mirror at this massive transformation.

Rigo raised a fist and shook it, face set like a large-mouth bass; the scar from the years-old brain surgery phonily enraged into proud flesh. He shouted, "Gosh darn you kids!"

"Say 'God damn,' Rigo," said Dennis, but it was hopeless.

Rigo's life on disability consisted of hatching goofball schemes like this one. A stroll through the Castro, a drink at JJ's piano bar or the Twin Peaks. Dinner at the Galleon, maybe, and a souvenir cane at the end of the evening, which would come in handy in the real twilight of life, ever-swiftly approaching. Time was wasting: the three of them, suited up, struck out.

At JJ's, it would appear that Rigo began hitting on three boys all at once, young and slumming, by telling them one of his lousy clean jokes. "I was standing here the other day," he said, creakily, emphasizing his fake age, "and the bartender walked away, and I was alone and I heard this little voice. It said, 'Hey, handsome, that's a real nice suit!' Well, imagine how surprised I was. I looked around to see who was admiring me, but nobody was close by. Then this little voice said again, 'And that tie is pure silk, isn't it?' I looked at the bar and I saw these here peanuts," and Rigo pointed at the nuts on the bar in front of them. "I turned to the bartender and I said, 'Bartender, what's this?' and the bartender told me, 'Those are peanuts. They're complimentary.'"

The boys laughed, but in a superior way. It wasn't long before they were ignoring Rigo and thumping their chests. They were know-it-alls, born to a capital city and only on an extended sojourn to these provinces, bragging about their knowledge of the Mission District taquerias, as if they were the first ever to discover burritos—La Cumbre! Pancho Villa! Cancun! Ay! Ay! Ay!—they named those old joints one by one, for to name them was to invent them.

Rigo was smiling. He didn't care. So Dennis didn't care. Dennis surrounded himself with Rigos, the boys who did not sew quilt panels or mope through candlelight vigils, or even chain themselves to pharmaceutical companies in Silence Equals Deathwear; no, Dennis wanted some other note on the emotional scale other than that monotonous G for Gloom, which wasn't what he felt anyway. Rigo toddled away. He was on the make, flirting up a storm. Dennis and Jimmy ate the complimentary nuts and did two quick shots of scotch. Jimmy ordered a third, and he'd bought them all—he was okay with generosity as long as he was its beneficiary, too.

"So," said Dennis to Jimmy, trying to talk over the din of show tunes at JJ's, "Try and follow my reasoning: there are people who prefer to long rather than love. What I mean is—" What did he mean?—"that you remove the object of your desire."

"Are you talking about celibacy," asked Jimmy, "because I'm not interested in celibacy." For a moment, the teenaged werewolf face shone through the makeup as it had from under the wig that time at Rigo's going away party. Dennis thought, I've had wanton ways, but this man might have committed a crime at some point.

People were looking at them. Not as sex objects. Rigo returned momentarily and said, with a peculiar mix of amusement and disappointment, "We don't look old, we look like homeless people. JJ was almost going to ask us to leave." That irritated Dennis, but maybe what really bugged him was the sing-along to "Gigi."

"Homeless people don't order single malt scotch," said Jimmy, then. Now, though, he was protesting for another of the great pleasures.

"I'm not talking about celibacy," said Dennis.

"Oh no," said Jimmy, ordering another one. "You're talking about *longing*."

"Sailors did it. Longed. Whether they knew what they were doing, that's another question, but they conjured up all sorts of excuses for the people at home. They were looking for a new passage to the Orient, or El Dorado, or a better place to live. Sometimes they accidentally accomplished those goals, but mostly they just wanted to go go go, sit on deck and watch the horizon fade forever and forever from their view."

"That's Tennyson."

"God, that's why I love you."

"You don't love me, you're too busy *longing*."

"That's right, but shut up. I'm having deep thoughts."

"You're having scotch, a whole bunch of it."

"In vino veritas."

"It's scotch."

Dennis drank. He quaffed. His fake nose hairs tickled the rim of the glass. "Tennyson did it, he longed. But poets said they did it for the Lost Lenore or whoever. Dante's Beatrice strikes me as a lover of convenience. They'd get all mad, like Tennyson did when he was surprised by joy—feeling real good when his daughter was dead dead dead."

"Ah yes! I rememb-air it well," Jimmy sang along in a bad French accent. Dennis had told Jimmy all about his adventures with Isabelle. They'd been corresponding, and she'd invited the two of them to her mother's chateau to eat salmon and store-bought sorbet. Jimmy's French was much better than Dennis's.

61

And in his geriatric outfit, he looked a little like Maurice Chevalier. Dennis determined that Jimmy sang to avoid these not-so-deep observations.

"And do you see the worth of longing?" Dennis insisted. "It's revitalizing, it's a fountain of youth. Even for the ones who claimed to be seeking the fountain of youth."

"Am I getting old?" Jimmy sang the question.

"Oh no! Not you," Rigo hollered back from across the room—he wanted to be closer to the piano, where he'd planted himself.

"But I've strayed from my point," said Dennis.

"You have a point?" Jimmy said, betraying himself. He *had* been listening.

"My point is this. Can't you agree that, if there is such a thing as longing, that if passion and love could be made more elastic and active until you die, then its opposite might exist as well?"

"By opposite, do you mean 'hate'?"

"Yes! Don't you think that a man could hate without there being an object of hatred? Think how harmless and pretty hatred could be."

Now they were singing "The Night They Invented Champagne." The player was plinking on all the keys at the high end of the piano. Good God, it was a Gigi *montage*.

Jimmy stopped listening, but then, Dennis had stopped talking. He thought: What hatred is, is loved turned away. It's like not feeding your children, in hopes that they might build up an appreciation for food. "But it doesn't work that way," he said out loud.

"You're going to get us kicked out for being homeless," Jimmy said.

Dennis kept the rest to himself: I want to dedicate the rest of my life to longing's opposite, which is not greed, but something, I don't know, *unnameable*. And since I thought of it, I feel entitled to name it, like a new comet or an island. Later, when he looked back on this night they invented champagne in old man drag, he would see it as the night he first thought he ought to be a priest.

⌒

Dennis was late for the clinic appointment, which was not entirely his fault. On Muni, filled with morning commuters, the only one seat left was next to a ferocious-looking homeless man, one who might have been sane at some point (sane enough to pay and sit still for a handful of artistically accomplished tattoos) but was no longer. The seat was not exactly vacant: the homeless guy had his duffel bag on it. The homeless, with their shopping carts filled with stuff, bags full of bags full of bags like nested Russian dolls, filled with the true meaning of riches. An ivory chess set with a missing pawn was useless, and the cornucopia of life seemed a step away from the *sheol*-emptiness of death. He'd seen another homeless woman with sores on her face hog a phone booth at the bus stop, jabbering away about this and that, and the more she talked, the more Dennis was sure she was speaking to a dial tone. This man with the duffel bag was as tan as any retired movie star spending a luxurious life on the beach. Plenitude, mocked, Dennis thought.

Dennis looked down at the duffel bag and then to the scary tattooed guy. People around him stared, too; as Dennis had done, two or three people had chosen to stand rather than ask for the seat. The homeless guy took the duffel and dropped it at his feet. He had two different shoes. Dennis sat. The bus lumbered, wireless, using gas like sheer willpower. People continued to stare at Dennis. Consorting with the poor? Then he looked down into the duffel bag. Its zipper was broken, so it sagged open like a seed pod too fecund, bursting. Inside were several packages—gifts? mail?—tied individually with string. They were of a uniform color, deep red, purple, in shiny cellophane. A vague steely smell came from it. *Meat*. It was meat, all sorts of cuts of meat, not fresh at all, and carefully packed in to get the most use from the duffel bag.

"Would you like some?" said the tattooed madman, in the nicest voice.

He looked at the man with the meat, said no thank you, and then thought, the madness of men is mistaken in the way vertigo is often misunderstood. Vertigo, after all, was not a fear of high places, but the imagined fall from a high place. Madness was not the torture of too many thoughts, but the thought that the thoughts were too small, and the mind suggested now and then its possible greater abilities—and saddened the heart unto melancholia.

These thoughts didn't console enough. Dennis had to get off the bus and walk the rest of the way, and was late for the clinic appointment.

⌒

This is how they inserted the dock: first Zoe shaved the hair on their arms, and then she found the best vein available, and she swabbed it with alcohol, and dried it carefully. "When I stick you, you know, it's not the sticking that stings you, it's the burn of the alcohol in your blood if I don't dry you off enough." Sufficiently distracted, Dennis allowed her to slide the thick needle under his skin. There was only the smallest pinching feeling. Which word made him feel ickier—Install? Port? Usually Rigo did this thing, but here, on this day of days, he was not here.

"Is Rigo out sick?" Dennis's question tiptoeing near terrible probability. "I was just out with him on Saturday."

"You didn't hear?" Zoe said.

"Oh no, what?" How much of his dread was real and how much staged?

"Brain tumor." Brain tumor, how melodramatic. It's what soap opera characters got diagnosed with at the end of an episode, when their contract was up for re-newal and there were some questions of money.

"Brain tumor, after the lymphoma," she said. She looked into his eyes and the two of them almost burst out laughing, and then felt suddenly and truly terrible, both of them. For both of them now, after all these years, were indifferent to the various blades of pleasure and pain.

"Just last week, we were doing old man drag."

"What?" she asked, taping down the dock. I, Robot, he thought. Costumes, masks, they used to stay on the surface—now they were in his veins. How long could you live with a dock in your arm? He explained to Zoe about the geriatric disguises.

She sighed and pursed her lips and shook her finger, imitating moral rectitude. "Why must you be so vulgar? Why can't you be kind?" she squawked, but smiled. She was wrapping surgical tape round and round his forearm. "Why can't you give up sugar and coffee and ride in the AIDS Ride and be Shanti volunteers?"

Dennis wanted to tell her that he didn't want to be told how to feel. But then he thought of Rigo, who had, last month, to give away his dog to PAWS, because it wouldn't have anything to do with him, because it was an animal, Dennis knew, and animals always knew when somebody was going to croak, and Rigo had been always about to croak for five years, and the dog was now terrified of him. Dennis said to Zoe, "Because there was never a day of ordinary kindness to begin with. Why should I participate in regular human emotion if it was denied from the start?" Being *not allowed* to have something was not an act of generosity, either, he told himself.

Now she unexpectedly smiled, and all his resentment crumbled with hers. He didn't want to think bad thoughts about her. Wasn't it important to her, as well, that all things be brought down to zero? They had everything in common.

"Are you Catholic?" he asked her.

"Jewish," she said.

"An Old Testament girl."

"An only testament girl. Torah girl. Woman."

"Sure, sometimes I think I could do just as well without all that forgiveness and transcendence," said Dennis. She was putting lights in his ears, thumping his back, tapping his knee. He was as ripe as a pumpkin. "I'm happier seeing thunderclouds of blue smoke, the manifestation of the Sodom that is good old San Francisco. I need judgment. I need closure."

"But Dennis, starting next year, you're not allowed to smoke in California."

"I'm thinking of becoming clergy. Do you think I should become a man of the cloth, nice Jewish girl? Woman?"

They talked a lot that day, because there wasn't much else to do. Dennis and Jimmy had volunteered for this, the umpteenth study for yet another wonder drug, and it was in Phase II trials—that meant dosage. Straws were randomly drawn, and the shortest got one tablet of the drug, medium got two tablets, long got

67

three tablets. Because Dennis was late from the incident on the bus with the meat guy, he got the last straw. It was long.

The pills were pink and powdery, sissified, and had to be eaten with a stale bagel. Dennis didn't really think about it. This one didn't make him nauseous, though, so it wasn't like the usual junk. Immediately after taking the drugs, blood was drawn, and again every hour for eight hours. They'd return the next day, too, and repeat the process. That's why they had the docks installed, to save on the veins.

Jimmy and Dennis knew the clinic too well now. It had the cheeriness sad places often displayed, a constant parade of frosted sheet cakes, taped-up greeting cards, shiny Mylar helium balloons.

Dennis and Jimmy signed their waivers. It felt dangerous every time they did this, because they were risking their lives. "Don't you want to read it?" asked Zoe.

Dennis said, "Zoe, three years ago, we promised to hand our lives over to science. We're the rhesus monkeys. We're your lab rats. Fill us full of toxins. Take what you need."

She smiled, but not that tight-lipped vacant smile. "You watch too much television." He blushed. More and more often, doing good things seemed scripted. Could he ever do something kind without it having a moral?

They were allowed to go outside. He plowed through all the magazines in reception. There was a copy of

Midnight in the Garden of Good and Evil, but he'd already read it, before it became the big blah-blah deal sweeping the nation. They had junky videos in the lounge and since Dennis was also sick of bagels, he went back out to the bench next to the annoying corporate garden. He'd go in for the blood draw, and come back out. All he'd done all day was sit on this bench and look out on this shiny new city, but he felt haggard, achey in the shoulder joints, as if he'd been sitting all day on one of those transatlantic flights he and Jimmy had been taking more and more often. His body was a sheen of oily sweat, and it covered him like the old man makeup, and the nausea over the tied-up meat. It was the same sort of skin that formed on boiled milk or cold oatmeal.

In the garden of little good and lots of evil, the corporation had begun uprooting gladiolas. Tonight, Dennis swore, he was coming back here with grocery bags, and he would rescue them, replant them in his own little garden.

Jimmy came running out. "Dennis! Dennis!"

What was going on? Did somebody pass out? Were the drugs killing them off?

"Our first results are coming in! From the first draw. You won't believe what's happening. Come now!"

Jimmy pulled at his arm, the one with the dock in it. This caused the tape on his arm to pull and the dock to leak. A small orangeish trail of blood followed the inside rill of a crease in the tape. They hustled in, past reception, into the lab.

"Look," Jimmy pointed to a chart, printed from a computer logarithm on one of those fancy new color printers, taped to the door like final exam grades. "JT," it said, Jimmy's initials. Only it wasn't a final exam, but the trail of a stock market crash, or an ill-managed company. This line represented the viral load, the number they wanted to disappear, and it was plummeting. Dennis perceived some kind of miracle so foreign as to be nearly unrecognizable. He even believed it to be bad news until Zoe taped up four more charts. One was labeled "DB" and it was he, Dennis Bacchus. His also crashed, even harder.

"We're going to live," Jimmy murmured, and his quietness reminded Dennis of the way the earthquake in 1989 had started as a low temblor tremor.

Zoe was excited, too. The whole roomful of study participants had pooled their money and bought the lottery ticket for the jackpot. The race was on. Wind was blowing through the room, from velocity. They were all standing very still.

In the lab, behind a big swirling ominous "biohazard" symbol that Dennis recognized from barrels of toxic waste and the defiant biceps of HIV-positive men in grungy gay bars, Zoe couldn't get the test tubes full of blood draws into the centrifuge quickly enough. With a dozen spinning merrily on that vampiric carousel, she cheered them on, come on, hurry, hurry! She wanted immediate results, magic beans for an overnight beanstalk after a decade of famine. She wanted it for them, for Dennis, for Jimmy.

Dennis peeked around the corner to watch her shriek, half angrily, half joyously, at the centrifuge. "Damn you, hurry up!" she smacked her hand hard against it and beat it with a clipboard. Half of the test tubes full of tainted blood, his blood, shattered, and Dennis could see from where he stood that, of the several shards that spun at her, only six or seven of them hit her hand. Maybe only one or two of those actually broke her skin. But she was bleeding, that was the thing. Her blood and the other blood were all mixed up, and she'd been exposed. At least, Dennis thought, when he got infected, he was having a little fun.

Hagiography

Carcassonne, France, March 1995

For somebody lukewarm about France, Jimmy expressed surprise that Dennis was so eager to be back within two years of his last visit, when he'd met Isabelle on the train. Jimmy had wanted to go, too, one of their "last hurrah" voyages, even though Jimmy reminded them both that the term no longer applied.

They'd had a shared interest in the South of France, and Dennis especially wanted to visit the ruins of the Cathar castles. "I would have made a great Catharist," Dennis told Jimmy while handing him a history book about that twelfth-century heresy that held that every earthly thing was created by the devil, and any source of power was Satanic in origin.

After reading the dust jacket of the book and showing that he'd seen enough, Jimmy handed it back and said, "Yes, you'd make great pope fodder." For the church had felt threatened by Manichaeism and had Catharism wiped out, leaving behind nothing but the ghostly strongholds on the tops of volcanic pilings.

Jimmy wanted to go for the wine. He also wanted to meet Isabelle, in or out of underwear.

Dennis had tried for days on this trip to dig into Saint Augustine—he'd been taking religious classes and this was his spring break—but he was starting to quarrel with the master, who kept exhorting him not to step outside of the self, a basic tirade about the sinfulness of travel and experience. This from a man who traveled and experienced widely before giving it all up, the annoying self-righteousness of the prodigal son turned ascetic who went around telling others not to do what he had done. Perhaps travel was a luxury Dennis was no longer entitled to, if you were a religious, but he would preach just the opposite to any disciple: go out and see the world, or you'll end up coming to confession every week with the kinds of peccadillos muttered by little old ladies ("I failed to clean the kitchen") and children ("I was mean to my sister"), and the greatest sin of all is boring the daylights out of those shut-up priests doomed to sit out life in little confessional booths.

Dennis looked up Isabelle again. She'd slipped him her address when they'd arrived in Paris. Dennis and Jimmy went to the Languedoc and took rooms in Isabelle's mother's chateau, which was just perfect in its run-down state. The friendship between Jimmy and Dennis still felt strong. Dennis cared what Jimmy might think of the wild sassy French girl. But on her home turf, Isabelle was twenty-four, restless, and bored. The chateau, though it had room for at least six roomfuls of guests, they had to themselves. Isabelle's mother, with dyed hair fixed to highlight her noble forehead, stuffed them with good bread and wine, tiny dark-green lentils, platters of fish and raclette, potatoes beaten with cheese until they were a ropey, gooey paste. All of it seemed to disprove Isabelle's comment about her mother serving store-bought sorbet.

They let the family dog, Jana, sit by them during dinner, and she loved to play fetch until everybody fled her to avoid yet another merry retrieval. Jimmy loved Jana. "Jana and I are een loav," he told Dennis, "bot hair mothair disapproves, for I am poor, and alas, she eez a dog." Jimmy amused Dennis during these years, though he chain-smoked for a while (this he gave up in the late nineties, apparently in exchange for uglier habits).

The friendship between Jimmy and Dennis then was, well, real and nice, like that middle section of fifty or sixty pages of a big fat good novel you're reading when the book stays open on the table without your having to hold it or weigh the spread down with a butter knife, and you could read it while eating dinner.

Isabelle had nothing to do, she complained in her tiny English. She was bored, bored, bored. Jimmy asked her if she would like to join them on one of their sightseeing excursions from the house, and she nodded with pleasure. "I will take you to my favorite place, if you like?"

They were more than happy to follow her, although they did not anticipate her driving them fifty miles, hardly even in Catalan country anymore, to a place that neither of them could ever again find on a map. Nor did they anticipate her twenty-four-year-old crazy French girl driving, her screaming obscenities, challenges, and encouragements (all sounding suspiciously the same) to cars she passed or nearly hit.

Her favorite place turned out to be a church and a monastery dedicated to the cult of Saint Roque. When Dennis saw it, he gave Isabelle a significant look: she had not slept through his story on the train.

"He's not going to be a bloody gorefest, is he," Jimmy wanted to know, "like the usual French saints, like that Saint Denis guy?" Jimmy had teased Dennis about the headless namesake patron of France, represented everywhere carrying his own decapitated pate in the crook of his arm. As if to balance the world, every day Dennis became more serious about his Catholicism, Jimmy became more jaunty. But Dennis was attracted to Roque from the very moment he set eyes on him. Dressed as a pilgrim (walking staff, hat, cloak, a gourd full of water), with that small dog at his side (this one looked more ferocious, a wolf, maybe) holding a loaf of bread in his mouth for his master, he was shown lifting up his skirts to reveal a wound on his inner thigh. Roque pointed out his own nasty gash, in case anybody missed it.

Isabelle practiced her English by telling them the story of Roque. "But the Lord would not let him die, and he sent to his pilgrim a little dog each day with a loaf of bread, and slowly he grew stronger until he could resume his journey and his good works."

Dennis smiled, "And he went to Rome and found his God."

Isabelle pouted, bad news to break: *"Je suis désoleé,"* she said, "for a wicked uncle put him into prison and he was died there." Jimmy thought this was just high-larious.

The church of Saint Roque, patron of plague victims, turned out to be historically a large operation. There was a tremendous monastery for monks, the kind that hid themselves away from the world, the kind you could get pastries from by putting money on a lazy Susan and out would swing your food—or perhaps you might plop a bastard child on the swiveling table and poof, it'd disappear.

At least that's what Isabelle told them. "What would they do with the foundlings?" Dennis was concerned.

"How do you think the French make such great strawberry jam?" Dennis, even two years ago, hoped Isabelle's English would never improve.

Now, as the guidebooks always put it so simply, the monastery's vast legions had been "reduced to a handful." There were six or seven aged monks and they had sublet huge portions of the monastery to a day care center. Amidst the gloomy cloisters with dark crevices and tiles worn down and gargoyle faces, incongruous children shrieked like gulls stealing bait.

Isabelle asked a tiny woman in an office at the entrance if she would give them a tour. An aged lady, a fourth of their group, shuffled along from chapel to chapel as fast as she could, but could not keep up with their zealous docent.

The tiny tour guide rattled on about the trashing of the church during the revolution and the refinding of certain statues in devoted households after many years. She said some things about Napoleon's troops Dennis never quite got a grip on, and Jimmy had to help her unlatch some closed-up retableaux when the clasp was too high for her to reach—but when she did, they beheld wondrous and well-preserved depictions of Saint Roque.

They had to hustle up a long steep flight of stairs to get to the upper reaches, and it was like following the white rabbit. Dennis noticed that their fourth, the aged madame, gave up. Only he looked back at her sad countenance at the foot of the stairs, and she had a look of betrayal and relief, like one of the children from the day care center left behind.

He forgot, though, looking at an excellent painting of Roque (from the school of Tiepolo? For though rooted to firm ground, the view was dog's-eye, and Roque's head swam amidst cotton candy clouds).

"But where is the madame?" the docent suddenly stopped her fluid background narrative.

"She couldn't walk up the stairs," Dennis said.

The woman looked at him as if he were personally responsible for the feeble. Then she shrugged and muttered, "They are not that steep."

"Look," snickered Jimmy, close to Dennis's ear after

the fifth or sixth rendering of Saint Roque, "every time we see him, he's hiking up his skirt just a little bit higher. Pretty soon, he's gonna be flashing his boner."

Dennis smiled but he said, "Shh!"

Jimmy pushed him in the shoulder, "Oh, these people don't know the meaning of the word *boner*." He said the word at room temperature as they marched along a corridor—"Bo-*ner,* bo-*ner,* bo-*ner*!"

Only Dennis blanched. Jimmy tortured him down the halls, past the ancient infirmaries and kitchens and refectories, a little cadence: "Bo-*ner,* bo-*ner,* bo-*ner.*" They'd been on a bus two years before that in Italy, with nuns in the front and teenagers blasting a tape player in the back. *"Prego! Prego!"* thumped the song, *"Prego! Prego!* I like the way your pussy tastes! *Prego! Prego!* I like the way you sit on my face!"

Dennis whirled around in his seat, glaring at the kids. Not those words, not with nuns on the bus! But he could see the English words meant nothing to them, and certainly even less to the nuns. They were pleased enough to snap their fingers and shimmy their shoulders to their favorite pop song.

Here in the monastery of Saint Roque, they were shown to the place where, in ages past, the private monks took mass behind an iron grillwork while the rest of the village sat up front. That room was full of pews, mostly unused now except the place where three old men prayed in a corner. Praying for what? Dennis always wanted to know what other people prayed for. More friends? An end to this dying tradition?

The docent, her short little legs almost as noisy as her whisper, explained to them how the priest gave them communion through these little bars, that little curtain.

She led them out the other side, and escorted the group through a hall at the far end of which sat a monk with so many dewlaps hanging from his jowls he seemed diseased. He seemed to have sat there forever, with a strong newfangled metal cane, one that banded around his upper arm like a crutch and gave him a handle to grip further down.

Dennis could see a few terra cotta statues on a table before the decrepit monk. He had smeared out a line of paint blobs, acrylic colors, and with one of those palsied hands he worked an assembly line of Saint Roques. He had painted all the brown things on the half dozen statues, Roque's cloak and three-cornered hat, his dog, his sandals. He'd dabbed on gold, too, the crossed keys on the hat, the bread in the dog's mouth, his gourd full of water. Now he was working on the red things, Roque's lips and the horrid gash on the leg. Watching him paint, Dennis thought of a surgeon trying to perform on a ship in a squall.

Across from the artist monk of Saint Roque was a tall cabinet, eight feet high, with shelves and shelves of already-painted figurines. Those of the Blessed Virgin Mary looked as if they had put on their makeup without a mirror. There were luridly slathered Sacred Hearts and *"Ite ad Joseph's"* that slung lambs around their shoulders like stoles, whose painted fleece were nowhere near as white as snow. Mostly, though, the monk was selling Saint Roque statues, and Dennis had to have one.

"How much?"

Hardly anything, about four bucks. The old monk was overjoyed, got up from his painting, used his crutch to move painfully across the way, and grabbed onto the monumental cabinet for support.

Dennis felt he was choosing a single goldfish from a tank filled with hundreds, all looking vaguely the same, but he liked in particular one on the highest shelf, because instead of the keys to Rome on his hat, he wore the cockleshell of a pilgrim to Santiago. A minor heresy only he would care about. The palsied monk handed his crutch to the little docent woman for momentary safekeeping. There was, in the gesture, a lifetime's relationship, one that had not run smoothly. She was antsy to get to two more chapels; she had work to do. After the old monk had reached up and pulled down Saint Roque, Dennis gave him the francs and told him to keep the change.

The docent glared at Dennis, not for the first time. Was it a twitch or a real wink that the shivery monk gave him: we must suffer fools.

The docent marched ahead even while the monk wrapped Dennis's statuette in pages from *Paris Match*. She was going on about something that happened here during the Vichy government, but for Dennis, this tour was complete.

"Madame, madame!" shouted Jimmy to their

guide. He pointed back so that they all noticed how the old monk was clinging to his towering curio cabinet for dear life. Preoccupied, the docent had walked off with the lame man's crutch. She looked at it as if she'd just discovered a secret weapon she never knew she had, and then offered up a peal of laughter.

So did Isabelle. So did Jimmy. She hurried quickly enough to the brother and helped him back to his table, but Dennis thought on all this, the old woman who could not make the stairs, the crutches of the lame, the patron of plague victims. The kingdom of the well had no use for Saint Roque or his followers.

Back at the chateau, Jimmy begged Dennis to un-wrap his new fetish so that he and Isabelle could study it.

Isabelle pointed to the slopped-on black eyes. "He looks as if he wears mascara!"

Jimmy added, "And look at his dog! He looks more like a raccoon! And what is that in the raccoon's mouth? He's like one of those African tribal dogs with a disc under his lip."

Dennis laughed just as much as the rest, and even added that the ghastly wound on his thigh looked like cake frosting. But secretly, he never loved anything, any object anyway, more than this poorly realized depiction of lameness.

En Passant

San Francisco, August 1995

Zoe had called his home number, but it was for business; it turned into a social call after that. She was almost as chipper as the night she gave Rigo his memorial award, and that made Dennis nervous. "Dennis, it's just incredible." The words rushed. She had one of those cell phones everybody was getting now, and since she wasn't good at using it, her words, especially the loud and multisyllabic ones, were fragmented and smeared; of course, who needed the clear articulation of the word *incredible*? It was more an animal noise than human speech, a goose protecting its young. "The drug company is ending the study!"

"That's great?" he said, also pointless, just the sound of the question mark enough for them both. His head was even shaking "No?" but she couldn't see that.

"Eat a lemon, it'll sweeten your disposition," said Zoe. He was ruining her day. He could hear that. "It *is* great, it means the drug works, the drug will keep working for you, and no more sitting around getting blood draws every other day down at the clinic."

It was only twice a month, but her exaggeration's rationale came through over the static. In his mind, he matched her hyperbole: now I'll be paying millions of bucks a month for meds I used to get for free. "That's great," he said.

"We should celebrate! But I think the funeral parlor is booked today. Dennis, you were more fun to talk to when I told you you were positive."

"Well, now what kind of excuse will I have to come talk with you?"

The cell phone signal was getting weaker, and sometimes he couldn't even hear static. He wondered if he was talking to himself. "Are you asking me on a date?" she finally said.

"I don't date anymore." There was another pause, and he almost hung up and waited for her to redial, but in a last-ditch effort, he said, "Not even boys."

"I heard about that. Rigo told me all about your big God thing."

For a moment, the phone's signal was perfectly fine, but Dennis paused anyway. "I'm not going to talk about it on a stupid cellular phone," he said. "I don't want important things to get eaten up by all your static. We can discuss it on our date."

Maybe the signal had cut out, because she said, "Are you in training to be like one of those superstitious fundamentalists? My static won't hurt you, Dennis. And: what date?"

～

Rigo had decided to become an artist. It was a natural step after old man makeup: that business dried up quickly. Rigo had had a skinny artist friend who dressed in women's corsets and fishnet stockings and painted with mascara, eyeliner, lipstick. Dennis had met him at the award party the night he had tested positive. Now he was dead, and Rigo had inherited the art supplies and studio (as he'd inherited all sorts of secondhand items—cars, love letters, dried flowers, other people's keepsakes; Jimmy said Rigo had five toasters). The art-work was going for skillions of dollars, and people shook their heads—that skinny queen was going to be great, cut down in his prime. What if he had had a chance to really develop?

Rigo's art, on the other hand, was terrible. He'd invited Dennis one morning to his studio, which was the sun room on the back of a sex club; all the other windows in the entire house had been blocked off with black garbage bags. After walking down long hallways of dim bulbs and gloomy Clean Team workers wet-vac-ing the carpeting (sex club carpeting!!! Dennis exclaimed within himself), the northern exposure streaming down on Rigo's gloppy disproportionate depictions of streets and boats and pudenda made Dennis's eyes dilate.

84

"I call this one *Night Owl*," Rigo said. "Do you recognize that bus line? The one that runs twenty-four hours?" The muddy colors had more texture than form, layers of pasty paint built up, Braille.

Dennis wasn't a priest yet, so he felt he could lie. "It's beautiful. But it's only the back part of the bus. How come only the back part of the bus?"

"Crikies, Dennis, I am so glad you asked that! I am so interested in this technique my art teacher calls *'en passant.'* You speak French with that little French girl, don't you? You know what *en passant* is?"

"In passing."

"That's right!" There was paint everywhere. Paint, and liquid paper and mascara and eyeliner and rouge and blush and lipstick, and long snaky mascara brushes to apply it all. Dennis thought, he is using the wrong tools for the job. But there were so many other reasons why the paintings were ugly. It seemed a feeble thing, just the front of the Night Owl bus that was the impossibility of Rigo being an artist, and so Dennis didn't even start. Rigo said, "This one is called *Oceanique, en Passant*."

He'd cut This One into an oval, like a long mirror, but except for a tiny corner of blue at the top, it was a smear of inept brush strokes, brown, black, and whatever the color was when brown and black mixed— black, Dennis decided, Kindergarten Black. "I don't see the ocean."

"That's because it's *en passant*. You only show a little

85

part of the thing, so that you, the viewer, trigger your imagination—what you see in your imagination is always bigger than the actual thing."

Dennis would have to agree. The ocean in his mind was bigger than the two inches of blue at the top of the painting.

"It really works," Rigo said. "My painting teacher stimulates me so much. I believe in it." He sighed. "I remember getting show tune albums before I even saw the show. *Les Miserables, Evita, Sweeney Todd.* I would listen and listen, and in my head I had created a fabulous musical, one of those big Busby Berkeley spectaculars. And when I finally saw the show, it was so rinky-dink, I couldn't believe they had such tiny imaginations. Somebody should do a whole Broadway series where the actors just sing one song, offstage, and call it *Evita en Passant, Kiss Me Kate en Passant, Oklahoma! en Passant.* I'd go."

Dennis went from painting to painting. The trouble was, he couldn't even tell what he was supposed to be seeing, *en passant.* Rigo grabbed a canvas from his easel, and a pair of fabric-cutting shears.

"So what I've been doing is painting the whole thing on a big honkin' piece of canvas and then I just get out my scissors and I cut off one piece of it. It's my own technique! The guys down at Sweet Inspiration promised me I could have a show there in November. It gives me something to shoot for."

"It's good to have goals." Rigo leaned over to move

another of his half-finished works. They looked better when they weren't finished, Dennis decided. Rigo's shirt fell open and Dennis stole a look at the shunt doctors had installed in him, to drain fluids from him, the ones that built up in him from the Kaposi's sarcoma. Dennis suddenly realized that he had never seen Rigo express pain—only painfulness: shunts, muddy oils, lesions, bad jokes.

Rigo sat on a wooden cube. Dennis was alarmed that one of them would sit in a gob of wet . . . lip gloss. "Are you feeling empty, Dennis?" Now he had seized upon an unfinished portion of another of his works; how it seemed unfinished was a mystery, especially in a painting purposefully incomplete. "Because I could understand that. We've all been forced to walk away from our religions because they've walked away from us. What does that leave you with? Goll-dang science! And pills? Of course you want more than pills." Dennis looked him over. Rigo was what they were calling, these days, "a Salvage Case," his body a strip mine zone that needed new topsoil and erosion walls. Just the exact number of pills that kept him quick and wouldn't make his liver fall out and stopped the virus from mutating into some newer, fiercer dragon. "Come to yoga class with me. It's hot yoga—it's the rage! And Elliot is the hot hot yoga instructor!"

The naming of Elliot in the air made Dennis notice the name Elliot on the wall. On another canvas, there was written in mascara in big bleeding letters the name

Elliot—otElliotElliotElliotElliotElliotElliotElliot-
ElliotEl—in rows and rows, big, small, cursive, print.
En passant, indeed. He stared at it for so long the name
fell apart in front of him, stopped being a word, became a series of shapes, a body of some sort. This felt
erotic, as if the word had taken off its mask, or clothes.

"I don't want to take classes in soul."

"Oooh, so now you're a biggy-biggy-wow-wow
know-it-all about the soul! Do you see any paintings in
here you'd like? It would be my gift to you."

The idea of having one of these paintings, of dis-
playing one, made Dennis hope his room in the seminary would be very small, no space for art. But then,
how long could Rigo last? He'd show the painting until
Rigo was gone—on loan from the permanent collection. And perhaps, despite everything, this awful stuff
would appreciate in value.

"I like the one that says 'Elliot.'"

"Any painting except that. And what would the
monsignor say if he saw you with my big sexy *Elliot*
portrait?"

Portrait? "I meant the one with Elliot's name written a thousand times."

"So did I. Not available. It's for my show at Sweet
Inspiration."

Dennis felt that softening in himself, which he'd
come to recognize as an event that made him do dangerous things, sign contracts, eat iffy food. "Is painting
good for your soul?" he asked.

"Dennis, I can't begin to tell you. So much to think about, meditate on. I sometimes start to sweat, like I'm doing my hot yoga. Just come to yoga with me, Dennis, or art class. It helps."

"Sure it does, Rigo. But I want something more complete."

Rigo tore at another canvas, tore until he had a piece of painting small enough to patch a hole in blue jeans. There were so many paintings on so many easels and on the floor—he was painting thirty things at once. "More complete? Here's complete. Why do you want something to seem complete? Do you have to find new ways to feel so small? You were saved from eradication, and now you want to be eradicated? Or put into an envelope?" He pointed to a jar of ashes, the ashes of the dead painter from whom he'd inherited his supplies.

Dennis wanted to be part of something. Attached. Attached, okay, offstage, *Dennis en Passant*. But because he didn't pursue Rigo's challenge, Rigo gave up, and instead, told the joke about the man who joined the order of monks with a vow of silence, who could speak only once every seven years. After seven years, he went to the monsignor and he was praised for his good work and adherence to the rules. "Do you have anything to say?" asked his superior. "My bed is lumpy," said the monk, and went back to his cell. Seven more years passed, full of good work and prayer, and the monsignor rewarded him again: "Do you have anything to say?" "The food is terrible." And in the twenty-first year of poverty and silence, during which the monk was exemplary, the monsignor asked him to return a third time: "It's been another seven years. Do you have anything to say?" "The floor is cold on my bare feet." The monsignor then stood, and gravely said, "I'm sorry, but we are going to have to ask you to leave our order." "Why?" asked the incredulous monk.

"And the monsignor said, 'All you do is complain!'" Rigo bumped Dennis down with his hip, chicka*boom* on the punch line, and Dennis landed on a wet mascara brush.

⌒

"There is a gathering of wisdom, and there is a gathering of experience," said Monsignor Hardy, and Dennis knew it was the path of humility and obedience he really needed to learn how to embrace when he thought of the priest in his impeccable cassock, his own future superior: what does this man know about experience? But he gave the posture of obeisance while he noted that the monsignor had the remains of a former handsomeness about him. Dennis wondered if he'd ever let anybody enjoy it. "What does ecstasy teach us? What is it for?"

"Oh well, it's for the soul!" Dennis said too quickly.

"Oh, the soul," said the monsignor, and it could have been sarcasm or disbelief or jealousy or envy; Dennis would never know.

"You would think it would be detrimental, feeling so good, but if you do it right—"

"You're not special here, Dennis," Monsignor Hardy put his hands together in both a prayer and a wall. "You're coming to us aged and alone and damaged."

"Damaged?" He closed his mouth. Savage tribes-people often closed their mouths and pinched their noses to prevent the soul from escaping.

The monsignor held up the manila folder that contained his application, dossier, letters of recommendation, various business. This meeting was about his acceptance into the seminary, the conversation they needed to have about "the calling," as they put it, the voice in a religious man's head. Dennis thought of the tiny magnets in birds' brains that helped them migrate. Was there such a pull toward God for him? Was that what the soul was? Some kind of magnet? There was something calling him, and it might have been God.

Monsignor Hardy put his finger on the line that said "HIV Positive" after flipping about to his State of Health form. "The church will cover these medicines you need. We have one doctor to deal with the several of you with this condition. But don't think yourself superior to us."

Superior? "Superior?"

"Worldliness, self-testing. Ecstasy."

Neither of them said anything. This was a trial, wasn't it? Dennis was supposed to say something reassuring, but he didn't know what it was supposed to be.

Something about memory; perhaps the monsignor didn't understand about memory. There had been an Irish spy, in olden days, Casement, who kept or had planted upon him the "black diaries," records of how many boys he'd slept with in all his travels. To read it was to be bored to death, like staring at notches in a bedpost; it was a useless book except that it was used as evidence against him when it came time to execute him as a counterspy. Dennis had tried to read the pages of this journal and they were rudimentary, inventory: one blond, tall, mustache; red-headed twins, smooth; Persian, from the marketplace—*storyless,* anonymous, not enough of a detail to fill in the rest, to evoke Rigo's *en passant.*

In a certain way, Casement was innocent, unable to recall anything about the encounters, except for tallies of spilled fluids. Dennis was guilty by association, memory of everyone, heapings of pleasure: the blond boy who giggled uncontrollably when he came, the Latino who would engage in only a horizontal position. The man who told him that he never wore a belt, because it was too much to fumble with. They were not always good, but they were always good for a story.

In a storefront church full of folding chairs, at the edge of a swamp with the shoes half-mucked, on a precarious slatted fire escape four stories up, in a hot corncrib, in a tent, its walls flapping in a storm; the fresh breeze under an oak in the wine country, the sticky heat of Rome after even the Pope had abandoned the city, under eiderdown in Christmas Vienna, the man who would not let him touch him there or there, his body a game of Operation, his nose lighting up in alarm when he tried to remove the funny bone or the bread basket; the breeze over sweating skin at midday, the moon and Venus and a small plane in alignment just at dusk and climax, the discovery of some scar in a nether corner of the body—the *discovery*—the screamer, the guilt-ridden, the talented, the cheat, the sad, the drunk, the deaf, the skinny, the fat, the insatiable.

And which one of these was Dennis? What did they remember of him? He did not think he was remembered, for they all the rest of them threw away their dance cards. Some were dead, true, but what hurt Dennis most in the world of promiscuity was the amnesia of it. He remembered and was guilty and they forgot and resumed a blessed innocence, and his used heart was always alone.

Monsignor Hardy had allowed him to be quiet for long enough, and perhaps it was the frown Dennis made at that last thought that made him say, "And you'll have to get rid of most of your things. Or put them in storage. Your room will be very small, and worldly possessions stand between you and the loving contemplation of Jesus Christ."

But this was no task of self-denial, Dennis thought, just a pleasure. He'd been trying to get away from all his stuff for years now, the things, the friends, the sex, the freedom burdens all. But oh, the pleasures, still manufactured by his faculties of memory, another little toxic factory within him not unlike the one that churned out the virus, the result of a life's worth of sybaritic living. There were no pills to take to quell pleasure's memory, because pleasure could not be extricated from pain, wrapped like phages around normal DNA in the same way—kill the virus and kill the patient. But Dennis loved the pleasure and its attending pain: the bee's sting that is the price of honeycomb, tickling, the rose and its thorns, attempting to tell a joke to Isabelle in French, buttfucking, a productive cough, horror films, cracking walnuts to get their meat, the goofy, funny last words of a dying friend, the spectacular crash to the floor of an ornate antique dish.

"Are you sure you want to make this commitment, Dennis?"

⌒

"*Bon jour, Saint Denis!* What time is it there?"

"Not too early, eight hours earlier than you."

"It is still early here. My mothair has not yet opened thee can oav Deenty Moore boeuf bourguignon for thee guests of thee evening."

"Your mother is a scandal. More scandalous than even you."

"Don't say such terrible things, Denis. I do not want to have any competition! I am the most scandalous. Promise me, Denis! That I am the most scandalous!"

"Well, Isabelle, that's why I'm calling."

"What? You are in a scandalous situation? Are you in the prison?"

"No! Why would I be in prison? Do I seem like the kind that would go to prison?"

"I don't know, eet's crazy. Perhaps I have some hope for you."

"Then what I'm about to tell you may seem scandalous to you. I've been accepted into the seminary and I'll finally do it. Next month, I'll begin my studies to be a priest."

"What kind of school? Do they teach you how to pray?"

"I taught myself how to pray, long ago."

"You teach yourself! You would be a great teacher to othairs. That is what you should be. The teacher. Just be the teacher."

"The connection to France is very good. It's like you're right down the street. I have friends down the street who have cellular phones and they sound like they're in France."

"Everybody should have the cellular phone, Denis, then we can always pretend that we are able to talk to many lands far away, even when we are not. To be a teacher is a noble profession."

"Isabelle, teaching isn't enough for me."

"I thought you wanted to be generous. This does not sound like generous."

"Your English is improving, isn't it?"

"You are in trouble. That is the thing, isn't it? What kind of trouble are you in?"

"There's no trouble! I'm not in jail! You sound just like a nurse! Always thinking everybody else is in trouble when you're the ones who need the rescuing. You're the ones getting me into big trouble!"

"So you are in trouble."

"I won't ever be in any kind of trouble when I give up all this troublemaking."

"That is what you think, Denis. It is a pretty idea. But it is too late. In your life there have been too many of the sword fights and dancing in the oubliettes and—beating?—pounding?—hurting? Of the antlers. They will find you, even in prison."

"I'm not going to prison!"

"Monsieur Dunsany is my mathematiques teacher. I love my mathematiques teacher. He loves mathematiques. And he has helped me."

"I will probably be a teacher, too. I'll be a Jesuit. They teach."

"Oh, *merde.* The Jeh-zoo-eets. Now I will not ever speak to you again."

"You'll be able to speak to me. I won't be one of those monks at Saint Roque, hidden away, not talking. I'll still be able to travel with you."

"*Non, non,* I mean that I will refuse to speak to you."

"Because I'll be a Jesuit."

"I know you Jeh-zoo-eets. You will want to hit me with sticks and scream at me and make me write the journals and the poems. I hate the poems. Stupid Jeh-zoo-eets and the stupid poems."

"The Jesuits are different here in the States, Isabelle."

"Oh! When can I come see you in the States?"

⌒

Dennis took Jimmy to the Motherlode. It was a bar in San Francisco's Tenderloin where drag queens, transvestites, transsexuals, and their admirers went to see and be seen. Though in a seedy neighborhood, the Motherlode had a cheerful, old-world charm to it. The men who loved these ersatz ladies were gentle-men. They pulled out a seat for a girl. They bought her a drink. They stood when one entered or exited a room. They yielded the urinal to her.

This was the fantasy, that the women were real and the men were also real—heterosexual. But it was theater, and couldn't exist without the stage where the queens lip-synced pop songs and a special light that hid as much as it revealed.

He had told Jimmy that he'd answered his calling earlier in the day.

"The calling? Who's calling? You have call waiting? I can hold."

Dennis didn't want to say "God is calling" even though that's what he was thinking, that's what was really happening, except that it didn't translate well

97

into the secular language; in that tongue, it wasn't of-
fensive, just tacky, like white belts and tube socks. He
said, "I'm going to enter the seminary."

And Jimmy responded: "You've got to check out the
Motherlode. I'll pick you up at ten tonight. Take a disco
nap in the afternoon. It may be your last." And now that
they were both here, Jimmy said, "If you want to get
into a costume, why don't you become a drag queen?"

~

Since neither of them had a car, Zoe and Dennis took
BART under the bay and stepped directly out of the
Ashby station into the flea market shantytown. The
weather was soft. San Francisco was easy to see but
seemed far away. It felt as if it had been snatched momentarily away from Dennis, or could be escaped easily.

Zoe said, "My parents kept me pretty true to my Ju-
daism. I had no idea there was anything other than
being Jewish, when I was five or six years old. Then
our family took a vacation, I think up to Montreal
or something, and we visited the Church of Saint
Anne de Whatever. My parents decided that the best
way to admit the existence of Christianity was through
tourism—my brother and I would take it in like the
local cuisine, or the birthplace of Lincoln. So imagine
we're walking into this humongous cathedral, all those
steps, all those people sitting around with rosaries in
their hands praying, all that incense, and up there over
the altar is a pretty bloody Christ, writhing on the

cross, blood just everywhere, a look of real emaciated agony just, just *ripping* across his face." She stopped them in their walk, held Dennis by the wrist. "The family story goes, though I don't remember it, that this six-year-old nice Jewish girl—"

"Woman."

"—woman boomed into this silent church with my big Jewish voice, 'What happened to *him*?' We were hustled right outa there, you can bet."

Dennis smiled, and they continued through the aisles of cheap plastic toys, packets of hair nets, and bundles of kitchen utensils. Zoe said the good stuff was all in the back of the lot. "My Jewish friends are loud," he said.

"In the grave it will be silent," she said, which was probably Talmud or Midrash, but Dennis didn't know. As if it were the appropriate way to broach the subject, she said, "So you're really going to become a priest?"

"I like your hair that way," he said to Zoe. It was growing long and so thick it was almost matted. She'd pulled it into a wad at the top of her head with a pencil, and three exhausted neck-curls had fallen out so far.

"I've never grown it out this long before. I feel different."

They were celebrating, the two of them, because the protease inhibitors had continued to work, the study was over, and Zoe had had a second blood test proving that she had not seroconverted. She'd dosed herself daily with AZT for weeks after the catastrophe with the centrifuge. That drug ruined her appetite and burned like poison, but perhaps the virus in the test tubes had all been killed off with those drugs that gave new life to Dennis and Jimmy.

She kept apologizing for the card tables full of aged porno tapes, scratched vinyl record albums, overhandled cassettes, piles of human discontent; she apologized as if she owned them herself. Who would want such things, Dennis wondered, and then repeated the question out loud for Zoe to answer.

She took it personally. "It's like any other love or art, Dennis," she said. "I'm looking to make order out of the disorder. I think it's why forty-niners came to this area all those years ago, panning for gold—finding wealth in the mud." She told him that her favorite thing to do was buy a whole box of books for fifty cents, in hopes that there would be one first edition worth a bundle. "Plus," she said after a pause, "I'm in love." As she said this, they came upon a large truck with a man hauling cardboard boxes out of the deep recesses, dropping them onto the tailgate, where he would transfer them to the card tables all around them.

"I got your call, Cash," Zoe yelled up.

"Hello, Zoe! You're going to be the highlight of my day."

Dennis knew all about it: this guy Cash kept himself in business roving through estate sales during the week, and he could already see that he had classier junk, that they were in the region of classier junk.

While Zoe negotiated with Cash, Dennis ran his fingers over things: this china is crazed, this fabric is crewelled, that frame is dovetailed. Going through a box of antique doorknobs, he sorted out the ones that had big fat many-faceted jewel faces for handles. He wrote names for them on masking tape. "Koh-I-Noor" was one, "Hope," "Moonstone." These diamonds were cursed.

"In the market for some door hardware?" said Cash, grinning, teeth stained, furry, an ancient graveyard of crooked tombstones. He held up a doorknob in a stubby hand, his fingernails painted an unfortunate shade of forest green. His name was Cash, which might have seemed like an affectation, Dennis thought, but was probably just another unvendable casualty of the flea market junkyard, one perfect cufflink, a door-knob without a door. Cash's first name had been weakened from dis- or too much use, snapped off like a car antenna.

He remembered something Zoe once told him: "The clinic also works with the Shoe and Glove Society, a club in which people with a missing limb can find another person with the opposite missing limb, to buy foot and handwear, and split the cost."

Zoe had an eye for the broken, and could make things whole again. "Look what Cash found for me!" she ran to Dennis with a thick, scuffed album. "It's her scrapbook."

"Whose scrapbook?"

"My true love!"

When Cash sidled up, Dennis got a closer look. Parts of tattoos poked out of the sleeves of his shirt, something similar in the corner of his collar, done with the same panache Rigo exhibited in his studio. "Nice tats," he said, because he'd been caught looking.

"You like them?" Cash asked. Though he had a powerhouse of a body, his face was lumpy and swollen, with landscapes of scar and permanent bruise; here, you could drive a truck through one of his pores, there, the skin gripped his skull. "Had this one done in San Quentin. Guy used the E-string from a guitar, took him three months. Hell, I wasn't going anywhere." He was saturated with nicotine and bad breath. What hair he had had not been washed. Dennis found himself resenting Cash, who'd cultivated ugliness with vanity. A peacock more proud of his scaly black feet than his fan of feathers.

"Cash, this is my friend Dennis. He's going to become a priest."

"Well, all right, my man! What's the occasion? Going on the straight and narrow? Once was lost, now was found? Amen to that, bro. What did you do that was so bad you gotta clean up your act?"

"Nothing! Why does everybody think I'm going to prison?"

"I can tell you all about prison. Been in San Quentin. Been in Corcoran. Assisted a priest there in San Quentin and all the guys thought I was a holy man. I'd be in the yard doing exercises, just trying to keep in a warm patch of sun, and the boys would think I was doing some kind of ritual. They stay away from you if they think you're a holy man."

Zoe said, "Cash has been through a lot, haven't you Cash? Drug addiction, gangs. He's got HIV, too."

"You too, man?" said Cash, suddenly eager to shake his blood brother's hand. "Now I see."

No, you don't! Dennis wanted to say, but given the choice of prolonging this conversation with a scoundrel in order to set him straight, or keeping it to the bare minimum, he stayed quiet, or rather, said, "So what have you found for Zoe today?"

"Zo's my favorite customer," Cash said, giving her a squeeze. The first time she'd come there, he explained, she was looking through the bins of old photographs and had come across a photo booth strip, with a pretty girl in the 1940s holding a small dog. In the last of the four pictures, the dog sat alone for the picture, on its hind legs. It was a trick the dog could do.

"The next week I came back, I found a photo of a grown man in a clown suit with five little dogs each standing on a barrel in the same position. I recognize the dog from Clarice's photo strip."

"Clarice?" asked Dennis, "her name is Clarice?"

"That's when Zo here started talkin' to me," said Cash. "It's nice when a pretty lady talks to an ex-con. Makes you feel all fuckin' warm inside."

"Oh, you boys," she said. "I asked Cash to be on the

lookout for any more pictures of the dogs or the pretty girl. I gave him my number, because by then I was in love."

"With me?" Cash said. "You gave me your number because you were in love with me?"

"Oh, you boys."

Slowly, Zoe had accumulated little bits of evidence of Clarice, which was her name because she found a picture of her on a poster advertising a traveling family circus. The man in clown suit, Zoe had divined, was Clarice's father, and trained the little dogs. But Clarice—oh, Clarice. *She* was the main attraction, the contortionist of the circus. In the poster, Clarice was standing on her hands, and her chin rested upon her own crossed legs, flipped backward. "How could I not be in love?" asked Zoe.

And today, Cash had found her the big score: Clarice's scrapbook. The three of them sat on the tailgate of Cash's truck, marveling together. It told a story through photos, yellowed newspaper articles, commemorative cards. It showed Clarice as a little girl just getting started, doing simple acrobatic stunts; after that, a basic highwire act; and then a growing limberness that seemed something only one's ancestors could exhibit in these faraway photos; one needed, it seemed, a flapper's bob in order to fold oneself into an accordion.

There were other stories, too, one about the elephant, Peanuts, who fell in love with a cow in one town they performed in and busted down his stall three times and ran away for his own true love, until the circus family had to buy the cow in order to move on. They had given a glorious series of performances in Cuba. They were interviewed, giving a sense of Clarice's growing fame and, no doubt, a troubled consternation in her own father, whose doggy act was marginalized as his daughter became the toast of the sawdust ring. "How do you like the show business?" an interviewer asked Clarice when she was nineteen years old, and, over Zoe's shoulder, Dennis could see how Clarice was growing weary of it all, the traveling, the never settling down, the wintering in the Wisconsin Dells with other circus troupes, a place one could not call home. In an interview with her father, pasted side by side, the ringmaster grumbled about "giving Clarice the room she needed for her skill and ability."

"He ain't happy about that girl's skill and ability," said Cash.

Zoe turned the page. Dennis read out loud to her, over her shoulder, some poems Clarice had written, doggerel, really, full of pathetic fallacies and syntax as contorted as their author. Clarice had begun to pursue, it would seem, an inner life, and published it in papers where her fame in other artistic feats was known. Dennis thought to himself, I could write better poems than these.

"Isn't it romantic?" Zoe said, and turned the page again.

For five more pages, Clarice had pasted in strip after strip of photo booth photos of herself with all the little dogs, artfully arranged. Many of them featured only her small flexible hand, holding the dog steady, or just an eye, or a lock of hair—she was not the main event, did not want to be so for these pictures. When she did make an appearance among the shots, sometimes she smiled, sometimes she didn't. Her thickly applied lipstick came off black in the black and white photos, as black as her hair. On the last page of these, in a scrap of published newsprint the size of a fortune cookie fortune, glued in upside down so that it might have been missed (for whom? Why would she almost hide this?), Dennis caught one line: "Missing: Miss Clarice Barlow. She was with the Barlow Family Circus. If you know her whereabouts, please contact her mother, care of this paper." And that was all. Zoe turned the page, and they found a photo of the Radio City Rockettes, a glossy eight-by-five, a souvenir, full of posed leggy dames smiling in that same black lipstick. The three of them looked and looked, but none of them could recognize Clarice Barlow. "I think I want to cry," said Zoe, earnestly.

"Most people run away to join the circus," said Cash, who could have been a carny in any traveling attraction.

"I can see how you'd get tired of being in a circus," said Dennis.

Dennis decided Zoe needed some time alone with

her perfect impossible love, so he spent an hour putting some of Cash's junk in order. He thought about Zoe's lucky, fragmented love, as incomplete as Rigo's paintings, only better, and it occurred to him that truncation, foreshortening, had a wonderful romance to it. His previous life, the one where he could almost see the means and time of his death, had an elegant shape to it. Along came the drugs.

He just let Cash talk at him about this and that. After Dennis made the mistake of telling him that they had been in the same study for the same protease inhibitor, Cash felt they had been buds for life.

"I miss that study, man," said Cash.

"Why's that?" Dennis asked, because he did too, but he didn't want Cash to know they had another damn thing in common.

"I miss having my life written down on paper." His words were perfumed with cigarette ash and grease. "I liked somebody keeping tabs on me, I felt *certified*. Proof of purchase, you know, bro? Redeemable at the counter."

Dennis said that he thought he could see his point, but inside he thought, "Oh, you are so very right."

"I want to confess something to you, Father," Cash said, while Zoe's eyes adored her new book, "since I'm a Catholic. I have a secret I need to tell somebody. Promise you won't tell Zo?"

"What's that?" Already offering the sacrament of confession, practicing without a license.

"I've been in some jails, but I've never been in San Quentin. Corcoran neither. Never been in prison. Promise not to tell?"

⌒

An expert here at the Motherlode, Jimmy was happy to explain the masonic details, the way somebody might show the proper way to eat sushi, or judge the quality of a matador. "What I like to do," he said, "is nod and smile a little if one of the girls fools me, even for a moment. That makes them feel good, that they've done really nice work with their makeup and their outfit." He pointed to one over in the corner, a slight white thing in a pink dress. She really could pass, at least in this room. Jimmy nodded and lipped the word, "Pretty." She giggled and blushed and blew him a kiss.

Dennis decided to try it himself. There was a Latina in a smart Marimekko number at the bar. She was petite and not gaudy. Ringlets of hair framed her face. The dress so blue, cobalt blue. Dennis nodded: "Good job."

But she misunderstood the compliment—she stared back at him as if he were her next pickup, one of the men who loved the theatrical story of boy meets girl with a surprise twist at the end.

Jimmy said, "Oh, she likes you. You're already giving off priest vibes. You're forbidden fruit. You should buy her a drink."

Dennis slugged him in the arm, which probably looked very manly to She Who Held Court at the bar.

For twenty minutes he had to stare into his beer, and whenever he looked up, he saw her eyes locked on him like a laser beam.

"Buy her a drink," teased Jimmy.

"Shut up, shut up, shut up," Dennis returned, all lips-over-clenched-teeth. But she did not take a hint. He sensed her urgency. A half hour went by, and the beers had run through him. He needed to pee very badly. But to go to the confusing restrooms meant having to talk to her.

Jimmy used this moment of weakness to address what he believed to be Dennis's madness. He said, "I don't know what you're trying to prove by this, Dennis, but from here, it looks like a circus spectacle."

In the same tone of voice, a short man was hectoring advice to a tall younger man. "Does she pay for her therapy all by herself? Or does her health care provide? Is she making you pay? You shouldn't pay. That's bullshit." The tall younger one at the other end of this was trying to look older, wearing a thrift store trench coat and a porkpie hat—younger, or straighter. The shorter guy with a lot of advice to give was trying to look young—younger, or more important, in the crisp white dress shirt and silk tie investment bankers and photocopy machine repairmen wore. He was tan, evenly tan, tanning-salon tan, so that one could not see so easily how he would never get that bright pink flush along the cheekbone, which that other guy at the table had, and could not hide. "Have you guys come up with a budget? It takes a lot of work to live with somebody. Like, for instance, how are you about dishes in the sink? Dishes in the sink, that drives me nuts."

Dennis couldn't hear what the tall one said, but he guessed: mopey, made-up answers, the answers filled into pop quizzes when a student was not prepared.

"I couldn't take that shit," said the know-it-all. "You sure you want to be with her?"

Jimmy said, "Do you have any idea how hard celibacy really is? I don't think you do. I can't even imagine. It would be like dying. It's how they say birds of prey die not of old age, but because they starve to death. You'll starve, Dennis." Little Miss So-and-So at the bar was still boring holes into his heart, pants, wallet. He could feel it by just stealing glimpses at a little bit of her, the part closest to the floor, the highest heels he'd ever seen.

Dennis suddenly wondered whether the Xerox repairman was talking about a relationship between this lost pink boy and a trannie, a male-to-female, a post-op. Dishes in the sink would be the least of his worries. The guy yammered, "God, you guys have to learn how to sit down and talk things out. Have you talked things out? Have you set up a budget?" And then Dennis suddenly wondered how this guy could be giving advice about relationships when obviously it would be sheer hell being in a relationship with him, like attending the seminar of a self-help guru every damn day of your life.

Years later, Dennis wondered whether he would have listened more attentively to Jimmy's argument against becoming a priest if they hadn't been sitting between ersatz sex and ersatz relationship counseling.

Finally, Cobalt Blueberg gave up with a sigh and a slap on the bar. Dennis watched her stand and mix into the crowd, and he saw her make her exit onto the Tenderloin streets. His bladder wouldn't wait any longer, and he excused himself for the men's room.

"Excuse me," he said, nearly running into somebody. There were mirrors everywhere in this bar. They were wall-sized mirrors. The walls *were* mirrors. They made this hole-in-the-wall saloon look silvery and palatial, and the girls looked special, too, in the dim twinkly light. He had nearly run into a wall, and said again, to his own reflection, "Excuse me." He hadn't even recognized himself.

Halfway to the john, he felt the hand on his shoulder. "Hello, Dennis. You don't remember me, do you?"

He turned at his name. It was his girlfriend, all smiles, nails, long, long lashes. "Remember you?"

"I'm Monica, but you know me as Miguel."

Dennis keened his eyes to gaze at her, the way he went about recognizing himself reflected in that estranged way in the huge mirror, odd yet familiar. "Miguel?" Seven years before, he had dated for a few months a man who swam in his lane at the YMCA. He was strong and bony, with a bow and arrow tattoo next to his left nipple that may or may not have been executed with a ballpoint pen. Miguel worked in a bookstore, was well read. On each date, he lavished upon Dennis gift books.

He told Dennis he was pre-op but mostly ready for the complete change (did Dennis momentarily grab his right nipple, responding to the ghostly twinge of scalpeled flesh?). Miguel had breasts and estrogen and a pearly little clutch purse. He conceded this: as Monica, his face was best suited. Her cheekbones were high and almost to the sides of her close-set eyes. Her mouth was small and her nose, too, all in a quiet line down the center of her economical face. "And are you still working at the bookstore?"

"Oh no," said Monica. "I'm a maid at the Hyatt."

She had taken the whole package, the fantasy cruise, and disappeared into the woodwork, evaporated into thin air. She had all the accessories for being a woman except the last thing, which was, for Dennis anyway, merely academic.

She put a soft hand on him. She probably wore gloves while she cleaned. "What about you, Dennis? How is life treating you?"

Dennis decided and said, "I'm a priest now."

Decadence

Santa Clara, California, November 1995

From the window of his simple room in the Jesuit seminary, Dennis watched the stones that made up the building opposite become polka-dotted with intermittent rain. Even here in Santa Clara, California, the trees looked dead—blown in a uniform direction like lines of fright wigs. Over the ocean, which he made a point to go to as often as was allowed, he liked to watch the sunlight stream through rushing cloud banks onto the water, like klieg lights searching for enemy planes.

It had been raining more and more these past few years. Dennis recalled not seven years before when that long drought in San Francisco had forced him to shower next to a bucket, using the extra water to flush. He missed lack. Even now, the habits of that time were still with him, and he never flushed the toilet if he didn't have to, even, absentmindedly, at Rigo's last-hurrah party—"If it's yellow, let it mellow," he'd told a fellow seminary student, gangly lolloping Danny, a twenty-two-year-old who'd attended alongside him. Danny thought this catchphrase deliciously naughty and hysterical.

"I love poetry," he said, when Dennis added the concluding verse about brown flushing down.

Dennis knew Danny didn't conserve water because he always showered at the same time in the morning and Dennis would be in, out, and nearly finished shaving at the big dormitory mirror when Danny finally stepped out of the stall, tall, lanky, and hunched, inverted for Dennis in the mirror's reflection.

Danny was some kind of reflective opposite in many ways, youth to Dennis's age, voracious when Dennis felt sated, terrified while Dennis had little left to fear.

Dennis remembered the first time he became aware of Danny. In the morning, they'd get up before dawn for matins, no light yet through the stained glass and no other source but a few candles on the altar. Dennis had dragged himself to the place among the pews where the other seminary students congregated in a loose group. After all, this was a time of silent prayer, yet even when one was alone, some sort of vague need to be together made magnets of people, even the most misanthropic of them. Dennis had seen the attraction on lone stretches of deserted freeway when four cars would bunch together with nothing else forever, before and after.

That first day Dennis took a pew just behind his superior, the only silhouetted head he could recognize in the dim cavern. Monsignor Hardy was letting his hair grow long. In the candlelight, his forehead gleamed like wax fruit. Not a minute later, another student entered Dennis's pew and sat oddly too close to him. In a movie theater, Dennis would have considered the move an attempted pickup. Perhaps the guy was European; they had different ideas about personal space (Isabelle, in the crowded coach with the Dutch couple, on an otherwise empty train!).

Then Dennis realized why this unknown man in the dank was pushing the accepted cultural norms—he smelled alcohol. The guy was inebriated! And in church! And before dawn! Perhaps he'd gotten pickled the night before and the hooch reeked through his pores. It was a processed alcoholic smell, unpleasant, unhealthy.

Dennis's sense of smell was always strong in the morning. Even now, with the layers of incense, smoke, and candle tallow, this new smell was like a shout, an inappropriate word—"What happened to *him*?"—on hallowed ground.

Oh God! And there was Monsignor Hardy! He'd think it was Dennis, the new guy, who was a lush. And so would all the other seminarians within smell-shot. To pray, to concentrate now was hopeless.

He wanted to exude his own odor to make it clear that he was sober, soapy, even. Smell was an amorphous cloud. Sight and sound came in rays, offending pains of ear, eye, even finger came like needles. The blunter the smell, the more awful.

Who was this guy? An alcoholic who'd turned to God to find some kind of control or replacement? How sad, how very last resort. Dennis recalled how all the psychology majors in college were the most screwed up, trying to find their diagnosis in class. What sort of priest would this guy make? He'd be into the sacramental wine in no time; when his parishioners started burdening him with their troubles, he'd have to numb himself to the pain.

Dawn came, hit the stained glass mosaic pieces, and they seemed to melt like icicles. They had the delicious sparkle of windowpane candy.

After a handful of Hail Marys the light came in full bodied, a wine. Dennis dared to look to his left at the drunkard. A kid! Tall, stooping, Dennis could see somehow that he wasn't inebriated at all, but steady, perhaps even a teetotaler type. How could he see that even in the dimness? It was the posture of inexperience, the bowed head of undivided attention, the untried muscles of a man whose mind was more cared for than the body.

And then: it wasn't liquor at all—the smell of blotto was actually the smell of rubbing alcohol—oh dear!—of acne medication. The boy was struggling with pimples.

And after all those overlong showers, Dennis would watch Danny pale and sunken and slouching at the mirror, rubbing the astringent medicine over his face and forehead with a cotton ball and, when he thought Dennis wasn't watching, his shoulders and chest, too.

"Do you think I'm vain?" he said, once, when he realized he was being watched.

Oh, moral issues. Dennis was now faced with a daily contemplation of them, though usually this was painless, a voyage without an end, round and round and round the mind could wrap around the deadly sins, the virtues, the mysteries, the glories, freed from having to actually participate in the laboratory of their activity. Dennis loved praying the rosary, the here-we-go-around-the-mulberry-bush endlessness of it, he could pray forever.

But if somebody asked him whether he was being vain, and by corollary asking whether he were sinning, Dennis would rather not answer.

"As I remember, acne can be very painful," said Dennis. He looked at Danny's face as if he needed to in order to figure out whether the guy really was sinning. It allowed him to wonder, is he cute or is he homely? Two older gay men in his dormitory said that Danny was "definitely a babe," but Dennis wouldn't believe these guys. They were confusing youth with beauty, which Dennis tended to do as he got older, since both were things equally out of reach. But Dennis liked to look at a face and try to guess what it would look like after it had aged.

He'd had practice at this, seen so many good friends age before his eyes, shrivel and compress, wrinkle and gray and die, all before their time. Death, when realized through HIV, was a Hollywood special effects

117

scene of rapid deterioration. He would study death in his own face, contemplate it in the same bathroom mirror from which he spied upon water-wasting Danny. Was that vanity?

Danny looked goony, so tall and stooped and thin; he had droopy turtle eyes and bangs, thin hair (thin but not thinning; his forehead was a short, almost Neanderthal overhang) that looked as if it grew in small tufts, installed as it is in cheap dolls. His face was flat against the bone, and would have looked impassive if it weren't always rearranging itself in exaggerated expressions—eyebrows, ears, nostrils, lips all had their mechanical rotations.

Dennis, on the other hand, had over the years become poker faced, fierce. These were the days before he grew the beard in order to hide the severity. And many of the other seminary students thought him too, as he overheard one guy observe in a hallway, "ummm, *dark*."

But good jokes are best told by the deadpan, and when Dennis told Danny that when it was yellow, he ought to let it mellow, drought or no, Danny laughed and adored Dennis's straight face.

Yes, adored, in hindsight, it was true, though Dennis didn't think Danny was gay. He was somehow sexless, or, as the mirror inversion would have it, Danny might be keeping under wraps a reservoir of desire, building dikes and levees and canals in order to transform the flowing water of want into something else—namely, study, and as an occasional treat, poetry: "If it's brown, flush it down."

Danny adored Dennis's world-weariness, he even listened with pleasure to the lost-sheep-found stuff of a man who'd had sensual pleasures to excess, the sex, food, and drink. "What was it like?" he asked, not in so many words, "what do you recall?"

What Dennis recalled were numbers, unless he forced himself to conjure all those sensual episodes. He was a calculator full of facts and figures, estimated body counts. Without even trying, he was teaching Danny a lesson; he was an effortless moralist.

"And travel, man, you've been everywhere," Danny would say when Dennis, perhaps vainly, recalled the last-hurrah trips with Jimmy.

"You would like Isabelle," Dennis said to Danny once, telling him all about France and Saint Roque.

"I don't know," he said, as if he were being forced to make a decision about this.

"Don't get me wrong," said Dennis, "I don't usually like the French." He told Danny about the arrogant ticket sellers at Gare du Nord who slammed their windows shut on his feeble French, of the unbelievable chauvinism, even in Isabelle, when she asked him earnestly, on that first trip to Languedoc, "Do you have fruit in your country?"

When Jimmy and Dennis left the chateau, great friends with Isabelle and of Jana the dog and all the family, Isabelle's mother had handed her card to Dennis and said that they must come to France again but that she did not need his address because after all, "I never have to publicize my chateau and I will not need to see your country ever." No, Dennis told Jimmy on the plane ride home, nor would they get a Christmas card.

The food, the wine, the cheese, the artistes, these French things are worthy of praise, Dennis told Danny, "but in general, the French are abominable."

"I don't like them either," said Danny. This bothered Dennis, despite its being said in solidarity. Danny couldn't be sure of liking Isabelle, whom he had never met but whom Dennis swore by, but Danny could dismiss an entire population he had never encountered. How could a person know the difference between good and bad without first investigating it?

"I do like Baudelaire," Danny said, and seemed to prefer all the indulgent decadent writers and painters, Rimbaud, Odilon Redon. *"Luxe, calme, et volupté,"* Danny recited, enraptured, from "Invitation au Voyage," a poem Dennis considered a dreamy, deadly, mocking paean to travel, which Danny had done none of, "What more could you ask for?"

Sometimes Dennis thought Danny was practicing to be some kind of mystic, a Teresa of Avila or something, a guy who might go into a trance when he should be making soup. But mostly, the kid was bookish. Because he'd read twice as much as Dennis in half the time, Dennis was embarrassed.

It was the only thing Dennis was competitive about in seminary, and it had been the uncompetitive nature of seminary that was perhaps the biggest reason he stuck it out. After a whole adult life living in San Francisco, the City of Thirty-Year-Olds (where did they go after thirty? Marriage, suburbs, death), of jockeying for position, keeping up in all those ways with the Joneses, he was thrilled and pacified to join older men who had let that oily film that was anxious drive burn off. There was *luxe, calme, et volupté*, somehow, in long prayer and in men in no big hurry to get from mass to dormitory to refectory, but got there all the same.

Seminary was a stark place with a disembodied warmth, not anything spiritual so much as mechanical, heat caused by regular function that might grow cold if the general mechanics were to close down. Dennis found a pleasure to this impersonal heat, the purr of the heavy zipper on his rucksack every morning, the heaving and stuttering of the water pumping through the pipes when Danny squandered water in the shower and Dennis shaved.

The rooms they lived in might have depressed Dennis ten years before. When Danny stopped by one evening to see that there was no difference among the tiny cells, each one big enough to handle a bed, a single-burner stove, a sink, and a closet with a rough ugly brown curtain, Danny had said, "I see you're also living in a Jean Rhys novel."

Dennis luxuriated in one-upping his literature: "Last stop for May Bartram," deadpan again, but added, "Do you think glibness is a sin?"

Maybe not, but on most, it went unappreciated. Danny, however, enjoyed it.

"I've brought you Baudelaire," he offered, his excuse for dropping by that day. He had his finger marking a page, and he read from it. "'There are but three beings worthy of respect: the priest, the warrior, and the poet. To know, to kill, and to create.'"

Dennis took it from him. "Well, two out of three ain't bad. So do you always read such racy stuff?"

"Oh no, it gets me too hot and bothered." He said Baudelaire was his reward for reading Aristotle, Heraclitus, Saint Augustine. "And when I want to avoid drama altogether, I read older French formal poets." Danny loved the ordered rhymes of sonnets and the evolving repetitions of villanelle. This was the first time Dennis had heard of water songs. Danny had given him some to read and translate, and because they were so simple, Dennis understood the French. "They're good for us," said Danny, "for anybody who talks too much."

Did Dennis talk too much? At night, or even during prayers, Dennis's mind wandered to Danny, his eagerness. A boy his age and with such a mind had no business shutting himself away, at least not yet. He was all aquiver. So much a mirror version of somebody like Isabelle, who was a target, wide open, drawing fire.

Dennis decided Danny was secretly afraid of something in the world.

Ultimately, the two of them could only be so close. There was a wall between them, for Danny could talk only about books. When Dennis pressed him for information about his life, he was silent. Dennis thought Danny was being secretive for a short time. But then he guessed that, for the most part, there had been no personal life. Or a horrible, chaotic one full of screaming parents and unpaid bills.

For that brief time, Danny and Dennis grew together and Dennis would never say it aloud but he hoped he'd found for himself an experience of agape, of teacher and student, but what he really wanted to teach Danny was the need to live, at least for a while, a profligate life. Such a deeply religious idea!

Oh, but Danny would turn out just fine, he thought. He'd be incomplete, sure, full of academic knowledge and an appreciation of love and other passions gained only through troubadour lyrics and novels rather than experience, so he'd have compassion for sinners, perhaps even idealize their sins. Artificial flowers could be prettier, less blemished, at least, than real flowers.

And how could Dennis have ever been the one to convince Danny to go out and livelivelive? Early on he'd admitted, or narrated, the fact of his HIV status, to which Danny had responded (not in so many words), "How romantic," and wanted to know all the ways it had changed him, made him tick. But such an example of liveliveliving would tend to scare a guy off it.

Dennis felt like a crepuscular jade who'd run out of avenues for pleasure after ruining his stomach on too-rich food and hard drinking, disease-ridden sex. Compared to others he knew, he'd been conservative—but now he'd be the village priest, sitting behind the confessional screen discrediting sins: "You were mean to your sister? Sugar, that's *nothing.*" "Didn't clean your kitchen? Granny, those scouring chemicals are bad for the environment." "No, my dear, in fact, you're not vain enough." There would be a kind of pleasure egging others on, but perhaps that would have to be done anonymously.

The friendship ended some months later, when an aspect of Dennis's dyspeptic past was truly applied to Danny's own world. For once, there was benefit from bad judgment.

Danny came out of the shower stall one morning and grumbled, applying his astringent, "I think I've caught a toe fungus from these showers."

Dennis looked down to study it. "Just like mine!" he smiled. "The problems of adulthood. And it's hard to knock a fungus out, sometimes it's impossible. I've kept it at a minimum but the medicine for toe fungus is rough on your liver so, seeing as I'm already rough on my liver with all the miracle drugs, I can't take it. Death or toe fungus, that's the choice for me."

Danny frowned, admiring his own bulbous toe.

"But I'll tell you the secret cure Zoe told me about. I think it works. Pee on your toe in the shower every morning."

Danny looked at him with horror and dismay. Silently, he toweled off and left. Dennis watched this briskness, could see the boy thinking, "Human contact is poisonous, all of it, I'm better off a hermit in a hut." Had Dennis been too familiar? Were bodily functions so completely out of Danny's experience or vocabulary? Or maybe he blamed Dennis for spreading the toe fungus? Such a young boy, to be having a toe fungus.

Oh, the kid should've gotten over it: everything was communicable, in the end, especially in a place where there was little privacy. Isabelle had been so impressed with the idea of privacy in the United States, the pictures she saw of backyard patios and the unshared bedrooms of children. When Dennis had entered seminary, he feared losing his privacy, but quickly learned he felt alone enough in the presence of the other students of the seminary—in the showers, in the church, in the classrooms.

In fact, he felt that in the lack of privacy there was a kind of luxury. They were second-class citizens by the looks of tiny Jean Rhys rooms, by impoverished economies: a small excursion airline subletting terminal space, which meant one man handled the baggage, the peanuts and pretzels were off-brand, the wings were painted dull insane colors like yellow and orange, meant to suggest a quick getaway to sun and sea.

125

Dennis didn't feel responsible for Danny's toe fungus.

Later that afternoon, he was called into the monsignor's office. "It's come to my attention, Dennis, that you've been getting along well with Danny. You enjoy each other's company."

It was calm there, too—a shelf of books, antique hymnals, and calfbound Bibles with a soft beam of light carved up by the leaded colored image of Saint Ignatius Loyola stretched along the spines, the disjointed image that Silly Putty revealed of a comic book character.

The monsignor was speaking gently of the good of camaraderie, of sharing thoughts and prayers. The way he spoke reminded Dennis of a time when he was in the third grade and was called to the principal's office to see Mrs. Sherwin. He had not been interested in kickball or the monkey bars in grade school recesses. He'd taken a girl named Laura out into the grass behind a big tree and kissed her, all experiment, all more important than games. Playground monitors must have seen him and not known how to handle such grown-up activity instigated by such a young boy.

He'd been sitting in front of Mrs. Sherwin, a bulgy woman with wattles of flesh, arms and legs in segments like clay tied tight with dental floss, all swinging out of her Soviet-realist sack dress. "This . . . touching . . ." she was trying to describe it, and Dennis did not try to help her out, "isn't appropriate, not at your age." She described it and yet could not say exactly why it was wrong, but she made Dennis admit that it was, and before he knew it, she was spanking him with the big wooden paddle, the one she used on bullies—gently, but still, it had shock value, for Dennis was known as an impeccably good boy.

Now Monsignor Hardy was doing the same. "There are some who aren't comfortable with your closeness with Daniel Converse. I'm asking you to do me a favor. Will you try to spend some time apart?"

"Of course," said Dennis. That was easy.

"And please say a novena to contemplate the sin of it."

Dennis did spend quite a bit of time apart from Danny: the rest of it. And he spent a long time thinking about it in his Jean Rhys room. Dennis and Danny were not homosexual lovers, no, but Danny might have found his faith shaken if he had come upon open Isabelle.

She would have really screwed him up, Dennis fantasized. She'd have made of Danny's life something out of a bodice ripper, or a Mitteleuropean existential tale of horror. She would have slipped into Danny's cell and forgotten her panties or stolen Danny's own underwear, and Danny would have crumbled, easy as that. Dennis sat around for a little while and conjured these scenes for himself now and then, Isabelle teaching Danny how to kiss when he was supposed to be at vespers, her expecting a posy of wildflowers slipped through the fence

127

of the seminary, his Abelard-like letters of yearning, her growing disinterest, his broken heart—yes, and *then* he could become a priest, then he'd know for sure. Dennis wished he could have been so selfless as to provide Danny with Isabelle.

Religious Experience
Minneapolis, January 1999

He could see Mary Jane Draper through the front porch window, ungainly, determined, and dangerously perched on a stepladder. This made Dennis Bacchus wonder who was supporting whom. It made him laugh to think about this new life, in which he spent the better part of his mornings doing just what they'd said he'd be doing: guessing how many angels could dance on the head of a pin.

Mary Jane wasn't dancing, nor was she angelic, but what made angels angels? He'd been reading Dante's *Paradiso,* the first time ever, that story of storyless perfection. He was near the end, and all the angels were dancing around and around the warm light that was the Face of God. "The light of God illumines all of the angels each in a different way," he read, "and this is why (because affection follows the act of knowledge) the intensity of love's sweetness appears unequally." There were better angels than others, Dennis realized—the closer to God, the brighter they were. And how to get closer to God? Apparently, good deeds.

He put the book down, drank skunky black coffee. He was concerned. Mary Jane, even she, was taking down the Draper family Christmas decorations: that's how long ago the holidays had passed. It would take her all day, and the undertaking coincided with a decision on his part to end his own last little yuletide holdover, to put it away, himself, to do a good deed.

He checked her again. There she was on the head of her pin, unstringing her first drape of lights. He made these periodic glances because he had set her day's task as a measure of his own, a deadline, a race against him she didn't know she was competing in. Then she caught him glancing, and the world shifted: he felt of himself her boss.

So he opened the window and said, "Where did you get those extra wise men?" and he had to be careful not to seem to accuse her of sinning—for she was a member of the altar society and one of her sons was still an altar boy. But they'd had him over for Christmas dinner, so they were familiar with one another.

"At the Schmelzer garage sale—an incomplete set," she said, and pulled up a particle board Rudolph by its pronged stakes. "Two babies, though!" Dennis was learning that here there were hierarchies of nobility, and that true wealth was found in those who had so much stuff that they cycled through possessions, in Goodwill bins, church jumbles, eBay. The Schmelzers were royalty. They brought in the most money for the Saint Matthias bazaar back in October, when Dennis had first arrived.

The Draper house was also blessed. So many of everything, stuffed in the nooks and crannies of their brick bungalow—jolly snowmen in each window, full sleigh and reindeer on the roof (although Santa reappeared here, in the attic window, an apparent hostage, and here, in jointed cardboard at the door, and here, on the front step as a figurine, a doorstop), and lights, lights everywhere. She had turned it all on so she could make sure not to miss any, and the day was gloomy, and what tired January rays hit this part of the planet couldn't even attempt to pierce the veil of clouds, so that frantic trills of red and green and white made Mary Jane's house look like a casino, or bordello: something belonging in Nevada. With a string lassoed from her hand to her elbow, she seemed a power source for the twinkle. If his periodic glances were quick enough, the lively blinking made it easy for him to pretend she was putting them up rather than taking them down— and that bought him time to accomplish his own task. Another sip of the coffee and he said, "You have your work cut out for you."

And she said, "And Les will be so disappointed if I don't do it now while he's at work—he never wants me to take them down. He'd just start drinking if I rubbed his nose in it. Besides, it's supposed to snow today, finally."

Her husband, Les, had been out on this same stepladder the day after Halloween, pulling down cardboard skeletons with eyelets for joints and Frankenstein faces. Yes, faces, because Mary Jane and Les were cut from the same cloth, the sort who benefited most from the more-is-more of American plenty, who knew that the only thing scarier than a Frankenstein face taped to the window was *five* Frankenstein faces taped, in regimental order, to the living room window. For now, two sets of illuminated nearly life-size wise men, six in all, sat in the winter-brown grass obstructed from epiphany only by Saint Nick himself, who glowed in less sober robes, naughty, tarted-up in all his red gluttony.

The present for Jimmy, which had migrated from under Dennis's modest Christmas tree to a place separate from the display of his own unwrapped loot to the top of the spice rack in the kitchen when the tree came down, had to be moved again to make sure it wasn't spattered by kitchen work. He was sure he was going to see Jimmy during the holidays, all the lost found, and even though he was in San Francisco, which Dennis was glad to leave for a while, Jimmy's mother lived two towns over here in Minnesota, and Jimmy had promised to visit. Then in October, Jimmy's mother died. And the get-together, the holiday drink, did not happen. Now even Epiphany was past, and, like the plastic wise men in Mary Jane Draper's yard, the gift would not reach its hallowed recipient.

⌒

"Can I get you anything while I'm on the town, Mary Jane?" he asked, but she said she was just fine, thanks. It was ten thirty. Now he was on the street in his hopeful boots, even though they trod on blanched grass, tender inside, brittle with hoarfrost outside. He had a list of errands and one grand goal.

Dennis Bacchus was landlocked in Minneapolis, about as far away from the ocean as anywhere. Brick bungalows instead of Victorians, hunkered down close to the ground, wise little pigs, permanent pigs, rather than the giddy ones making their houses of sticks in San Francisco. Not even seagulls, but crows, which bent on the tips of oak branches like the withered plugs of unpicked fruit. They screamed bad advice to each other and passersby. There'd been no snow yet. Forecasters were calling for it today, almost with ecstasy; people here seemed to thrive on harshness. Me too, thought Dennis. "Now that I am a representative of the church," he said out loud but to himself, as if he had escaped something.

Back There, where Jimmy still lived, it was carnival. Here, he had a job to protect parishioners like Mary Jane and Les from a certain kind of danger—sin, poison ivy, temptation, snapping turtles, tent worms, bald snow tires, secular humanism; one of Mary Jane's daughters had told him that they always reserved a page in the high school yearbook to be dedicated to whatever boy was killed in a farming accident. Faith had to be sour, a leavening for plentitude.

He wished it would snow, too. Something had to be done to shake off this feeling of *stuck,* this after-Christmas *saudade.* It seemed that any enterprising blues singer could make a fortune writing laments about January, but perhaps that same tar pit sucked all the singing out of people, too. Dennis said so to his barber, Jay, who ran the Original Palace Barber Shop ("All Styles").

He'd ducked in when he saw nobody waiting in the extra chairs, because he hated feeling shaggy, and Jay, despite having his business in what was once a massive, airy showroom for luxury automobile sales, was cheap, cheap, cheap—twelve bucks!

Dennis, in the fifteen years of his nonclerical life, had always gone to a salon, dropped a wad. Now he went to barbers, and loved this new thing, too. Aging men lolling about on stacks of dated newspapers, the piles of hair, the friendly sniping, the scissors snipping. The fleet of five barbers fought over the men who came in cold, but it was a posturing game, puffed up peacocks bred to breed more peacocks.

"We're in the same line, aren't we, Padre?" said Jay, who was Lutheran, fastening the smock around Dennis's neck. "Always hearing confessions." He snipped a bit, combed it again, snipped again, not apparently ready to *act.* "Years of them." Whenever somebody put scissors down or spoke, the sound reverberated, because they had the entire barber shop huddled at the front of the car showroom, leaving acres of empty space to let sound ring and amplify and distort; it seemed only natural, in a world of too much plenty, as it seemed natural for guests at a house party to congregate in the tight steamy confines of the kitchen, leaving the living room empty.

"I'm pretty new at this," Dennis admitted, and realized he felt shame for being so green. He'd stopped studying his image in the mirror and looked now at the floor at shocks of hair, apostrophes quoting the floor tiles. His eyes trailed to a stack of 1972 *Penthouse* magazines. Up, to the fuzzy black and white television showing game shows. Over, to the faded photo placards in the windows, the framed testimonials. Unsold bottles of high-end shampoo, five nonfunctioning credit card machines, an eye-dropper full of mineral oil for the clippers, a bowl, a disused strop. "And mostly, I just teach at the university."

"No, you won't betray your race if you become a priest," Jimmy had said, over the din, when Dennis had broken the news to him years before while they debated the choice surrounded by the trannies of the Motherlode: I'm going to seminary. "But you'll be wasting your time. You'll be one of the clergy who sits around arguing over how many angels can dance on the head of a pin, crap like that." Maybe another reason Dennis was avoiding Jimmy now. Dave, the organist at Saint Matthias, and Dennis had been reading *The*

Divine Comedy together, and while the *Inferno* had been a romp (Dennis had found a place for himself at nearly every circle of hell, a schismatic like Mohammed, lustful as Paolo and Francesca, a thief, a glutton, a fence-sitter, a politically cunning animal, and of course, a sodomite. Only simony and suicide remained), *Purgatory* was a slog and *Paradise,* while pretty, was inert. Or so Dennis had decided, until Dave disagreed.

"Look at the angels close to God," he recommended. "They're spinning around so fast they create a kind of music of the spheres, and some spin faster when they approach God, and some go slower, depending on who knows God better."

Dave heard music, Dennis saw light. Here in Minneapolis, Dennis had met many exotics, like Les and Mary Jane, like Dave the organist, like Jay the barber. Between Mary Jane's yard decorations and Jay's scissors, he'd even encountered African American Hare Krishnas, who explained, to a girl he passed while walking along a lake, the basics of reincarnation: "You be ant, you be good ant, you die, you come back pig. You be good pig, you die, you come back human. You eat pig, you *be* pig."

The girl had not been convinced. "How can you be a good ant?"

The brother shrugged his saffron-clad shoulders. "You do good ant *things.*"

Is goodness, Dennis wondered now of Dante's vision of the angels, as Jay used the electric clippers, based only on deeds? As usual, Dennis felt more comfortable among the sinners—even in heaven, he felt sympathy for the dimmest ring of angels around heaven, who spun slower; it was the best good that he could do, sometimes, to recognize goodness, if not commit acts of goodness. This was the counting of angels. This was the contemplative life.

Jay said, "I'm okay about the confessions, Padre. I bet people don't know why you'd go and become a priest at this point in your life, but I get that. I used to be a mortician, can you believe that? I've always been a people person. I respect you and your relationship with God. Except, I'm sorry, Padre, but I just like the ladies too much."

Dennis smiled. This caused some snippings to tumble a little down his face, making his nose itch. "It's not as tough as you think."

Since Dennis made himself seem open to the question, Jay felt free to be tactless. "So I've always wondered. What do you do about the sex thing, Padre?"

The question was casually asked, as if the answer didn't matter, as if it would be just another confession. The question went out into the barren showroom like a kite in a strong headwind, in need of a tail, rattling this way and that, charging into the air and down to the ground, ready to fly apart soon. So Dennis said, "I stare at words on a page until they don't make sense anymore."

Jay didn't tell him this was a weird thing to say, but

he began to cut his hair faster. Dennis regretted saying it, but only because he liked a nice long haircut. Anymore, it was the only time Dennis could be touched by another man. It was a time to gossip with men, to have a man run his fingers through his hair. To be vain for a moment, and look into a mirror and study himself, and get a glimpse of the back of himself.

He did not want a nosy barber. He valued his privacy as much as anybody. But Jay was part of the little-celebrated community of the semistranger. Dennis was just like him for that reason, too. The friendship with Jay was the most distant of sorts, one of the dimmer rings of angels in his personal heaven. Jay didn't even know Dennis's name. But Jay knew *of* Dennis. He could tell by the friendly nod of recognition, the hand ushering him into the chair. Jay the barber was somebody who smiled and said, good to see you're still alive, and yes, you got your haircut someplace else last time and yes, you're still losing your hair, but don't worry, because I'd notice if something were *really* wrong. Anything more would be presumptuous, or sleazy.

When he was through cutting, Jay held a hand mirror out to Dennis, so that he could inspect the work. "Hello, my nape," said Dennis. And then, "It looks great tapered instead of blocked." It was the first time he had had it tapered instead of blocked for many years. Jay had talked him into it. Dennis had said, "You don't think it will make me look like I'm trying to look young?"

Now Jay said, "You look more natural this way." He kept the mirror up longer, as if he expected Dennis to study it for a while.

But Dennis didn't like looking too long. Now he was thinking about the big sheet mirror that covered the entire wall against the bank of barber chairs, all filled with men his age, all getting cuts. There was a wall of mirror on the opposite side, too, where the barbers kept their scissors in little surgical green baths. The light and images bounced between the two opposing mirrors and reflected back and back as images echoed into infinity, head upon head upon head, an army of men getting haircuts. The reflections at the deepest telescoped point were bathed in green like the instruments, and Dennis was struck with a notion—it was only at such a distance, after the first image had been copied a hundred times, deep down in the most distorted depths, that the true nature of the overhead light, neon or halogen or whatever they put into those long tubes, the true quality of the light, the true color, was revealed. It was green. They were living in green light all the time, and they never knew it. "Look how green the light in here really is," Dennis said to Jay. "Sometimes you have to get some distance on a thing to get the truth of a thing."

One of the men down at the end of the row of chairs was talking to his barber. He said, "Well, those Florida Gators just pissed me off this year."

Dennis had thought he had said, "Well, those fornicators just pissed me off this year." He figured it out when the other barber said, "They need new coaches." Jay had smoothed his new hair down with a spicy pomade, but Dennis put a hat on top of it. He overtipped Jay, and waved to everybody as he walked out.

～

Snow was beginning to fall as he stepped out of Jay's. He'd smashed down his new haircut with the hat, but once he was out of eyeshot of the barbershop, he took his hat off again. The sensation of cold air running across his exposed scalp thrilled him. Soon, he was shivering, and he put his hat on again. It wasn't enough— he felt chilled through now, and needed to warm up. He was going to head for the post office with the little package, he had a piece of paper with Jimmy's address wrapped around it, all he'd have to do is slip it into one of those mailers they dispense, and it would be done. But now he realized that he was going to walk right by the university, and the university had a gym, and he had a free membership because he taught one class there this semester. They had a pool, and also a dry and wet sauna. Small bits of hair had fallen onto his shoulders and into his ears, and a warm shower and a rest in the steam room seemed both a kind of reward and a sensible thing to do. Jimmy's present would have to wait. And an idea was paddling back more often, now that he had thought of it: Shouldn't he unwrap it and keep it for himself?

At the gym, they gave him two towels. They gave him a locker key. That practice reminded him of the old bathhouses, only now he was a representative of the church, now it was a college gym. With men twenty years younger than he. They were taking off their clothes all around Dennis. He kept his eyes on his own hands, but the glow of their skin, a kind of solar tawniness persisting even in the dead of winter, caught his eyes. How could an angel not gravitate to the sunny face of God, he wondered. He thought all sorts of things like this in order not to think about sex. He thought about Mary Jane and knew he was behind her in their imagined race, because she'd have the lights all down by now and at least one set of wise men twisty-tied into lawn-clipping-sized garbage bags, and he thought about Jimmy's undelivered gift—so pathetically small, really, not worth sending on—and the practice of mailing a present seemed an insult, especially now, an afterthought.

Wrapping the towel around his own stringy haunches, he tiptoed toward the showers. Confident undergraduate boys slapped their feet; *they* would never slip and fall. If they fell, they wouldn't hurt so much and the bruises would heal sooner. It wasn't the pain of growing older that bothered Dennis, it was the ability to remember the prior elasticity that had informed his own body.

When he was a boy on Whidby Island he used to go to a beach that was stony where the water lapped. He loved the feel of those stones under himself, worn round by waves, each one fitting like an egg into the arches of his feet. He would walk on those stones, then. He would run on those stones, he would "scamper," as they called it, something only small dogs and welterweight children can do. A year ago he'd been back to the island, taken off his shoes, and walked along those stones. He could barely stand it, the pain shooting up through his legs as the stones bit to the bone, his own weight pressing him ever down on what might as well have been jagged fields of glass. This was during a break from seminary; when he returned to his studies he found himself able to pray, for after the rocky walk he had put his shoes back on and spent hours on shore sitting, submitting, and concentrating, watching the sun set on his family's summer home.

He was tiptoeing across tame institutional tile now. A student, one of those who went to his own hipper barber to have his mop of top hair tipped blond, narrowed his eyes at Dennis. Dennis thought about how he must look, the boy functioning like the barber's infinitely receding mirrors revealing the true nature of light: he wasn't tiptoeing, he was *stalking*.

He hung his towel on a hook, and felt suddenly feeble as he grabbed the Hot knob to steady himself. He let go, at the feeble feeling. He looked around, not to see whether there were handsome naked men, but to see if he'd looked like a fool. Nobody cared. The blond-tipped boy was not in the showers.

Oh, but he also liked how the students were hell-bent on shocking their teacher-priests. One came into his classroom at the beginning of this semester, his smartest one, in a T-shirt, which accentuated the unseasonably warm weather they'd been having, with an iron-on graphic of a Corvette, and beneath it, the slogan, "Wrap Your Ass in Fiberglass!" They all wore their various allegiances and determinations on T-shirts like this, while Dennis was reduced to a single allegiance. Now and then Dennis shocked them all back, bringing houseplants into his seminar room, or by quoting Tallulah Bankhead in some strange context to illustrate the effect of glacial dumps on Minnesotan topography. He made himself a fool in class, and he didn't care.

He let the warm water get warmer. When he'd had enough and felt grounded on slippery tile, he stalked into the anteroom and wrapped the towel again, stepping into the dry sauna, where he sat on the lowest tier, bowed like a question mark into his own thoughts. He thought about Jimmy, about how often they used to talk, every day they would blaze away, fired on agreements and disagreements, and now Jimmy was as far away as Neptune from his life, a cold planet he knew hardly anything about. But this was difficult for him to think about. Instead, an easier thing to think about was how long he could stay in the sauna and still get to the post office on time.

He also studied his feet in the sauna. Since being sent to the Midwest, he'd spent a lot of time looking at the ground. He was always looking up in California, up a hill, up over the ocean. They'd said America's

Landlocked Breadbasket was flat, but it was not. It lacked big hills, but the slopes and inclines of Northern California had been steep and smooth, while here the ground was always uneven, clumped, root-riddled. Even paved areas had been heaved up by the cycle of hot and cold seasons. Weather crumbled it all, and he found himself watching where he stepped all the time, like a penitent, or a man in a menial job, sorting buttons, writing numbers in columns, praying. Did he look as if he was praying right now? He looked up and around him at the hushed students in the sauna. When he was their age, he thought anybody in a surplice or wimple was thinking about God every single waking minute. Is that how the students saw all the Jesuits?

"I know what you're doing!" It was the blond-tipped boy. "I know why you're here, you fucking creep," he said this time, and Dennis knew he was being discussed in front of two, three, four other students in the constricted cedar box. "Quit staring at my dick!"

If he got up now, he'd be proving the kid right. But the longer he lingered, the more the bottle-blond pressed. "Keep your towels on, guys, or you'll be going straight to hell with the Holy Father here. You're all a bunch of freaks."

The other students didn't know how to respond, either. Maybe Dennis should stay and take the brunt of this, absorb the punishment on behalf of the men in his profession. Would that be martyrdom, the right thing to do, bring him one orbit closer in heaven's solar system? He sat there, not leaving the sauna, but it didn't feel like a moral act to stay—it just seemed like sitting there.

What he didn't anticipate was rescue. In the far corner, near the hot stones and the thermometer, a small guy, maybe older than the others, maybe a graduate student, spoke in a slow drawl. "I know what perverts look like," he said, standing up, "and I think you've got the wrong guy, chum." It came out evenly, it came out naturally. It didn't seem like standing up to a bully at all. It came out like fate, grace, unearned but inevitable. Even that word, "chum." "Maybe you've got the wrong guy? I don't think anybody here wants your sorry skinny ass, anyway."

This guy was not so substantial himself. His skin was very pale, interrupted by only a tufted triangle of red-brown hair in the middle of his narrow chest. He had warrior-short legs, however, probably a difficult man to knock over. Still, he seemed ghostlike, diaphanous, or perhaps made of a soft translucent stone like Egyptian alabaster.

The blond-tipped boy tightened his towel, huffed, and left, and after he slammed the sauna door shut, they could still hear him shout into the locker room at large, "You're all a bunch of faggots."

The two boys who did not speak for or against anything stirred after an appropriate time. That would befit well-socialized, repressed, taciturn Catholics,

Dennis felt, and they left quietly, leaving Dennis alone with his hero.

"Somebody just failed a midterm," the guy said, and then let out a low, modulated whistle, some mix of sexed-up catcall and appreciation of monumental achievement, or disaster.

"Thank you," said Dennis.

"You'd do the same for me if I was getting queer-bashed."

If Dennis were not already basted in the sauna and not already brushed a second coat of crimson from the embarrassing attack, this guy would have seen him blush, because he wasn't at all sure he would have done the same.

"I'm Greg," he said. "You teach that survey course on American Land Masses." It always unnerved Dennis that people knew who he was. He was trying to seem far away—but that only made it harder for him to see others, while they saw him just fine. Greg studied him. Then he said, "You *are* a big homo, aren't you?"

"No longer practicing," said Dennis. "Seriously," he added, just in case.

"It must be tough," Greg said. "I lived all my kid life alone on a farm down in Nebraska and nobody would touch me but a calf, maybe, if I put sugar on my dick, and I could maybe be a single man my entire life except that I need to get touched now and then."

There was something about him, Dennis realized now, that told him what Greg looked like as a boy, spending long periods of time alone on a farm. Talking to himself, making his own fun, telling himself goof-ball stories, singing made-up songs, coming up with that low, odd whistle to call a horse or cow closer.

"I touch folks for money," said Greg with a wise-guy smile, but couldn't even wait to let Dennis gasp or ask him whether he was a prostitute, "I'm a masseur."

"I used to have a regular masseuse, when I had money," said Dennis.

"I give serious massage, now. No hanky-panky."

Nobody was coming into the sauna. Dennis was sure that word was getting around out there. But Greg didn't seem to care. They were the prophets of the Lord, in Nebuchadnezzar's furnace, oblivious. Dennis leaned back confidently and enjoyed the smell of hot cedar. The boards against his back were something like a tease: stiff hands that might soften, form to him, comfort. Greg pressed. "You're no stranger to hanky-panky, are you, Father?"

"If this is some kind of candid camera thing," Dennis said, "it's not like I have a reputation to lose. But I really did give it up. And besides, even when I hadn't given it up, I never liked to mix my hanky-panky with other hanky-panky. My friend Jimmy used to drag me into Middle Eastern restaurants, but a belly dancer's navel ring in my couscous was no fun. Strip-pers and booze, nope. And Hooters? Ridiculous idea."

Greg moved down a shelf and scrambled himself into place next to Dennis. "Everything is pleasure if you look at it right. A warm room. Good conversation. A little hot oil. Even a little bit of wine. Some music? The spirit is in the body and the mind communes with both the soul and the loins."

Dennis nearly giggled. Greg had said this, had said words like *spirit* and *body* and *commune* and *pleasure,* and he was so far away from Northern California, where that lingo was invented to rebel against the bullshit of organized religion and simply became a new brand of bullshit. But Greg had gotten hold of these phrases, probably off some mass market paperback rack at the checkout stand in a grocery story in a small town in Nebraska several years ago and didn't know it was just as manufactured as anything else, and he believed, and now Dennis, for a moment believed, and that's why he didn't giggle, in the end.

But he didn't say anything, so Greg filled the sauna room—which had the very opposite acoustics of Jay's car dealership barbershop in that words came out broad and narrowed down precisely, so there was no mistaking what was said (that was perfectly clear when the blond-tipped boy delivered his lines to his small audience)—"You need some all-holy touching, don't you think? Especially after all that verbal abuse, don't you think? I can bring my table over to your place at six o'clock, don't you think? What's your address?"

Dennis wasn't thinking, however, when he told Greg the address. He felt naughty, thieving, forgetful. Was this some moral moment, once again, where he was supposed to act correctly? Despite contemplative prayer, the world was never going to be free of action, not until he was dead. "But I can't afford a massage."

"This one's on the house, Father. This one's for Jesus." Then he stood up again and stepped back up to the top shelf of the sauna and looked to where the sky might be, and he said, "That Christ may dwell in your hearts by faith; that ye, being rooted and grounded in love, may be able to comprehend with all saints what is the breadth, and length, and depth, and height; and to know the love of Christ, which passeth knowledge, that ye might be filled with the utter fullness of God."

Dennis marveled at this. He'd heard this affirmation of faith recently, from other lips, very different ones. But Greg said words like *ye* and *dwell* and *passeth* just as naturally as he had said *chum* and *spirit-body-mind*. "Six o'clock," said Greg the masseur.

⌒

Back on the street, it was colder, and the snow had accumulated enough to make people in cars and on foot move more quickly—this stuff would stick. Warm, even hot in his guts, Dennis resumed his meander toward the post office, a lunchtime hunger assuaged with a bag of potato chips from a university vending machine.

It was his mind, this time, that made him lose his way. Such regret for that episode. He had been so very careful about not looking. He did want to look, and that was the truth. Nobody ever saw that all of his not-looking muscles were flexed almost every moment of every priestly day. He thought it very funny that the thing one most naturally cared about needed hiding away, the way boys in high school ignored girls who declared their affection. Little Jennifer Schmelzer, the five-year-old daughter of the Garage Sale Schmelzers, had been cause for concern: they'd brought her in to see Dennis (not old Father Fitzgerald, the pastor of Saint Matthias, but him, the younger, more worldly Dennis), because Jennifer had written another kindergarten boy a rudimentary love letter and delivered it. "Dear Patrick," it said, "I love you Patrick. I mean it Patrick. Sincerely, Jennifer."

"And what did Patrick say to you when he got this letter?" Dennis had asked the little girl.

"He said, 'I'm going to kick you dead.'"

On these rare occasions when Dennis gave counsel, he bided his time caressing a small smooth stone that had been left by the previous priest who had occupied this office, never fully appointed because no priest served long assisting Father Fitz, who kept tight control, and hardly ever let his assisting priest preside over a mass, or give a sermon, or provide advice. Dennis told Jennifer's mother and father that things should be all right, but that she shouldn't be encouraged in this kind of . . . he almost said *promiscuity*, but that word was so charged. He wished it wasn't. He felt promiscuous so much more now, as a celibate man, being intimate in a very casual way with many more people than he ever had before, here in his office at this parent-child meeting, at the various dinners he was invited to at least three days a week. So casually intimate that he would preside over emotions, putting hands on shoulders, kissing, cooing, everything but the nasty—*getting around,* too, the way they said those girls in high school did, the ones who showed their affections for boys too easily—"she gets around." Dennis was going door to door, practically, with his little comfort factory, a street walker. The streets were flat here, though, which made his promiscuity easier. In San Francisco, he had lived at the top of a big hill, and there were hardly any crimes, no thefts—walking up a hill required work, the chastening influence of sweat. Sin was sloth.

Promiscuity, too, was a casual hunger for satiation, and what if that hunger was in the realm of knowledge, or spiritual fulfillment? Certainly nothing that could be unloaded at the church bazaar or into a Goodwill bin, but still, sometimes, junk, useless, a fire hazard. Little Jennifer sat in front of children's television programs and was told to love everybody in that adoring child way, equally, a cheap love easily accumulated, easily cluttering.

And now, wandering somewhere between sauna and post office, somebody tossed a spent cigarette out of their car window and on the bounces of impact with the sidewalk in front of him, it gave off sparks, a little cast-off firework that Dennis enjoyed.

It was in a promiscuous way that he had attended Christmas dinner more than a month ago with Mary Jane and Les and their family. He'd been excited—this would be the day, he thought, when he would discover exactly how big that big Catholic family was. He came to the dinner with egg nog, and Mary Jane took it out of his hands at the door and slipped it into the refrigerator, where it was forgotten. Les, a likably shameless man wearing an extra large polyester sweater with the word *Scrooged!* woven into the pattern, pulled him into the living room, where, judging from little charred corners of paper in the fireplace grating, most of the Christmas morning wrapping paper had been incinerated.

"So what do you do, Les, that I never see you?" Dennis asked Draper in order to be friendly, not quite steering clear of overhead mistletoe or double-edged questions that meant something different coming from him—more judgmental. Les handed him a sickeningly sweet blended highball. He didn't mean to point out that Les wasn't coming to church enough, which he wasn't, though Dennis didn't care, though that's the way it sounded. He swallowed half the drink.

Les didn't care either, though, apparently. "I tuck-point," he said.

Dennis clinked his glass against Les's—Les had caught up easily with him. Dennis was supposed to know what tuckpointing was. It sounded a fussy profession for such a burly man, like the tatting of socks, perhaps, or a skillful maneuver hotel maids used on impeccably made beds. But Dennis was pursuing the contemplative life, and he felt excused from the world of action at the moment, emboldened by sugary alcohol. "What's tuckpointing?"

Before Les answered, their oldest son, Mark, appeared in the living room like the Ghost of Christmas Present, gifts for kids and his mother in all his pockets, the video camera lashed by its cord in one fist, a seasonal beer in the other, so that he had to hug people instead of shake their hands.

"Father Bacchus!" he shouted, "I've heard a lot about you. Mom tells me everything. I'm *impressed*." Dennis smiled. An emotionally available straight man, he thought, easy with compliments. But what had impressed him? What had Mary Jane told him? "Hey, Dad, I saw Anne's car coming up behind me, she'll be here soon. Mom make her deviled eggs?"

Mary Jane poked her head into the living room, her apron downy with flour. "Sprinkled paprika on them just for you," she hollered to her son.

"For that finished look!" Mark shouted back. He turned to Dennis. "I saw that once on her recipe card. 'Sprinkle with paprika, for a finished look.'" Two of the smallest Drapers, maybe six and eight years old, tugged at his pant legs. Mark was the favorite older brother who always played billiards with them in the basement, and let them keep score with the sliding counter and win. "In a minute, you animals." They accepted this promise and ran toward the cellar stairs, presumably to remove the cover on the pool table and chalk up the cues.

"What do you do?" Dennis asked. What you did is what you were, he found in this inland nation. It also doubled as the question, "Are you married?"

"I paint," said Mark. "When I can."

"You have to take inspiration where you can get it," Dennis advised.

Mark said, "Yeah, and work, too. Tired of chasing after odd jobs." Dennis thought of Jimmy in San Francisco, freelancing articles to anybody who'd print them. The life of an artist seemed a hustle, selling the self, another kind of promiscuity. "I'm thinking of chuckin' it all and getting myself a desk job."

"Well, I hope you won't give it up completely. Think of it as a creative outlet."

Mark smirked. "I'm tired of getting up on ladders. I'm tired of sunburn on my bald-assed head. I'm tired of vinyl siding."

Oh, thought Dennis, *that* kind of painter. That's how different things were here.

"But I don't know. I like the guys, I like the talking. If I were sitting at a desk all day, I think I'd miss the socialism."

Mary Jane came through with a plateful of peanut brittle. Behind her was a young but grown woman. "Father Bacchus, this is our oldest daughter, Anne."

Sweet Mary Jane. She was old and charming and a little lame, which might have been caused by all sorts of domestic work, or from bearing so many, many children. Now she was built like a bird with clipped wings, a preferred chipped plate in the cupboard, a favorite record that skipped a bit. It could charm or it could irritate, thought Dennis, the way an overhead light, running out of its gas, flickered, trembled.

"How do you do," said Anne, who tried to minimize her precise beauty with close-cropped hair. She looked like the strong surviving girl in an action movie, or the supermodel designers always put into the haute couture.

Mark said, "Anne says she's going to be a nun, but I don't believe her. How can you guys live without, you know, it?"

Sometimes Dennis was annoyed by the repetitive inanity of the question, and all the questions about his life's decisions: "Why would you move to this weather when you lived in California?" or "You're gay? Don't you want to have children?" This time, Dennis said, "I like to look at maps."

Mark said, "I'm impressed. Maps? I'm impressed." Dennis felt pleased around Mark, as if he were always being slapped on the back. Dennis basked in his words' glow, as if he really had accomplished something by not doing anything. And then Mark said, "Maps, like in *National Geographic*? Maps, and native girls? That kind of maps?"

"No, just maps." Anne would understand, perhaps.

But she said, "You don't need anything, Mark, not even maps."

Mark stepped back. Dennis saw it: the older brother was afraid of his sister. His name was being called from the basement. "Gotta jet," he said, gratefully, and Dennis was alone in the room with Anne, though the television blared and Christmas carols competed on the stereo in the front room and Mary Jane commanded Les in the kitchen, so it didn't feel like an awkward silence at all.

"I've been working with the Poor Clares," she offered. "I've decided it's the only thing that will give me any sort of hope. You know, to just do something. Just go in every day and give them soup and teach them how to pray."

"That would be hard for me," said Dennis. He meant it to make sympathetic conversation, but judging from the look on her face, she thought she had found a kindred spirit, and was shocked to find, instead, a fake. He looked at her anew, as well, in cheap simple clothes, no makeup. But she was young and didn't need makeup, and her twenty-year-old heart beat power enough to light up a town, because that was what youth was: Plutonium-239. "I get tired just taking care of my own self, and my own business," he drank, but both of them could see that he was drinking from an empty glass.

"I get my strength from Christ," she said. She read

156

it from the catechism; he'd read the same materials. He'd watched the younger seminarians take to that line with much more zeal than he. Then Anne quoted Paul, who, Dennis realized, was a convert, and should have been his role model. He remembered the quote as it spilled from her mouth, and she expected him to recite it aloud like a poem with her, but he watched her be disappointed again when he didn't: "That Christ may dwell in your hearts by faith; that ye, being rooted and grounded in love, may be able to comprehend with all saints what is the breadth, and length, and depth, and height . . ." He could see it in her eyes: this priest was an imposter, and didn't spend enough time measuring the physical volume of God.

Her brother had emerged from the basement as she finished this recitation, and he said, "I'm *impressed*." Dennis was crestfallen—he had not been impressed by Dennis; it was just something he said, a gladhanding way of sidling up to another person, making them feel good about themselves. It was a harmless promiscuity, and it stung only when he realized it was meaningless.

"Come and get it!" Les yelled from the dining room.

Then they ate. They ate with some sort of faith that consuming was the fate of them, as it is with caterpillars who singlemindedly reduced leaves to a skeleton of veins, and converted destruction, self and otherwise, to beauty: *this,* the lacework of a leaf, *that,* the filigree of a butterfly. But, thought Dennis, as Les stripped from the turkey carcass another hunk, *that* is meat and *this* is a man, and what's left of one side is a filigree of bones, memento mori, and the other, an overlarded heart. He counted the Draper family to himself: five at the dinner table, three little ones at a card table in front of the television in the other room. Such plenty.

He was afraid that there would be dinner conversation in which he would have to speak up against racial slurs or animal torture or crappy movies or homophobia, ruining everything, but everybody was decent. They were even Democrats, even working-class Democrats, talking about the March primaries and speaking with informed zeal about this and that candidate. Dennis loved that people surprised him.

They retired to the living room, and Dennis joined them in the sleep of gluttony in front of that flickering light of the television, a pantomime of life projected on inert people, the light of which made the big soft patriarch a canvas, a photoplate upon which images were exposed, now fabric softener, now the Florida Gators losing the big bowl game, now Scrooge, now a mother and son embracing.

"I'm going to help out in a soup kitchen in Saint Paul this evening," Anne said, after distributing some small Guatemalan-made wooden toys to her younger brothers and sisters, which had none of the machine-mold fabulousness of packaged plastic Barbies and GI Joes and were therefore tossed aside. She gave him a small hand-carved crucifix when telling him her intentions. "Will you join me, Father?"

Dennis looked at her. He was drugged on wine and the turkey's tryptophan, and could not even conjure an excuse. "I can't, Anne. Thank you for inviting me. And thank you for this crucifix." He had nothing to give to her. As if he were the lazy village curate of an eighteenth century novel who spent his career mooching off his well-to-do parishioners and never lending a hand.

He knew this had been the impression he'd made on her when she left the house without saying good-bye to him. He had so much he wanted to say to her, about how much he admired her, how she reminded him of Zoe, the nurse practitioner, the best of all possible people, about how there were many rooms in his father's house.

A liberal evangelist, he thought, as he walked over to his own building in the warm winter that evening. He'd had *l'esprit de l'escalier*, something he should have said to her. He wanted to quote her back: "We cannot all be friars and there are many paths by which God takes his own to heaven." But that was not Paul, not the Bible at all. Not even Dante. That was what Don Quixote told Sancho Panza when Sancho asked him why he didn't become a priest instead of a knight-errant. Still, the words seemed holy, a true and right thing to say and believe. He should have said that to her. She need not be so self-righteous.

The moral act, however, performed too late, or thought of later—was it still a moral act? Can you always think of the right thing to do, immediately? Every day he was backing away a little more from the world of action, a less swiftly spinning angel, because he'd recklessly bashed through little moral situations like this and found himself wanting.

⌒

He was going to get to the post office now. He was going to do it. The wind whipped up, and it shocked him. He sang himself a blues song, his own words set to the tune of a song he already knew, to cheer himself up. "No, not until late January," he sang, "does ground give way, and while it's easy to set aside, to squelch a dream of a snowless year, hope curbs hard, stiffens and staunches, and this snow shocks us." As if in confirmation, his mouth filled with a few flakes, and when he reached into his pocket to get his gloves on, Jimmy's little gift fell onto the snow, and, wet, the inky address smeared into an unreadable blob, and the cheap wrapping paper mushed and the corners of the box pushed through here and here. He'd have to rewrap it, he'd have to get the address at home. He sang again: "Snow looks soft, feels sharp; it's like a bone broken, or worse, for bone and splint are indiscernible to touch. Who can dream of healing, new growth? How can burst limbs, a cracked thing, seal? Will this perfect cold break, ever?"

This snow was perfect on everything, but it made it hard for Dennis to think about the past. Jimmy and all of San Francisco, all his old life, was at the other end of the world, and at the other end of time. There had been another place where he had to do the moral thing, he realized. Were there times when there was more than one correct moral act? He could become a priest, or he could have done something else. What was that something else? He knew it would be obvious to anybody else, but it wasn't so obvious. They'd been close friends through so much, traveled, talked, compared, but they had never gotten naked before. He'd embraced the "impressed" Mark Draper more than he'd ever embraced Jimmy. He wasn't avoiding anything: all right, yes, duh, he loved Jimmy, but that way, that non-agape way? That choice was not a choice, not anymore.

He sang again. "The trees leaves, now gone, have everything to do with this. Must they leave me? Rot? Fade? Grow like ghosts? Must they—how dare they—any of them, Disappear? The dead, the loved, To loam, to bone, to other lovers?" He stopped singing. Anywhere other than here, they go, that was the answer to his own blues. A person needs so little, he had learned in this vow of poverty and chastity, but one little, palpable thing. Maybe this gift in his pocket, gummy-wet now, would do? Or even less, for he really should mail this. He could do with a few small clues: the scent of that desired one on another, for instance, because Greg the masseur who was coming later used the same deodorant Jimmy always used. So, less than that: rags, candle nubs, receipts, a menu from a restaurant that had closed down, a laundry list, a soap sliver, unstrung blue beads from my old rosary. That's all, no more.

He'd come to an open lot. Because the building next to it blocked the wind, it had not been carpeted with snow yet. It was like a brown bereft field. Dennis walked into the middle of it, and leaned down to pick up the husks of leaves, nearly decayed now to mulch. He fingered them anyway, picked clean by worms and wet, a brown delicate lace, but whole for one last time, a kind of proof before the snow got them. He felt a meager joy (a mortal joy, he'd have said, if he had had an opportunity to talk about joy in a sermon that he'd never be permitted to give at Saint Matthias) and realized that he was allowed, even encouraged in this world, to forget things but that he didn't live long enough, being a human being, to forget. If he were a God, if he were immortal, then it would be a sin to forget. The wind shifted and snow was finally settling and sticking on this lot, because it was coming steadily, and it was getting colder as the weak sun set, snow like a hopeless joy without a dream of spring. He stood up, dropped the leaves, and realized how strange it was that the snow, even this late in the overcast day, made things brighter, gathered and multiplied what little light there was in the day.

Fooled, however! He glanced at his watch—Greg the masseur would come to his house in an hour and a half. No time to go to the post office today. In his haste, one of the gloves fell into the leaves and joined a used pregnancy test he'd at first mistaken for an old toothbrush, the outcome of which was indeterminate now,

162

having been left out in the weather, where the sun could leech away the color of misery or happiness.

⁓

Back at home, more detritus. Mary Jane, victorious in the race she did not know she'd run, had completely dismantled Christmas, but she had placed a Country Clutter sign, something Les had made in his basement workshop with pine and whitewash and cornflower-blue paint, Welcome Winter! decorated with three merry blue snowflakes. Next to this sign, their usual Neighborhood Watch sign—hidden by the illuminated Virgin in the manger scene before and now revealed—that read We Call Police. This was the way, here, ferocious privacy, cheery niceness, two sides of the same coin. He still didn't know whether Mark was married or what tuckpointing was.

Before going inside, he went to the dumpster on the side of his building to peel off the soggy holiday paper from his gift that would not go, not ever, to Jimmy. In the dumpster, Mary Jane had thrown two broken clapboard candy canes and a couple of burnt-out strings of Christmas lights. He added the wrapping paper. There were dried-up pine boughs there, too, which had adorned her outdoor manger. The trash was fragrant. Over the dumpster, he realized that he'd lost his glove.

So many hazards here, and retreating from the world would never be enough. How could he have anticipated the blond-tipped student, without first experiencing

163

him? There were hazards one couldn't anticipate until they had already happened. Certain safety measures and emergency preparedness could not be implemented until the calamity had already happened at least once: the insides of some fast-food restaurants' hot apple pie, the cleaning of dead leaves out of the eaves to avoid roof leaks. And in this cold weather, the fingers numb and the gloves desensitizing the hand to touch, gloves that covered up wedding bands and past lives, you never know what you have dropped until it is too late.

⌒

Greg had set up his table, after lugging it up three flights of stairs, in Dennis's empty breakfast nook. It was nighttime outside, but snow reflected the moon so that through the windows it seemed brighter than it had all day. Greg commandeered quietly, set a pan of water to boil, and put his massage oil into the pan. "It must be hard not to be touched," he said, while hooking a doughnut-shaped extension to the end of the table, for the face to rest into; this was the right version of the question Dennis had to answer every day, "What do you do without sex?"

"Anything can be pleasure," Dennis smiled. "Any ordinary thing can just suddenly give you goose bumps. Suddenly seeing the design of the land in a map, or how three words in the right order make poetry, or watching that meaning fall apart if you just keep on staring, doing nothing about the design."

"I hear you," said Greg, and he told Dennis to strip, and rest on his belly on his table. It was covered in sheepskin. Dennis fit his face into the padded doughnut and closed his eyes. He could hear Greg taking off his clothes, too. And Greg worked in Dennis's breakfast nook, the lights off. Maybe he shouldn't have the lights off, he thought, except that he didn't want to move, he wanted to be touched and he wanted to listen.

While Greg kneaded and pushed at Dennis's back muscles, pulling his arms back to expose the wing of scapula, or distending the neck muscles, letting warm oil console his calves and inner thighs, he whispered a mix of Eastern chakra tenets, Wizard of Oz metaphors, and the prayer of Saint Francis. Dennis let his mind drift to the phone conversation he'd last had with Jimmy a week before Christmas.

"I'm not coming," Jimmy said, "I have to come in a couple of weeks to deal with her house and all her stuff, and I don't want to do it yet. I'll let you know when I come. Besides, I'm writing this big exposé on a sleazy real estate developer in Marin, and the story is going to be great." Dennis could have guessed. Whatever story Jimmy was working on, the subject informed the way he saw the world.

Dennis understood, he said. But now he didn't, so much. He had decided for the past month that this last conversation had been "nice," though Jimmy, full of his own metaphors of urban sprawl, said that he felt Dennis had abandoned him in California, like a corrupt developer, like an empty strip mall. It was some version of fundamentalism Dennis had retreated to in a world of action and change, Jimmy said.

"I'm dealing with the unknown every day," Dennis defended himself. "Everything here is new."

It was new, and it had an erotic charge for him. Dennis was supposed to be a staid village priest, but he felt uninhibited, capable of anything, stimulated by anything now, maps and words, yes, but any *body*, any source of light and heat and music. Maybe a previous life of promiscuity had made gestures any ordinary person made to him—pantomimes, shadows, emblems of real intimacy (Mark, clapping him on the back, impressed; Jay's hand scratching hair oil into his scalp)—seem enough to make him capable of lunging at them, perhaps at a frail woman, perhaps at a fat child, and kiss them, with full tongue.

Greg moved a hand down the inside of his left leg. Somehow, Dennis thought, the possibility of love had not vanished, but expanded, washed, like a spring flood over a river's banks, to include anybody, even a dog. Or Jimmy. And also, Dennis wondered about what it must be like off the coast of some cold continent, where, over the ocean, the sweet snowflakes might put out a little of the burn of sea salt.

"Roll onto your back now," Greg said. Dennis was surprised—he thought after this long and careful attention to each of his limbs, to his neck and back and fingers and joints, Greg was done. He rolled over and was afraid he'd catch cold, but before his chest or belly or groin could contend with the air as cold as the glass at which the snow sifted, Greg lay his own body down upon Dennis. Dennis knew he could never tell anybody about this moment—not because it was sex, but because it was not sex, and nobody would believe him.

As Greg placed his body over Dennis and pressed him, matching him limb to limb, Dennis said, "Quote Paul to me again."

Greg gave that low whistle of his, which didn't sound strange or lascivious this time, but perhaps an approximation of the soul celebrating, praising. Greg said it quietly, because his mouth was up against Dennis's left ear: "that ye, being rooted and grounded in love, may be able to comprehend with all saints what is the breadth, and length, and depth, and height; and to know the love of Christ, which passeth knowledge, that ye might be filled with the utter fullness of God."

Dennis thought, *utterfulness,* one word, the utterfulness of God, that it had to be uttered. Greg was done, done with the Letter of Paul to the Ephesians, done with the massage. He slipped off of Dennis and stood in the window, lit by snowlight. In the room, Dennis realized that Greg was not diaphanous, like a sylph, as he had seen him in the sauna when he saved him from that humiliation, but that he emanated some low fire, the kind that came from the coil on an electric stove set at simmer.

After Dennis had told Jay the barber that he found

it interesting to see how the green light of the infinitely regressing mirror reflections revealed the true nature of the light in the room, Jay had corrected him. "Naw, Padre, it just shows you how dirty my mirrors are. It's cheap glass."

Greg was dressing now, and Dennis lay there. "You don't have to move at all, Father."

But Dennis sat up on the table and rubbed his eyes—having had them closed for so long, even the snow was dazzling. He slipped off and pulled on a ratty terry robe. Greg was grinning.

Dennis went to the coat closet and pulled out of his jacket pocket the little box with Jimmy's Christmas present. He handed it to Greg. "It's just a little thing," he said. "It's just a corkscrew. But anything can be pleasure, can't it? A little wine, a little conversation?" He was almost able to say spirit, body, mind, groin, but he couldn't quite make the words not sound ridiculous.

Greg didn't open it, which disappointed Dennis just a little because it was a nice corkscrew. Greg only said, "Peace," but it was his eyes that gave him away, drinking in a generosity that wasn't there. If grace was something unearned, could the bestower of grace also be undeserving? Dennis was just a guy, Greg hardly knew him. He had taken from Greg, he had received pleasure, and the gift he gave wasn't really meant for the boy.

Anymore, in this land of plenty, nobody knew when they were giving out the thing that was *needed*. And money, and obligation, these were the cheap things, these were the promiscuous, tawdry measures of men. A twelve-dollar haircut meant more to Dennis than a night in a deluxe hotel. And a quote from Ephesians from the mouth of a farmboy was worth more than the same words out of the mouth of a nun-to-be who meant to move the world. But if he had an opportunity to give a homily sometime at Saint Matthias, which of course he wouldn't, Dennis would inform his congregation that maybe everybody was forever moving closer and farther away from God by design and accident, and sometimes the angels that seemed dimmest would, for hardly any reason at all, begin to blaze and throb.

Land of Lakes

Mankato, Minnesota, June 1999

Land of Lakes, Dennis had written in his little black journal, and then:

> The stillness of a lake
> A lesser kind of doom
> The act of standing still
> Seems stuck in muck and gloom,
> This water will not slake.
>
> The physicist will say,
> Of work, there has been none
> If nothing has been moved
> Stagnation's "do" is done
> No lake has sprayed or played.
>
> I want water that runs
> That's living in its splash
> An age of weeds and silt
> Has clotted in this ... oh ...

"Oh," he had written, and then said out loud, "forget it," and left the thing unfinished. Dennis Bacchus's recitation of occasional blues had evolved into lyric, and he had attempted, lately, to write for himself a series of water songs, because he loved water, and missed water, and how could that be in the land of ten thousand lakes? Minnesota was nothing like the Pacific Northwest, where he was from. It was buggier, for one thing.

Things had not really improved in Minneapolis, and Father Fitzgerald, seeing his assistant siphon off parishioners, continued to limit Dennis's role in the church. He was attached to Saint Matthias and its community in name only, and had instead pitched himself at teaching, where he had impressed his department chair and the students (except, of course, the blond-tipped boy, who never showed himself again).

Dennis had tried, he really had, to make this inland empire a home, but he was rebuffed at every stroke. He mustered courage and decided to take his prescriptions to a mom and pop pharmacy in the neighborhood rather than the impersonal chain that was admittedly closer to the rectory. He would support the independents.

He felt bold and good about himself, walking along the street in the late afternoon with three separate slips of paper with three separate prescriptions scrawled on them. It was the hour of the day when the gang scratchiti show up best on the plate glass of shop windows. He made a point of looking at himself in the reflection.

Dennis had successfully handed over all the duties of vanity to others—Jay the barber gave him the twelve-dollar haircut he thought best suited Dennis; the optometrist suggested a pair of passable, nondesigner glasses; on mail-order clothing calls, Dennis would ask the woman taking his order what she thought was the best color for the pants he requested.

The one last act of vanity was love of life, for in essence, the flow of pills could never be cut off, or the cottonmouth venom that had been for a couple of years held at bay might regain the strength to strike and kill—Dennis's life was held in his own hands.

But the pharmacy, dusty, full of loose tiles and the acrid tang of leaky rubbing alcohol bottles, customerless and sour, brought down his buoyancy.

The pharmacist was an old man who lived in the neighborhood, a member of Saint Matthias. Dennis could not be invisible in here. He was very nervous. What would the man think of him, of a religious man with HIV? Would he ask probing questions? Gossip? Dennis practiced answers, scenarios: No, they were tasteless and had no side effects. Yes, it was sometimes scary to think how close he'd been to death. No, he wasn't ashamed. Yes, he was a representative of the church. Probably, he was a man of the church because of the pills. No, it wasn't just that. Yes, he was celibate now. No, he didn't miss it.

The pharmacist, however, took Dennis's slips and was unimpressed. Like the apothecary in Shakespeare, he was not a dim angel but earthly, merely an acolyte, one of the many who were supposed to be watchers— the taxi drivers, the notary publics, the night guards— too bored with the sameness of aberration, who had stopped watching.

Heartlessly, the man reached up onto a shelf and pulled down three bottles, typed labels, and dropped it all into a bag.

"Can I just call in with refills?" Dennis asked, putting his pills into his coat pocket.

"No, I don't keep this stuff on hand regularly. You'll have to give me a week's notice." After that, Dennis returned, probably unnoticed, to the convenience and anonymity of the chain drugstore.

⌒

Jimmy didn't get in touch with Dennis until early summer, telling him he was coming out finally to take care of his mother's things. Could Dennis give him a hand? Dennis had to laugh thinking about how ridiculous his little corkscrew gift would have seemed, as far away from Christmas as the weather could possibly get.

He was about as far away from Jimmy. Sweet water for salt water. Dennis never felt so particular. Lakes wouldn't do it, nor an ocean alone, nor a river. The languidness of open sea and placid ponds was not what he was ready for. And now this—this!—the true meaning of the word *backwater*.

Jimmy rented a car at the airport and picked Dennis

up. They drove an hour to the Blue Earth of Mankato. After Jimmy showed Dennis the huge statue of the Jolly Green Giant, they drove to the Thornton house where Jimmy set to work organizing a garage sale. Dennis spent the day or two putting ridiculous prices on pieces of masking tape. Neighbors who knew Jimmy's mother came and glared at the two of them—how dare these outsiders liquidate this sweet woman's assets? But they snapped up the crockery, the labor-saving devices, the bagfuls of romance novels. Dennis set aside a few things for Mary Jane Draper. After two days, the only thing left was a box of bistro-style plates and the occasional piece of junk. Three or four things Jimmy saved for himself, including a beautiful knife with a polished bone handle and an inlaid metal design of a bumblebee. The blade was stainless steel and it folded up nicely. Dennis liked it very much. "That's a beautiful knife," he said.

"You want it?"

"No, no. I was just saying."

"You want it." But Jimmy put it into his own pocket.

It was also during this reunion that Dennis noted the first hints of Jimmy's full revival from the meds he'd been taking. He was acting like a child: he played mumbledy-peg with the nice knife, he spun his mother's Johnny Cash albums on a turntable in the spirit of camp, he gleefully incinerated baby pictures.

Dennis would often lift his nose and smell the air.

Boggy, mucky. Just behind the house and through a huge forest there was a large lake.

In the basement, behind the Christmas decorations, too late for the garage sale, they found one other box. Jimmy's father had made extra money by writing a how-to booklet for hunters who wanted to skin and clean their own deer. It was illustrated with lurid, matter-of-fact photographs. The genius of the thing was that it was printed on a kind of cloth, so that it could be hosed down after use; no deer blood and guts would remain. "My whole life, these big hunters came to our door with ten dollar bills, buying my dad's skin-a-deer manual."

Jimmy told him that he came from a long line of plate throwers. His father had been in the military, and each year their family was given a stipend for dishware. For plate throwers, a budget for new dishes was nothing but an invitation.

"It was November and my parents were fighting again," he explained, "probably about their sissy son. My mother was like an opera singer; she would get louder and louder until she picked up a plate. This time, she was about to throw a flowery saucer at my father like they were a Chinese acrobat team doing a difficult maneuver, and my father screamed, 'Stop!— We've run out of our dish budget.' And my mother put the plate down without breaking it. Then I realized it was all a drama they made for each other."

"Are you a plate thrower?"

"I think so. I don't know. There hasn't been any-body to throw plates at. Look at all of my mother's left-over plates now. After my dad died, she never threw again. Maybe if I had visited her more." Then Jimmy went out in the garage and pulled out the box of his mother's unsold plates. He looked at one for maybe a whole second, then tossed it with all his might.

Dennis watched. Each plate was a thought, a re-morseful thought. Jimmy methodically broke every sin-gle plate, one by one, by flinging them like Frisbees to the corners of the garage. Dennis heard that Jimmy was weeping, sobbing wordless sobs, grief's end being, after all, wordless. And at the foot of the walls all around the two of them were piled shards of French Bistro, a de-sign, Dennis later told Jimmy, that was his favorite.

"Oh, I'm sorry," Jimmy said, snapping out of it. "And I didn't even invite you to help me. God, here. Take this knife." He pulled the beautiful blade out. Dennis reached out for it, but Jimmy pulled it away again. "For a dollar."

Dennis snorted and went into the dead mother's house. He'd found among the romance novels a copy of Longfellow's "Song of Hiawatha," a poem, Jimmy used to say, "of his people." He'd recite long passages of it over dinner while they were in Mankato. "By the shores of Gitche Gumee," he'd drone, "by the shining big-sea-water."

By then, they were arguing about everything. Paul Bunyan was a Pacific Northwest hero, Hiawatha was a

Great Lakes hero, Paul Bunyan was gay, Hiawatha was a racist white invention, they were both shit, Dennis was a racist, no Jimmy was a racist. Jimmy was also an Indian giver, Dennis said, referring to the knife. He was glad he'd never mentioned the Christmas gift.

The broken plates seemed to have broken something else, something inside them: now Jimmy couldn't stop. So what were simple disagreements escalated rapidly into a series of coffee cups being chucked back and forth. It was as if they were fighting in two different spirits, Jimmy to trash his own muddled past, Dennis to make room for himself in this claustrophobic huge foreign world. Jimmy threw a cheap vase. Dennis grabbed an opalescent shot glass.

"No, not that!" Jimmy said. "Save that for my tears."

Unable to break the thing he wanted to break, Dennis felt himself shrinking, waning as Jimmy waxed. He examined the unbroken shot glass in his hand.

"All these nice things," he said out loud. "Neither of us know how to take care of nice things." Dennis had had practically nothing to take along with him to seminary. There were a few items, like a lace tablecloth that he just stuck in the washing machine one time and found it had unraveled in a dozen different places. The one photo he had of his parents was flyblown, faded, water damaged. Now Jimmy was selling and shattering every family heirloom in his path. The two of them might've stopped dying, at least for now, but they still acted as if they were dying. Minnesota was turning into a disaster. His new life was turning into a disaster. Jimmy was a walking disaster area.

"Speak for yourself," said Jimmy.

Dennis glared, then stormed out of the house. Jimmy was just behind him, heading for the woods, calling after Dennis, "What did I do?" he nagged. "What?"

Where were they? They must be near a boathouse on the lake, because he could smell live bait and boat engine gasoline along with muck and trees. Jimmy caught up with him. They were both genuinely angry, or frustrated. Both. "What is your problem?"

"You're an Indian giver, for one thing. You say you want to give me a knife and then turn around and ask for money?"

"That's a tradition, you boob. You avoid bad luck by selling a knife. It's bad luck to give somebody a knife as a gift, haven't you heard? All you had to do was give a dollar, or, what?, a kiss, and that would have been enough payment. It was something token, is all."

There was nothing in the woods to throw. Sticks wouldn't break. Dennis wasn't willing to pick up a rock.

"I'm sick of chasing after you," said Jimmy, chasing after him. Dennis was sick of it, too, so why was he doing it? That's what he asked Jimmy. He marched on.

"All right," said Jimmy, "I'll stop." And he took a path in another direction from Dennis, one that led as quickly away from him as possible. Dennis was relieved, but he was also concerned that Jimmy's was the trail out of the forest.

Out of pride, he forged on down the same path. The trail became thinner. Sticktights collected in his shoelaces. Wicked seed dispersal systems, they were general all over these parts. He thought nettles stung him once. Oh, that was just perfect.

He stormed along, nursing fury, despair, disappointment, sadness. The woods looked ugly, raggedy. All of these emotions, any one of them alone was like a tape loop that played his anger over and over, and if Dennis had allowed himself to see any beauty in them, he felt it would sully his pure bad mood. There was poison in Dennis, nettles, a black lace filigreed with all of Jimmy's faults. He would like to have arranged each of Jimmy's sins like rosary beads and clutched them to himself as if they were a string of emeralds.

Fifteen minutes went by, twenty. The smell of the lake and the bait and gasoline went away. Frogs were making their froggy sounds, more confident, with nobody around. Dennis fumed. His life had been so perfectly miserably quiet since he'd moved to Minnesota, until Jimmy insisted that he come to this place. How was anybody supposed to react when what little control they had in the world was suddenly taken away?

About forty minutes later, having tried three different trails and found himself heading for the other side of the lake, Dennis got nervous. What side of trees was moss supposed to grow on? No doubt Jimmy had done this on purpose—he knew the right way to go and left Dennis stranded.

The sun was setting. It wasn't half as bright as it had been when they went out, the sky steeping like tea. He decided to go back the way he came. After two wrong turns, he found the fork in the road, but it was nearly dusk and he could hardly see his hand in front of his face. Oh, for a map, a soothing, orienting map!

Somebody else was sitting at the fork—what if it were a maniac? He should've taken those Community United Against Violence self-defense classes all those years ago. Who could it be this far out? Was some dope going to mistake him for a deer? He had a fleeting image of his carcass hung in Jimmy's father's *Kill It and Grill It* book where the deer ought to be.

"Who is that?"

It was Jimmy. He was confused with relief and spite. "Jimmy," he said. And when Dennis came closer, he saw that Jimmy was soaking wet, covered in muck, and shivering.

"I'm glad to see you," he chattered.

The feeling was mutual, but should Dennis tell him so? He thought about how he hadn't recognized him at first, even when he knew it was Jimmy. Jimmy was a foreign country. Was Dennis doomed to always forget beauty? "You fell in the water, didn't you?"

"I couldn't see."

Dennis took off his coat and gave it to him, it was like some scene from the Holy Bible. "Do you have any idea where we are?"

"No."

But they walked and didn't know together, tourists in a terra incognita.

"I wish I had Hiawatha's moccasins," Jimmy said.

"What?"

"Hiawatha had moccasins that let him travel a mile with each step. They'd get us out of here a lot sooner."

"Where did he get special moccasins?"

"He had to challenge the West Wind, his father, for neglecting his mother. And then he fell in love with Laughing Water, Minnehaha, and he had to hurry to see her. But no matter that his moccasins could travel a mile in each step, for his heart went faster than that." They walked in silence for a while, and in the night trees, they heard the sound of what might have been an exotic bird. It had a pure, clear, long sound that eventually tapered into a less lovely croak.

"That's Wawa, the wild goose," said Jimmy.

Dennis was more interested in listening to the syncopated rhythms of their footsteps on the trail than talking about Wawa. Jimmy's strides were a little longer than his, but a little slower, too. He didn't want to walk in step with Jimmy; that would be too much of a sign of something.

The forest was getting more piney, and their ankles twisted now and then on cones. "Grow the firs with cones upon them," Jimmy recited, "Grow the black and gloomy pine trees." And then, "What do you miss, Dennis?" Jimmy suddenly wanted to know. "Home? Family? The mountains? The ocean? A lost love?"

Dennis wasn't going to answer. Perhaps sensing this, Jimmy answered his own question by saying something Dennis considered supremely stupid: "I miss Hiawatha."

"Hiawatha? How can you miss Hiawatha? He's a legend."

"In the days that are forgotten, in the unremembered ages. Do you know what happened to Hiawatha at the end of his song? He had a canoe that he could steer with his brains, and he got on the big Lake Superior and went westward, westward."

"People used to do that all the time," Dennis said. "Lately, though, they've been coming back this way."

It was getting very dark. Three lightning bugs limned a bush on their left, signaling, one, two, three. Dennis thought of Mary Jane Draper taking down Christmas lights, and he grasped Jimmy's arm: "My God! Did you see them?"

"Those are fireflies," Jimmy said. He told Dennis that in the summertime, he would come out on the lawn and fireflies would swarm him. They were a delight, even in the ordinary world, even when they were lost.

"Wah-wah-tay-see," Jimmy said. Now there were seven of the fireflies.

They must have been near the lake now, Jimmy said, fireflies living in the cattails and reeds. "They're easy to catch." One practically flew into Jimmy's cupped hands. It turned him into a miniature lantern. He brought it to Dennis.

"It's a miracle," Dennis said.

Jimmy shrugged. "It's science." Then, as if to make sure he understood it was not a miracle, Jimmy did something Dennis would always remember as the cruelest thing he'd ever done. He did it maybe not just to disprove miracles. Maybe he did it for another reason, like being lost, trapped, awakened, being alive again—he wasn't quite sure.

Jimmy squashed the firefly with a finger into his own palm. On the tip of the pestle of his index finger, he gathered up the glowing phosphor from the bug and smeared two streaks, one under each of his eyes, like a warrior with war paint. "I am the firefly god," he boomed. "You will worship me or I will call upon my minions!"

Dennis did fall back. "Will they bite?" He wanted to know.

"Maybe," Jimmy shrugged.

Dennis dared to touch one finger to the streak on Jimmy's cheek. He brought back a little of the powder on the tip. He could see his fingerprint clearly in the black night.

"Let's get more!" Jimmy said, and trotted up the trail.

"Wait," Dennis said. Don't kill any more, he wanted to say. He ran after him, through the black and gloomy pine trees.

It was dark, but Jimmy immediately recognized the place. He suddenly started prancing all over the place, withdrawn into his own little world as usual.

"It's the special place. The magic circle," he said to Dennis. In all the years he'd been searching, it was apparent that he'd never gotten lost enough to find it. For Dennis, it was miraculous for any number of reasons: suddenly, no more gloomy pine trees, but eight catalpa trees, more or less in a circle. Their leaves were broad and shaped like the hearts in a deck of cards. And best of all, animals had come here, deer, maybe, to rub the velvet off their horns so that, over the years, the trees had grown inward to create a dome.

Jimmy told Dennis that his father had brought him here one summer, knowing that the shade from the catalpa trees was perfect for the deer to rest in, and when he showed it to his son, there were three of them resting underneath, the trees seemed to bow to them, enchanted deer.

Now there were no deer, but there was light, the gloom was dispelled, and compared with the gloom of tall pines, light from the stars shone down and gave the feeling of daytime. Dozens of fireflies twinkled under the dome. Jimmy had run into the middle. "We're lost," he whispered, "and found, too." He bowed to Dennis and Dennis involuntarily bowed back. Jimmy put his hand at Dennis's waist and took his other hand, and hummed some music. Then Dennis let him know that he could waltz. Round and round, and Dennis thought, Jimmy is a good dancer even if he's possessed and doing a demon dance. He had to contend only with Jimmy's firefly war paint.

"You're dancing with the god of the fireflies," Jimmy said. "To appease him. Do you think I should be appeased?"

Too bad they detested one another, Dennis thought, but thank God the two of them were grown up enough to look at something beautiful together, for a moment. That was a goodness in the world, there, that enemies could share a similar vision of romance, general romance, not erotic love.

They stopped because Dennis said, "You're still wet. Aren't you cold?"

"That's why I'm dancing."

They enjoyed the dome for a few more minutes, and then resumed being lost. But Jimmy guessed that if they stayed close to the lake, which they could see now, they could find their way.

"You know, Jimmy, you could have explained the knife thing. All you had to say was that it cost a dollar and I wouldn't have gotten so mad."

Jimmy pulled the knife out of his pocket again. He opened up Dennis's fisted hand and placed the object snuggly there, as if he were attaching it. "Not a dollar. A kiss."

Dennis rolled his eyes. But he wanted the knife. He leaned forward and planted one briefly on Jimmy's cheek. He'd been out of practice, but it seemed to have gone well.

"I tricked you," Jimmy said.

"Why?" Was he going to embarrass Dennis again?

"Because you already gave me something in exchange, you gave me this coat."

"Hey. I want the coat back. The coat's not yours."

And it didn't seem terribly long before they were back home where they dried their clothes and drank whiskey served in the little opalescent glasses meant for Jimmy's tears. When looking for the liquor, Jimmy found another, larger set of dishes, but they didn't break them.

When they were warming up with the whiskey shots, Jimmy pulled out some old photo albums and sat down next to Dennis. "You haven't seen these," he said. He opened up a volume and began to point out snapshots.

The familiar made strange: in shot after shot, he saw Jimmy standing next to Isabelle—but not in France. These were taken here. There were the two of them fishing on a dock. Isabelle posing next to a hot rod at a car show. Jimmy pretending to be a muscle man with some dumbbells. Pictures with big pine trees, blue sky, good weather.

"Why didn't you tell me Isabelle came to see you? When did this happen?"

Jimmy looked surprised. "She didn't tell you about it? It was two years ago, when you were in seminary. We couldn't get ahold of you. She came here for a week. She loved Minnesota." He pointed out another picture of his mother, dressed with Isabelle in matching blue kimonos, the two of them made up like geishas.

"Don't they look happy? I love to see people in pictures being happy." Jimmy was grinning at Dennis, sure he'd agree.

But Dennis closed the album into Jimmy's lap. He finished his whiskey and went to his room.

Pain Management

Santa Clara, August 1999

The room is jaundiced, he thought, and caught the mistake—Dennis couldn't help himself. To give emotions to things made him feel hysterical, like a character out of a Tennessee Williams play; to personify this room's curtains or running water made him seem a child in a fairy tale; to see the world through his clunky metaphors was leading him nowhere—or worse, to story, to continuation, to wanting and scheming. But that room was jaundiced, sick yellow light.

In the jaundiced light, everything looked red. Even the communicant, there—although Dennis wanted to call him a patient, communicable. He sat on a couch in shiny burgundy silk pajamas, and in any other light, he'd look like Fred Astaire ready to dance.

There was nothing he could catch, Dennis assured himself. There were many other reasons why Dennis felt ill here. The man in the pajamas said, "All of my nerve endings are right under my skin now. There's nothing, no fat, no flesh, no nothing that can protect me. I can't do anything but feel." He seemed to have surprised himself with this fact.

Dennis was back in California, assisting a real priest, going from door to door among the sick to give them the communion. It was some final test, humiliating, ridiculous: not actually caring for the shut-ins, but giving them everlasting life, if Dennis believed, if they believed.

This man in the pajamas was also HIV positive, but the drugs had not saved him. Or rather, they had kept him alive, but because of his own body's reaction to the drugs, all of the fat had migrated away from his extremities and made his skin so profoundly sensitive that every touch, every movement, every breeze was painful. He was confined to this yellow room, a low grade fever of pain.

~

If that room was sulfur-yellow, the monsignor's library had been royal purple. It was a place for pomp, but Monsignor Hardy looked dissipated. Without robes, in a raspberry-colored dress shirt streaked with cigarette ashes half brushed away, gray oily hair slicked back in lank locks, the corner of his glasses taped together, he bent down now to aim his stick, and said, "You don't think about Christ enough," while he motioned with his head and cue: Eight ball, corner pocket. He sunk it, no problem.

Dennis didn't answer while they listened to the ball roll beneath the length of the table to join the rest of the billiard balls. Dennis should have been thinking about other things, but he couldn't help noting that according to the official rules of Eight Ball, his opponent should have explained verbally which pocket the ball was going to go into. But Dennis, at the moment, was in big trouble. The less said, the better.

The monsignor didn't acknowledge his victory, either. He simply reached into the table and took three balls in each splayed hand, a gesture people used at the grocery store to transfer tomatoes to the shopping cart. He had pulled the balls out again and placed them in formation for another game. "I can't look at the cross," Dennis confessed. Over the pool table, there was a large one. Christ was shown in yet another attitude of agony. Every artist of every crucifix used the occasion as a way to express another kind of pain. Dennis had a good memory for all the crucifixes, so there was a cumulative effect. Dennis had trouble breathing around pain. And praying before the cross became a kind of long, slow asphyxiation. He thought of Rigo's *en passant* art. Maybe Dennis could pray to *parts* of the crucifix—the two nailed feet, the lanced side, maybe the crown of thorns—but all at once: that, that was the horror of memory. "The pain," Dennis said.

For some reason, this pleased the monsignor. He smiled, and then he remembered himself, and frowned. "Dennis. What you have done is inexcusable. In the eyes of God. In the eyes of Jesus Christ His son. In the eyes of the Holy Spirit. In the eyes of all those people you fooled. The church. You have lied. You cause pain with your lies."

Dennis looked away from the cross. He had not really lied, he wanted to say; he had just neglected to tell the truth.

"Father Fitzgerald has suggested that you be sent away. I think he's right."

Father Fitz! That man had committed the other six deadly sins himself, every day, there in his Minnesota fiefdom. Dennis had done all the hard work while Fitz held the reins of power. Dennis made the social calls, called the caterers for the Knights of Columbus, got a plumber in when the boiler broke down. The only crime Dennis had committed was to let the congregation of Saint Matthias church, as well as Jay the barber and Greg the masseur, believe that he was a fully frocked Jesuit priest. They had called him "Father Dennis," and at first he enjoyed the name, which seemed almost true, and then, after a few days, it was too late to correct them.

Monsignor Hardy leaned over the green felt and hit the cue squarely. It broke the cluster of balls. A striped ball went into one pocket, then a solid went into another. "I call solids," he said.

⌐

The book was blue, he remembered, blue for sky. One of the big picture books from the *How and Why Wonder Book* series — *Wonder Book of Gems and Minerals,*

Wonder Book of Dinosaurs, Wonder Book of Wildflowers. The one he wanted, the one he'd seen in the store and now couldn't find anymore, was the *How and Why Wonder Book of Birds of Prey,* a clunky title that did not soar like a hawk, and so had to be doctored with blue sky.

He'd seen it once, and certain things about the book had stayed in his memory, probably in the wrong way. The hawks were arranged for a cumulative effect, too, from smallest to largest. Each two-page spread was devoted to a new bird—in the upper left, the hawk and its name, then a map of the world that showed the nesting regions in big colored blobs, then the bulleted facts: its habitat, its wingspan, its young, its rarity and plenitude; and in the lower right corner, the hawk in action, shown carrying its optimal payload.

At the front of the book, that lower right-hand picture showed owls with tiny mice in their clutches, the mouse bright-eyed, horrified, appealing directly to the reader for salvation. A sparrow hawk with a sparrow in its talons, some kind of eagle with a rabbit. Always, the victim was alive and struggling, its eyes rolling up into its head, a mouth anthropomorphic as Dennis's metaphors, sometimes, saying "Help! Help!"—not a sight for children. Dennis had, at that age, felt privileged and majestic to be able to see such a thing, even if it was only in a drawing. Nature, red in tooth and claw. It seemed like the truth, for a change. The secret world of adults.

The book had a velocity, or rather, it made Dennis want to turn its pages faster and faster, to watch the birds of prey grow bigger and stronger, the prey itself more and more substantial. He didn't even scrutinize or remember details of the birds themselves, only their victims—squirrels, then rabbits, then cats, then farmyard beasts, and then, there, there on the final page, a Chilean condor, its wings like an angel's or like something off a coin, and in its clutches, a girl, a blonde girl in a pink frock. Her eyes like the rabbit's, her hands clawing at the air, her body lifted off the ground, Zeus and Leda: a sudden rush.

When Dennis became an adult, he realized that no blonde girl in a frock would ever show up in the habitat of a Chilean condor. The illustration had been a pornographic science fiction fantasy. As a boy, he wanted to believe it. As a man, he wanted to see it again. He haunted used bookstores, hoping to find the book again. Nobody ever believed him when he told people about the girl in the thrall of the condor, whisked into the empty blue sky, not a puffy cloud around to soften her fate.

⌒

He let himself be led, one day, before he knew what power was, by an older boy, one he liked, along a green path, then through a field, near a farm he had always considered "far away." There was a fence, but it seemed like a mockery, at least to Dennis: just some stakes and a thin metal strand—not even the be-starred barbed wire that snagged your coat and got you grounded and reminded you of itself later when you had peeled away the zippered scar. The metal strand was threaded over and under plastic bobbins and rollers.

Dennis meant to slip under or step over, to keep up with the older boy, whose voice was already deep and resonant and commanding; but instead he grabbed the wire, leaned, and felt something happen, something not bad, not wrong, but an excited fizz, the kind mustard or ginger made in his mouth. A big idea felt like that, both freeing and distracting. Once a tentmate during a camping trip accidentally aimed the flashlight in his eye for a moment. In the garbage can outside the school that summer, something big was rotting. Just so, there was something in the wire, a burning current.

Dennis couldn't pull away. This is what electricity feels like, he thought, being partly current. The cows this fence was made for let themselves be stopped by it. He never touched a wire like that again—he didn't need to. And there was that older boy to catch up with, the one he admired.

Thirty years later and far away from home, Dennis walked by an open lot and put down his daypack, which he'd packed full of patens, linens, a little Ziploc bag full of the sacramental hosts, the body of Christ, Amen. He'd been caught in a strange rainstorm that had happened in the radius of this block; the rest of the town seemed to be under blue sky. But he, he had to take cover until the rain passed, let him pass. He'd be late, he realized, as he leaned down to hold the handles of the pack, because he wanted to keep it upright, trying to recall whether he'd packed anything inside that might spill.

That was when those same fingers that had tapped power in the electrified fence felt the spark again, the searing press against a hot teakettle. What was it?—something green. The empty lot was garden green. Just a brush with these steepled stalks, serrated teardrop-shaped leaves. He felt a quick throb, a lash across the knuckles. He looked down to see if something had bitten him. He saw only weeds, gewgawed with clusters of green berries. Of course, he remembered—nettles. He couldn't even summon the dignity needed to feel resentful. Nettles: not sneaking ivy, not the deceitful rosebush, just nettles, without any human emotion pressed upon them.

⌒

"Dennis," said the priest at the door, when they met, but that was all.

He didn't mention it, but after the rain clouds passed, Dennis could still feel the sting along his knuckles, the pain a chalky bite he tasted in a garlic clove, the altitude-changing blare of an organ chord in a quiet church, that thin metal strand of power.

He also didn't mention it because of the priest for whom he was assisting. He had stepped up to the door just as Dennis rang the bell. Dennis hadn't seen that boy—the man—for five years, and he was a Jesuit, if newly minted, succeeding where Dennis had so far failed. Danny's acne was gone, or it had been hidden away; in its place, Danny had grown and trimmed a complicated sort of facial hair that made Dennis think of French gardens and club kids, hip and fussy. "He's not coherent, so don't bother trying to listen to him too closely," Danny had said, just after saying hello, as if no reunion was happening, not at all. How much had Monsignor Hardy told Danny?

A voice belonging to what would turn out to be the man in the silk pajamas yelled from deep inside, "The door is unlocked."

Father Danny pushed it open before the sentence was out: he'd been here before. Knocking was a formality.

They opened satchels on the kitchen table, a realm for nurses and priests and Meals on Wheels, and very clean. "How have you been?" Dennis asked Danny as he helped prepare the water, the wine, the various stacking bits of chalices and napkins. It seemed that Danny would say nothing about their previous friendship. He was a businessman now.

"I'm well," Father Daniel said, "though mostly I'm restless, roaming all over doing God's work." Dennis couldn't tell if he was being sarcastic; he wasn't using any of the common cultural inflections of verbal irony that Dennis was familiar with. He guessed that Danny meant the task of giving communion to sick people was a work that made him want to continue roaming. Or that he hated God's work.

Danny's beat, it seemed from the list Dennis had been given by Monsignor Hardy, was made up of HIV patients. Dennis and he had been paired up not because they'd known each other before, but because Dennis could "relate." Dennis said, "I hope the church reimburses you for gas mileage."

"You're looking good. Healthy," said Danny, pausing to appraise his fellow seminarian, "though I can see that your medications are giving you a little of that lipodystrophy I keep seeing in many of my communicants." He reached out and, because of what he had just said, allowed himself to run three fingers along Dennis's cheek.

Dennis felt the words burn him right where Danny had caressed him. Nothing new had been revealed; well, yes—people could know that he had HIV just by looking at his wasting face, the frog belly made of all the fat that was slowly migrating from his extremities into a tight protective ball, and the small dowager's hump he'd developed ("home fat," Rigo called his, proudly, and kept his hair cut bristle-short to show it off). Danny's recognition of it didn't burn like nettles or truth-telling, but something more intimidating and brutal, like pure reason.

"How are you today, Father?" the man called from deep inside the house.

Father Daniel shouted over Dennis's shoulder, "I've brought an assistant today. I think you two will have a lot in common."

"Oh? A homo? A boyfriend? Another doctor? A witch doctor?" The suggestions were called out occasionally until Father Daniel and acolyte Dennis met him in the big yellow room, where the man, almost sexy in his fat-free state, reclined like a caliph on brocaded pillows, a copy of the visions of Julian of Norwich propped at his side.

Dennis picked it up, because he had loved this book. The man smiled, assuming that he was in the presence of another priest, not any of the assistants he had called out. He said, "Do you think it's true that we all have a natural will toward God?"

Dennis had to say yes, because he represented the liturgy. He couldn't tell whether Daniel, fussing with his missal, trying to find the part of the mass he already had memorized, was listening to this exchange.

"Even Hitler?" the man said. "Even Jeffrey Dahmer? My name is Oscar," he added.

~

The monsignor poured both of them glasses of apple juice. When he set it down next to Dennis's pool cue, Dennis thought it looked like a urine sample, until the monsignor dropped a tiny ice cube into it. "Dennis," he said, "do you really feel the call?" What he was saying was, this isn't working out. You're fired. The problem

198

for Dennis was that he had sworn poverty, chastity, and obedience, and so he could not protest. Dennis had come back from Minnesota a failure.

Monsignor Hardy handed Dennis his pool cue, because apparently he liked to watch Dennis lose. Dennis had failed so utterly that he was no longer asked to meet his mentor in the main office, but here in the library, full of hundreds of unread texts on dogma, all with titles smacking of socialist realist cant. There was a half-done five-thousand-piece jigsaw puzzle, the finished scene depicted on the box lid, propped against an overwrought chair reserved for a bishop. Only the billiard table in the middle of the room had not collected so much dust.

"I have nothing to say in my defense," said Dennis, "except that I was given no authority when I arrived in Minnesota, and people wanted to have some reason to respect me. I didn't mean to do any harm. I only wanted to help."

"What do you think I should do?"

"Please give me another chance."

The monsignor stood up. "Dennis, this is no work for you. There are many ways you can serve God without being a priest."

"When I was twenty and didn't know anything about anything," Dennis said, "I would go into the Catholic bookstore downtown, and the nuns would put propaganda in my hands, calling me to the priesthood. That's how hard up the church was then—snagging customers buying Bibles. Now I know better, now I could help people even more, and you all think I'm too old, too worldly."

"You are too worldly," Monsignor Hardy said. "You are an idol worshipper. You pray to saints more than you pray to Christ, to the Virgin." Dennis was silent, because it was true. The monsignor said, "Why is it that you do not pray to Christ, but indulge only in the cult of saints?" Everybody knew Dennis's devotion to Saint Roque. He had statues and prayer cards everywhere.

"Because the saints need my help. God does not seem to need any help. He can't get any help from me."

This was blasphemy, a heresy, a finishing stroke, he knew. He could give up all hope, now, of ever becoming a priest. But Monsignor Hardy said, "You want to help? Then you will help. I want you to spend the next six months assisting other priests who aid the sick and shut-in. It's not going to be glamorous work. I don't want you doing anything else during this time. No teaching."

"But I'm a good teacher!" Dennis wondered at this—taking away from him the thing that he was good at, and liked to do.

"Do you want this opportunity?"

⌒

Even in the dim jaundiced light, the room was an obstacle course of such little objects. Dennis and Danny had come to the room of a pharaoh, a man buried alive with his worldly possessions. There was an order to it, a little, although it seemed more of an inventory, a Catholic Church that had been around too long. He remembered a little game Rigo had taught him, and that he had passed on to Isabelle with pleasure: When you are dressed to go out, check yourself in the mirror, then turn away from it—then quick! look at the mirror again and the first thing you see on yourself, take it off. Dennis wanted to do this with Oscar's room. Ten or twenty times.

Father Daniel had everything in hand. He didn't really need any help: this was another humiliation for Dennis to endure. This kid! Danny could be Dennis's son! He could be the son of Oscar! And he was the one they had to call "Father." Oscar smiled at Dennis, and he had to grit and bare his teeth to smile, the skull's eternal smile.

Dennis said, "Would you like to pray?"

Oscar said, "Yes, but I don't like prayers of petition. I like to give thanks."

"What would you like to thank God for today?" Would they thank him for the nice day? For food? For children and puppy dogs? What other children's hymns did Dennis know?

"I would like to thank God for uncreating me. Just as he created me."

Father Daniel looked to Dennis and shook his head: don't encourage him—that's just the pain talking—that's enough. Dennis said, "Let's just share a prayer of thanksgiving. It feels good to say 'Hallelujah.'"

"Nothing feels good to me," said Oscar, although he didn't say it in a piteous voice. It was just a brutal view of his world. Dennis self-consciously touched his own cheek where Daniel had brushed it.

~

"Oh come on, what could be the harm?" Dennis said. He was sitting on the edge of Rigo's bathtub while Rigo painted the whole bathroom glossy black. It was a stupid idea. Dennis didn't even know why he was doing this; he had nothing in common with Rigo.

"I don't think so, Dennis. What would be the point? I'll be dead in a year. You want me to leave you everything in my will? Well, dang it, it's all yours. Poof! You're my primary beneficiary."

Two of those lantern lights workmen used in coal mines blazed in the black bathroom. It had the dark shine of stormtrooper boots and Greek olives. Dennis guessed that this bathroom was going to be sexy, in Rigo's mind.

Dennis had lied to Isabelle on that train ride they had taken so long ago. Dennis had, in this spring of 1990, if only momentarily, fallen in love with Rigo. He didn't know what to do about it. He decided to do what he would try to do ten years later when Monsignor Hardy was getting ready to end his studies to be a priest: he would cajole. "Come on. What else are you going to do? Have you already got another boyfriend? Two heads are better than one."

Rigo was not open to the idea, not at all. But he was a captive audience now, painted into a corner, not a metaphor for a change, but truly surrounded by glossy tarry black latex. There was a radio playing in the boxy claustrophobia of the bathroom, and between his appeals, Dennis heard "My soul is on fire, it has a hot desire," or something like that. For somebody who wanted an edgy life, Rigo's taste in music was tame, cruelly sentimental, something for single moms and unpopular office secretaries, soft rock. How many times, Dennis wondered, could they get away with rhyming fire with desire? "Is it really because of your HIV status?"

Rigo daubed the brush with jimmying clumsy strokes at a corner behind the sink, and laughed as if he knew something Dennis did not; this, Dennis later decided, was Rigo's confidence that Dennis was just as positive as Rigo.

"Because I'm not afraid of it. And if you think I'd ditch you the moment you got sick—" "Blue" and "true" the radio crooned, "away" and "stay."

Rigo was not showing any signs of consent, but listened, both unmoved and engrossed, the way a child tolerates a complicated bedtime story so as not to have to go to sleep yet. "Hand me that rag, will you?"

"Above" and "love"; the smell of plastic and turpentine. While reaching across the tub, Dennis nearly tripped on the big bucket Rigo used to recycle shower water into toilet-flushing water. If it's brown, they were saying all over town, flush it down. "Heart," the singer sang, then "apart." "Rigo, do you really want to be alone the rest of your life? Can't I appeal to you on a pragmatic level? Think of the time you'll save with a division of labor. You cook, I clean up. I do laundry, you vacuum."

"Sweetie, you've *only* appealed to me on a pragmatic level," Rigo said. "You're not built to be a romantic."

Dennis showed Rigo his own ebony evidence on an oily rag: "Neither are you."

Rigo frowned. He'd taken offense at this. Dennis felt that just then, he'd ruined his chances. "Birds." Then, "words." Dennis said, "I've never felt like this before." The radio mocked him: "implore." But it was true, he never had. There was real passion for Rigo, for his body and his soul, he wanted to be with him, live with him, even, even if he was painting his bathroom black and wore leather pants to work.

"I'm sorry I said that," Dennis backed up. "What I mean is, we're both romantic in unconventional ways."

"Oh, unconventional," Rigo said. "June" and "moon," of course.

"I sent you flowers!" He had. But they were nowhere in the house, he noticed, when he walked into the house to follow up on the gesture.

Dennis had some terrible feeling about this moment. It was supposed to be an important scene in his life, but he was ruining it, and he had no idea what could be said or done to save the day. The words had not been invented yet—and that thought made him

204

even more convinced that he was in love, of sorts, because the vocabulary didn't exist for it. If only he had been a poet, he would remember thinking.

"I could wait, if that's what it would take. Isn't that what real love is? Waiting for as long as it would take, because you know it was worth waiting for?"

Rigo smiled. "You'll be waiting for all eternity. Okay. That would be very romantic. But kind of stupid." They were on the third song of an uninterrupted set, the radio DJ announced. "Do to me" and "Misery."

Dennis wasn't sure when in the conversation he had started to hurt, though he noticed it when the stupid rhyming words in the easy listening songs started to have some meaning to him, when he couldn't be his usual independent skeptical self. Love made him feel weak, easy to harm. He'd make a note never to let it happen again.

"And what's wrong with pragmatism? Saving money and helping another person out." Rigo had dropped out of the conversation. Dennis said, "If you want an open relationship, I'm fine with that."

Rigo laughed again.

"I wish you wouldn't laugh at me."

"I'm not laughing at you, Dennis."

"Then just tell me why you won't be my boyfriend? Why won't you even give it a try? We have fun in the sack, we always have something to talk about. I'm helping you paint your bathroom black. What can't I provide that you need?"

Rigo pushed a cabinet door back in place and revealed a huge swath of white wall, just when he was hoping to be finished with his job. Dennis said, "Why can't I be your boyfriend?" "Please," and then the song rhymed the appeal, unbelievably, with the verb, "to please."

"Because, damn it. Because you can't do this," Rigo said, and he unbuttoned his smock. In the weakened light, Dennis could see vague discolorations on Rigo's arms. Sarcoma? No. Birthmarks? No. Rigo slipped the shirt over his shoulders and the move made him look exploited, tricked to expose himself, and Dennis saw more, the color and scattered pattern his paintbrush would make when it spattered wood stain. Because the black room absorbed all the light, Dennis had to lean in close. That's what made him feel trapped and implicated when he realized that what he was looking at were dozens of cigarette burns, in various stages of healing and not healed. Dennis winced. "Die," the singer cried, and finished with "cry."

⌒

Oscar had received the communion wafer. Father Daniel was packing up his kit. There were four other homes in which they had to serve communion. Danny had to take a confession, too. "We need to get going, Dennis," he said, when it was clear that Dennis wasn't moving.

"I want to stay here for a little while," Dennis said.

Danny turned on him, a disgusted businessman. Dennis guessed at a bad history between Father Daniel and Oscar. Or a challenge. Some sort of disappointment. Would Daniel report this to Monsignor Hardy? He needed to remember "obedience." He needed to look at the crucifix more often. He needed to pray to God even though God didn't seem to need him much. Love him, sure, God loved Dennis. But did he need Dennis? Oscar needed Dennis. Daniel, apparently, didn't need Dennis.

"Help me to the door, Dennis?" Daniel asked him, though he didn't need help there, either—he just wanted to tell him something in confidence. Even Oscar could see that.

They walked back to the kitchen. Father Daniel leaned over and with a stern upright finger he said, "Do you know what pain does to people?"

"What do you know about pain?" Dennis sputtered. That was his area of expertise. How dare this whippersnapper take over pain, too?

"I know that people gather it around themselves like a royal garment. They cherish it like jewels. When you are in pain, you are consumed, and you can't think about or feel anything else. It's not just physical, but mental. You can't think of anything, not even God. You can't attend to any of the other senses. You can't hear a pretty song or enjoy a pretty view. Even your imagination is consumed. You start to believe that your bones will shatter, your flesh will turn to jelly, and you can't avoid those imaginings, no matter how crazy they are. Oscar sees his pain as some kind of focus, as an ascetic experience. He thinks he's a monk. He's vain about it."

Dennis could hardly bear to listen to him. What pain had he ever felt in his life? Had he stubbed his toe, perhaps? The sting of an Oxy-5 pad on his pimpled face? Razor burn? Father Daniel saw the sour look on Dennis's face. But Dennis was in deep trouble; he had called himself a priest when he was not a priest, and Father Daniel knew it. He said, "Pain can become a kind of sin, it seems to me. Something that both humiliates you and makes you feel superior, too."

There was a tottering feeling in the room—Dennis's life could go either way. He could return to the fold and humble himself before his superior. Or he could speak up, and end this torture.

But before Dennis could decide, Daniel said, "Don't be too long," and walked out the front door.

Dennis would be walking again. He should have hitched a ride with Daniel, because it was probably still raining. He walked back down the hall, and watched walls grow yellow.

"Father Daniel isn't a happy man," Oscar said.

"Shh," said Dennis.

"You're not happy either. Even though you aren't as sick as I am, even though you've been luckier."

"I have a memory, though," Dennis said. "I remember all the sadness. How can I be happy when there's all the sadness. They're dancing in the streets out there, you know. Boys at the discos, orgies, and key parties again. Just like the old days. But nobody seems to remember how awful it was." He looked at Oscar, all nerve endings. "How awful it still is, now and then."

Oscar said, "Hallelujah, hallelujah."

Dennis looked up at a crucifix over the man. He hadn't seen it in the hour he'd been there, it was too much part of the clutter of the room; here in the yellow room, it wasn't as vivid, didn't stand out when it was with paintings and vases and pillows with tassels and figurines and dried flowers. Dennis could handle looking at it, in full, in all this inventory.

He let himself think: Oscar is a handsome man. The way the fat had gone away from his body had made him lean, taut. He was in pain, and he was beautiful to look at. Dennis put his fingers to the tight, sallow face, a gesture that made Oscar make a smile that was also a wince. "Put your hand down there, please," Oscar said, "please." Dennis knew that by grabbing the man's penis, he was throwing away his last chance to be a priest. Even more than his unwillingness to follow Daniel on his appointed rounds. He reached down, pulling the satin robe aside. The penis stiffened with blood—it was an organ that had always been hypersensitive to touch anyway. Dennis stroked it, and watched Oscar's face, which showed all sorts of pleasures and pains, and Dennis waited for Oscar to tell him to stop, but he didn't, not even to the bitter end. And Dennis comforted himself that he was sharing in some of Oscar's pain. With the vigor of his hand movement, he revived the tingling sting of the nettles whip: they endured the hurt together.

When Oscar came, there was such a strangled scream that Dennis had to think of something else, and he thought of being outdoors, and the blue sky, with no puffy forgiving clouds in it.

Water Song

The Pacific Northwest, September 1999

Portland-on-Columbia
Pacific waves pound clean
Though they're pike-gray, opaque
And corrugated tough
Ceramic glazed, and baked
A patina of green

The town's like that.
Wrought iron painted prime
Colonialish stuff
Built on lave, not lime
The tints of dings and dents …

These water songs, which he'd been working on lovingly and secretly now for a year, were work for the soul, Dennis decided, because they were entirely against his nature, just as clueless Danny had said. As a teacher-priest, he had no problem composing homilies and lectures and letters and papers. But the water song was made of lyric, short stanzas of light rhymes more successful as music than meaning. He liked the discipline of their construction. He liked discipline, after a lifetime of foregoing it.

Jimmy was not disciplined. Jimmy was sloppy. Even in those days after they'd first met, after Rigo's big rooftop party, Dennis had patiently held Jimmy's hand, reminded him of his visits to Sue-Zoe, taken him to the clinic, all of which he did because he knew there would be resolution, eventually. But as Jimmy's cheeks became roseate, his demeanor became more irritating, as if more t-cells gave him more of an attitude. After the episode in Minnesota, it seemed as if he'd let go of Jimmy's friendship too, which was just as well.

So it came as a surprise when Jimmy suddenly called in May, hey-hey-long-time-no-see. He was doing a series of articles on the religions of the Bay Area and wanted to talk to Dennis about the Jesuits.

Dennis met him in San Francisco. The city was now full of U-Hauls, reverse Joads fleeing California. Dumpsters were full of things too heavy to carry back east. Jimmy and Dennis met for a long lunch and it was more of a blab session than an interview, with Jimmy's handheld tape recorder catching every cappuccino reorder and the piped-in music. They talked about this and that, and Jimmy did ask what it was like being a gay man in a church that condemned the homosexual act.

Of course it was difficult, Dennis admitted, and he hoped to create change from within, but for the time being, he had taken the vow of celibacy and he was sticking to it.

The interview went off after that, the kind of meeting two former juvenile delinquents would have at a ten-year reunion, one gone straight and the other still a smart aleck.

Jimmy said, "So you've been born again."

"No, I am not born again. I'm Catholic."

"Of all the things," Jimmy sighed after he said, "Oh, pishaw" and waved him away like a bad odor, "couldn't you have been born again in some creative way? What about, say, reliving young love?" Jimmy went on and on. He'd felt unentitled, he said, to love or even have sex since he tested positive, but now things were changing.

Looking at Jimmy, Dennis thought he saw somebody who had been born again, himself. Or had gone after some kind of purity, the way fundamentalists of any sort went after it. Jimmy looked self-satisfied, confident, arrogant, sexy, a card-carrying member of the know-nothing party. Was he coming on to Dennis? Was this some kind of test of his celibacy? An attempt to convert him? Dennis couldn't stop watching Jimmy drum his fingers on the counter before the tape recorder. There'd be that sound on the tape, no doubt of battle drums, when he played it back to himself. It would probably drown out their voices, no accurate quotes available.

"You feel born again, don't you, Jimmy?" Dennis finally said it after the stalemate—one created not by awkward lacks but from sheer gusto: Jimmy did not drink his cappuccino, he dedicated it to gods of pleasure with each sip.

"Oh, Dennis, I do! It's like *It's a Wonderful Life!*"

It was Dennis's turn to fan away the bad odor. *It's a Wonderful Life,* my ass! He didn't believe people really changed, but circumstances (like, say, living fifty percent longer than expected) could bring out features in a man that were heretofore unseen. Dennis said, "And you're in love."

Jimmy shook his head, but not sadly. "No, but I could be. The world is full of possibility. And what have you done? Backed away from it. That's a kind of sin. You're the holy sinner. Don't you remember your first crush? First kiss? You could have that, if you want it."

But Dennis could not remember his first kiss. First contact had always been sex for him, ravenous, toothsome, a hunting. What so many others had had—magnetism, gentleness, desire deferred (okay, call it love, which lit up sex, so dark)—he had never had the patience for. And in terror that he might lose the ability to feel exquisite orgasm to the numbing influence of repetition, he plunged headlong into the sea of repetition. He'd surface now and then and ask himself, Do I still feel it? Do I still love it? Do I still believe that this is what living is all about? And he'd answer himself easily, sure is. But a first kiss? Nothing like that.

Jimmy said, "What good is celibacy? Are you trying to regain your virginity?"

"I made a promise."

"I don't believe that's what this is about."

That angered Dennis, because it was the truth. It was about a promise, and if Jimmy was entitled to have a Wonderful Life, then so was he. "What have you got against the church, really? Let's talk about what this interview is really about."

"The world is just temptation, isn't it Brother Bacchus? So you walk way from it rather than live in it. What was the name of the knight who wanted to join the Order of the Grail? When they told him he had to be celibate, he went behind a rock and cut off his dick? And the other knights said, 'Hey, that's not being celibate, that's just cutting off your dick.' And they wouldn't let him into the club after all? Didn't he become a villain?"

"I haven't cut anything off." A breeze blew through the restaurant. Dennis hadn't realized it was so stuffy. The little wind made him feel better and he wasn't in the mood to feel better. It wasn't that he'd been born again, no, it wasn't another life, it was more like a second life decoupaged over the original, a hassle for one person to handle, like balancing two bank accounts.

In the past six years, he'd found himself in many situations where he'd feel two or three feelings at once, and that was an uncomfortable sensation. Under Greg the masseur, refusing Zoe, smearing firefly warpaint with Jimmy, protecting Isabelle from the army boy—right now, even, out on the sidewalk, a man with an ancient arthritic dog was lifting bowser back onto its creaky legs, because it had collapsed right in foot traffic. Oh, take good care of that lovely beast, Dennis thought, as well as, kill it, make the pain stop, please, for it, for me.

Jimmy suddenly clicked his tape recorder off.

"Isabelle called me," he said.

Oh dear. He had kept Isabelle's visit and their Pacific Northwest trip plan from Jimmy. "Oh?"

"Why didn't you tell me?"

Later, Dennis tried to figure out whether he ever really thought he'd get away with it, just a duet expedition with Isabelle. Had he wanted to be discovered in the subterfuge? Did he do it simply to anger Jimmy? After all, Jimmy had basically done the same to him, once. But Jimmy didn't seem angry so much as puzzled. "Well, it was such short notice, I didn't think you could get the time off, or the money."

"I freelance, dummy," he dedicated his nectar to the gods again.

Wincing, caught in the act, regretful, mortified, and yet wondering how much Jimmy and Isabelle had discussed, Dennis said, "Would you like to go on a trip with us?"

Jimmy turned the tape recorder back on. "Of course."

⌒

216

"I heard you were back," Sue-Zoe said. "You don't write. You don't call." A year before, Dennis had capitulated to a cell phone. The church had issued it to him and paid its fees so that he could serve his parishioners better. Sue-Zoe had his number and phoned him now and then while he'd lived in Minnesota, but in the hubbub of moving back, he'd not found the time to talk with her.

"I'm sorry, I've been getting settled down here."

"Down where?" she accused. "Where are you?" This was the main topic of cell phone conversations: Where are you? It meant, "How fast can you get to me?" or "Can you stop and pick up my dry cleaning on the way here?" or "Who is listening to our private conversation?" or "You think you can hide from me by not being in your home, but I'll track you down like a dog." Modern appliances did not make Dennis's life more convenient; it made Dennis more convenient to others.

"I've got a little place in Santa Clara."

"Why are you living in Santa Clara? It's boring living in Santa Clara."

It hadn't been boring yet. He wasn't lying, much, because he'd spent most of his time unpacking. He was embarrassed when the shipping van stevedores carried his furniture in a stick at a time, and the one with the checklist of each lot number and its matching sticker cried out in the same tone of alarm Sue-Zoe expressed when Dennis told her he was living down here. He'd cried out because they had apparently brought the wrong furniture—the lot numbers on the little yellow stickers all read "78043" rather than "53002." Dennis explained that many of the things still had the stickers from the last move eastward. The stevedore had looked at him with contempt.

When they had left him with his boxes and mismatched furniture, he had felt a desolate sense of not belonging, not anywhere. In his zeal to settle into Minneapolis, he'd changed his driver's license, his voting registration, his bills and health care and subscription to the occasional concert or play. Even the junk mail that once went to Jimmy Bacchus had stopped finding its way to his mailbox. Dennis had mixed feelings about that. Was this a return home? Or had he just been on an extended leave?

"I hope you haven't signed some kind of crazy lease," said Sue, "because the mother-in-law unit in my house is made for you."

"Oh thanks, Zoe, Sue, but I need to be near the university, since I don't have a car and I need to establish myself here."

"But you don't know anybody in Santa Clara."

"That's all right. I'll come and visit you."

He'd learned the difference, now, between the silence of a cell phone cutting out and the silence of someone fuming. "Why are you so ungrateful?" she asked. "Don't you know that most people would give their eye teeth for a space that big, for so cheap?"

Didn't she see that that town was nothing but an

abandoned mansion to him now? Skeletons in the closets? Grave robbers? The living dead? He felt as if he were Abbott, or Costello, the pudgy frantic one, or a stooge, maybe (Larry, definitely Larry, the prosaic one), asked to stay one night in a haunted house, in order to get a million dollars. He thought: camp, horror—so close together. But horror had more depth to it, and he preferred horror.

"I'm too old," he explained, "I'm in exile."

"Oh, stop it, Dennis. You aren't going to impress me with your drama. I've got a subscription to Rigo for that. Do you know how much it costs me to hold this apartment empty for you? I could be getting sixteen hundred dollars a month. I'm offering it to you at the special clergy rate of nine hundred fifty."

"Well, don't hold that apartment open for me. Get top dollar. You deserve it."

"But I want a friend living downstairs. I don't want some crazy stranger. The whole town is full of strangers now."

"We'll make a standing date, we'll get together once a week."

"I'm not going to visit you there, Dennis. You'll have to come see me here if we're going to be seeing each other at all."

He tried to soothe her and promised it was easy to shuttle up into the city, but she sounded unconvinced. When Dennis hung up the phone, it occurred to him that the paradise he fashioned in his own private theology had everything to do with timing. For him, the essence of divinity was a being in which time was a place, one in which San Francisco would be his home, in which he lived in Sue's or Zoe's (whatever!) mother-in-law apartment, in which all sorts of crazy things happened: he was negative, he was a good man, he was paired off with Jimmy just as the junk mail said. Dennis had never been in love, but love might possibly be just more of that timing.

⌒

Dennis was not the first person to see the article Jimmy wrote after the interview about the Jesuits. Monsignor Hardy called Dennis into his office the moment he got in one morning. The paper sat on his desk, next to a globe, reminding Dennis that it wasn't until the late nineteenth century that the church had admitted, grudgingly, that Earth was not the center of the universe.

"Let me ask you something," his superior said. "Have you come to the order because you wanted to prove you could do it?"

"Well, yes, that's one reason. That's not a good reason?"

"Don't you think that's a kind of vanity?"

Dennis felt tugged in all directions. "James Thornton, the author of that article, accused me of being self-loathing. Which am I? Can I be both?"

"Don't you think you have a bad attitude, Dennis?"

220

Dennis was reading the article while he got read the riot act, so he felt pulled in two directions. Jimmy had portrayed Dennis as a former harlot who had become purified in the blood of the lamb. Jimmy did not like contradictions, and neither did Monsignor Hardy. "Do you do it because you love it, the people you serve, God?"

Dennis shrugged. He would not lie. He recalled, just after being humiliated by Mary Jane's daughter Anne on Christmas day, working in a soup kitchen with nuns. He was full of altruistic zeal, he was going to do Good Things. He was going to Help the Poor, just like Anne.

But the other nuns weren't zealous. When they handed out bread and ladled out soup, there was no love in it, nor pleasure. Maybe there had been at first, but now it was a mechanical act, as if Help were not borne of love or any emotion at all, just an undead drive that looked like some other incarnation of shopping at the mall. It had ambition, but mysteriously translated. Its outcome appeared more constructive and looked noble, though these nuns were cloistered away from everything, including Nobel prizes. He thought he could serve up soup and help in that driven way, and be a Jesuit with the same wound-up energy.

One of the sisters saw the drive and emotion he put into the job, and she smiled, handing him an empty stewpot, and said, "Short timer."

"This is my life's work," he protested. But he found after a few weeks of it that he didn't like it either, didn't have the reserves to love dually diagnosed homeless people, had no interest in their stories and excuses. He'd wanted to prove her wrong, and when he gave up, he could only think of her.

Monsignor Hardy said, "You aren't safe here, Dennis. If you've come to this place for shelter, we don't provide it. You're wide open." A phone call rang in, and it seemed the monsignor was finished with him, for he said, "I think you need to go," and picked up the receiver. He put his hand over the mouthpiece and said, "Close the door after you, Dennis?"

Go, or go? Best not to press the question. Dennis took the article with him, full of shock-jockey anti-clericalisms, none of which his superior had taken offense to. But he felt like a boy who'd broken a vase and thought himself well hidden in the backyard among the clotheslines strung with bedsheets, though his feet below the hem of the sheets were as plain as day.

⌒

The tide was very high. The three of them were paddling near the mouth of the Columbia River in the no-man's-land between Washington and Oregon. Dennis let himself think more pleasantly of how pretty the Columbia was. Here near its mouth, it was subject to the tides, a strange phenomenon in fresh water. He looked at sleepy docks and pilings nearly touching the surface of the water. People fastened their boats to moorings at low tide, and as the water rose, the rope slackened, and the river seemed populated by skiffs adrift.

Isabelle smacked a mosquito. Dennis pointed to the bag at the bottom of the canoe. "There's repellent in the backpack."

She shook her head. "I am enjoying them."

He was worried about Isabelle. She wanted the total travel experience, good and bad, or perhaps she wanted to be a polite guest. Either reason led to danger. She'd stayed with Dennis for two days before they embarked on this journey, and she'd been discovered chatting with the Jehovah's Witnesses in his modest home and listening intently to phone service sales calls.

They pulled up a slough and the silt on the shore was fine and packable. Dennis and Isabelle watched Jimmy roll up his pant legs and build a sand castle, with four towers and a moat. Isabelle pitched in when she saw his plans take shape. In the raggedy washed-up seaweed she found two anchovy-sized minnows that had dried up. From the look in their unblinking eyes, it had been a surprising and instantaneous moment, something done to them by a comic book supervillain with a ray gun. They were rigid as flagpoles. Isabelle stood them up in the two front towers of the castle.

Jimmy approved. "I am the Earl of Fishwich, and Isabelle, you're m'Lady of Fishwich." Isabelle laughed. Jimmy added, "And Brother Dennis, you can be the Vicar of Fishwich."

223

With the help of the surging tide, a wave lapped up and over one of the minnow-topped towers, and it crumbled. "The upkeep is horrendous," muttered the earl, and set to repairs. Isabelle abandoned the lost cause and went to pick wild iris, creamy yellow stalks that grew among the cattails. She returned to Dennis with a bouquet across the crook of her arm. She looked like Miss America, only French. "They grow by themselves."

"Sure," said Dennis.

"They grew here before the people came, they can grow alone. Everywhere in France is discovered land, nothing wild, every centimeter has a fence around it. You can not dig in the ground without finding stupid Roman coins. But this is wild." She scooped water with the coffee can they brought for bailing, and arranged her flowers in it.

They resumed their canoeing. "It's so peaceful," yelled Jimmy from the front, as if they were on opposite shores. "Maybe His Holiness should give us a sermon."

"His Holiness is on vacation," Dennis said.

"Is it possible that you are now truly a religious man?" asked Isabelle, in that tone of disbelief that only a girl who had slept against him in a train compartment without any underwear could ask.

"Well, you see, Isabelle," he explained, "when I was told I had HIV, I prayed to Our Lord and the Blessed Virgin Mary and to the angels and saints, especially Saint Roque, and I said to them all, if you let me live for ten years, I will dedicate my remaining life to you. And see how I got my prayer answered?"

Jimmy giggled. "It's corny, isn't it, Isabelle? Do you know what corny means? Brother Dennis is corny."

As if a man were a buffoon for keeping a promise. Even if his heart were no longer in it. Isabelle said, "Then that is good, you said you would do something and then you do it. It is an inspiration."

"Thanks, Isabelle."

"But you miss sex with Jimmy?"

Jimmy started laughing loudly, like a loon on the bank. "We have never had sex together," said Dennis.

Isabelle was genuinely surprised. "Oh, you are only friends? You should forgive me. I think for these six years that you fight like lovers."

Even Jimmy must feel it, Dennis thought: they had been friends and remained so out of a feeling that it was more dutiful to stand by one another when they assumed they would both die soon, and stuck to this friendship even when they discovered that they didn't like each other very much. The friendship should have ended prematurely with their lives, and now it was going on and on.

Isabelle pointed into the glassy black water. "My God, it scared me like a dream!" It scared Dennis too, when he looked where Isabelle gestured. Just below the surface of the river grew a field of yellow iris, tidally submerged and billowing as if in a wind and not a current. Their stalks and fronds plunged down into a murk. The prow of their aluminum canoe squeaked over one now and then, but when Dennis reached down into the river to pick one, they were too far away.

After the big goopy rice dish they ate for dinner when they returned to the cabin they'd rented, Dennis cleaned up another of Jimmy's messes in the kitchen while Isabelle found a cheap vase in the cupboard and put the yellow irises in it. Different kinds of bugs strolled out of the blooms and crawled in bee-lines away from the vase in a sunburst of directions. When she saw the bugs, she took a paper towel to clean up, very gently, the escapees from her bouquet. She walked to the door and shook them out like seeds from a packet. With her back to both of them, she said to the night, "So quiet, so private."

⌒

They had long, slow conversations in the car as they drove through hilly land that had a domestic tumbled look, like rugs that had crumpled and bunched up against a wall. Even though Isabelle wanted to drive, Dennis took the wheel and Isabelle sat in the passenger seat. On a sticker stuck to the glove compartment, she read, "Children can be KILLED or INJURED by Passenger Air Bag," and it puzzled her, for next to it was a large exclamation mark in a triangle, suggesting that this admonition was a suggestion, not a warning.

When they heard Jimmy snore in the back seat, Isabelle sighed. "I think I am in love."

"With me?"

She laughed. "I don't know if I should tell thee Vicair oav Feeshweech."

She was so young it made him squirm. She put her hand on his, on the steering wheel of the car. He said, "I am supposed to tell you something wise about love, like I'm supposed to tell you something wise about death at a funeral mass. I had so many friends who died, all of them, in fact—"

"All of them but Jeemmy."

"—and after they died, the only thing I have to say about it is, how stupid."

"Is that what you say about love?"

"I give people poems when they are at funerals or in love."

"Make me a poem for love," said Isabelle.

She was thinking of that gardener in the rose test garden in Portland, a weather-beaten, bandy-armed, lock-jawed man with brittle blond hair and smooth rangy legs. Watching Isabelle talk to him, sex tickled Dennis's mind, a stale anxiety, as if he were seeing the logo of a company that had fired him from a job long ago. Isabelle stooped to talk to the man while he raked in hydrangea bluing formula. He explained to her that they were in a memorial garden, but the names were all mixed up: Pink Lady, Father Oroñes, School Girl, Carol Jean, Sister Elizabeth, Madame Blavatsky, Mister Lincoln. "I don't know which ones memorialize real people and which ones are supposed to be picturesque."

227

Dennis watched Isabelle's face open, sensed how her heart distended and dilated. He smelled sweet perfumes of roses and clematis and wisteria, and thought of a hundred girls on a playground chewing bubble gum.

Isabelle skipped back to them. "He would like to have dinner with us tomorrow," she smiled. "He knows the most excellent restaurant, he knows the chef, and he will make special things. Here, I have his phone number."

Jimmy said, "She shoots, she scores!"

Dennis said, "But tomorrow we're driving to Washington, that's what our itinerary says."

Jimmy said, "Couldn't we stay one more day? It's not as if we're losing a reservation at your family's cabin."

Dennis shrugged. "I'd rather not miss a day." They left, and now Isabelle was in love.

Rainier's Rivers

High peaks catch clouds, make rain,
And then the music starts
The trickling down stone troughs
Like paper rolls—those parts
For player piano playing.

Along the inlets all
Plants fruit, weeds too, and hang
Or dangle, drooping, slough

Like droplets, bells that ring;
In currents, petals fall.

It's lyric, not ballade—
Like a church bell song
Strange-keyed but clear enough
Both delicate and strong.
This same way our souls are shod.

A sacred joy, to look below
And watch the flowers float
And with a song we laugh
And fold a paper boat
Then send it down the flow.

On Washington's Whidby Island, they had access to an even bigger house that belonged to Dennis's family. It technically belonged to his great aunt Margaret, but the whole family—courteously, it seemed, for he never heard of trouble—took turns coming here, enjoying it, cleaning it, maybe giving the deck a new coat of stain. Or perhaps everybody gave up on it, for there was termite damage everywhere, the newel posts of the stairway, the soft place under the bathroom linoleum. Generations of weekenders had unloaded crappy paperbacks and they rotted on hallway shelves.

It had been raining all day and more was predicted for the next day, and when Jimmy and Isabelle weren't reading books, they were playing one of a dozen board games in the house, all of which were the kind that drove Dennis crazy. Their favorite was Yahtzee, but at some point, they lamentably ran out of score sheets and they were using any scrap of paper to keep their scores.

Isabelle finally huffed and went to walk in a drizzle that was as insistent as garden weeds. She left Jimmy and Dennis quiet in the same room. Jimmy read his novel even more closely, a theatrical kind of absorption, which meant to Dennis that he was avoiding conversation.

Dennis had not yet confronted Jimmy about the article he wrote about his life among the Jesuits. If there was any way into the rehearsed announcement he wanted to make ("Jimmy, it seems to me that you and I have remained friends for no other reason than we had planned to die soon; now that we have not died, I feel this relationship has run its course, and you are hereby absolved from being in my life"), it was through that sneaky backstabbing piece of yellow dog journalism that had, well, mortified him.

Instead, he put water on for tea, arranged some seashells in a pattern, pondered how glaciers left a U-shaped valley while rivers left a V-shape. They gave each other the silent treatment, until Isabelle returned.

When she did, she was excited because just down the road she had found a tent revival, been born again, and met somebody. "I have seen the most wonderful of new friends, a little girl, a little black girl and she is here with her mother to save souls. I bought her a

Coca-Cola and she is now my comrade." Isabelle had no difficulty meeting people.

⌒

The weather finally cleared enough for them to do the thing Dennis wanted them to do: clam digging on the sound. Several people were out in the mud with buckets and spades, and Isabelle was in heaven, kicking up muck and pulling up the long pulpy geoducks.

Down in the sound, the air was briny and the rain, freshwater, pounded the salty mud. As a kid, Dennis had been out here and considered it fun, the way mowing the lawn the first couple of times is fun to a kid.

"Careful, Isabelle," Dennis said, and heard how annoyingly parental he sounded. "The mud will pull you under. It's soft. It's quick."

"Quick?" she said.

"Don't try to build Fishwich here," Dennis smiled.

Now she was talking to a dirty little girl, probably about nine years old, who just walked right up to Isabelle and started blabbing. Dennis listened in. It was the girl from the revival tent.

"Do you go to school?" Isabelle asked.

"Sometimes," the girl said. She was flinging mud at kingfishers, but not concentrating hard on that task.

"Do you like your teacher?"

"No! She so skinny, all she eat's those crumbly gunkies in her eyes." The girl demonstrated. Isabelle laughed.

231

"Do you have a boyfriend?"

"No. Alonzo was my boyfriend but kep making crosses out of ice cream sticks and nailing lizards all to them, and eating they tails. He retarded." The girl pointed at Dennis. "That you boyfriend?"

"No," Isabelle smiled. "Will you let me have Alonzo?"

"You can have him. He geoduck slops." She pointed at Dennis again. "That you daddy?"

Isabelle shook her head. "That is the Veekair oav Feeshweech," she explained. "He is a gayhomosexual."

"Ain't no such thing," said the girl.

To calm himself, Dennis concentrated on the king-fisher that would not leave despite the pitched mud balls. What a surprise he was, thought Dennis, he looks so ordinary at first, just another little brown jobby, and suddenly, you see some flash of pure black tail feathers under his brown speckled wings. And suddenly, the fisher raises an enormous crest. And suddenly, he stretches an impossibly long and graceful neck. And Dennis thought, how could I have been so mistaken?

⌒

Alone in the kitchen, the other two gone to bed, it was pill time. He always had to take food with his pills, so he rolled a slice of bread around an uncooked hot dog. It seemed both austere and fun, because it was the sort of thing he ate as a kid and liked, but which he made a face at as an adult.

232

A small round beetle landed next to his pile of pills on the dining room table, a table gummy from old finish. He reached for a Kleenex and covered the insect, held it there for a moment, and felt the bug's smooth sloped back beneath the thin tissue. When he pressed down, it made a grinding sound, and it made the room smell, for a moment, like the pulpy fresh scent of wet firewood. It was an ordinary bug, and didn't seem as sacred as the fireflies Jimmy had squashed in Minnesota. He wrapped it up and threw it in a wastebasket.

He looked around the room and noticed that somebody had wrapped a lot of the perishables in cellophane and plastic bags, the coffee, the sugar, some vegetables, a bag of flour. They were protected from the ants and beetles, and he thought they looked like gifts, ready to be opened.

He didn't notice that he'd rested his little blue pills in a small puddle of water on the table. The flowers Isabelle had picked while she'd been out on the sound dripped. His pills, nothing more than a powder stuck together with some sort of caking agent, had melted into little mounds of silly sand that might decorate the bottom of a fishbowl. Dennis had to scoop up the pastel mud with his forefinger and lick it off. Without thinking, he did it the way he used to take the last streak of cocaine off of a mirror: he rubbed the terrible-tasting muck over his gums. It left an unpleasant tang on the inside of his lips, the buzzing fizzing flavor of grapefruit pith.

Sweet Water, Salt Water

The water that is salt
The water that is sweet
They now and then converge.
These places where they meet
Are like a journey's halt.

From nothing rivers spring
To nothing do they end
Two kinds of water purge
All purity that blends
And muddled musics sing.

Is there a living thing
Of water, air, or land
That can swim in the merge
Of the salt-sweet new blend?
No, no creature, I think:

A salmon needs it fresh
A shark breathes in saline—
Should either fish diverge
From its true ways and means
They'd go the way of flesh.

About this poison blend
No sorrow do I feel
For I too know the urge
For fatal delta's deal
To swim to that wet end.

234

The city of Seattle had the exaggerated silence of places that were usually noisy: historic battlefields, shut-down factories, bars at ten in the morning, a roomful of kindergartners absorbed in coloring books. The three of them had spent the day wandering around downtown. Dennis got a haircut and Jimmy bought a fish cookbook. On a whim, they bought tickets to an all-male production of *Mourning Becomes Electra*. Jimmy and Isabelle thought it was screaming good fun, but Dennis talked about how these drag queens had somehow rescued the true meaning of the story from that dusty museum piece of a play by restoring its histrionics.

"You're just dying for a little drama, aren't you?" Jimmy needled. Then he pointed to a little dive and suggested they sample the local cuisine.

The place they chose had been decorated with crepe paper cutouts, the kind Dennis associated with taquerias in San Francisco. The clientele moved in and out quickly. There was a jukebox, and if nobody fed it quarters, it played by itself. When it lurched into a song, the sound was loud and abrupt, and the programmed songs were too high-energy, which seemed to clear the restaurant for a new cycle of people.

"We should get oysters," said Jimmy, and ordered them based on their names—Humboldt, Periwinkle, Fanny Bay. They ordered mussels and sea urchin roe and razor clams and littlenecks. It was an orgy of dangerous raw food.

A couple of years before, Jimmy and Dennis had flown to Mexico City. In the Cathedral of Our Lady of

Guadalupe, behind the great display of the beautiful shawl she gave to the anonymous soldier, there were huge vats of holy water to be dispensed to pilgrims. Dennis and Jimmy had brought their own drinking water, three big identical bottles in a backpack, untainted by Mexican amoebas. Dennis took the bottle and put it under the tap. A big sign over the urn said, Agua Non Potable. Later, back at the hotel, Dennis dumped the three bottles from the backpack onto the bed. They couldn't tell which of the three bottles had holy water.

"How ironic," giggled Jimmy. "We can't drink any of this water. It would be like playing Russian roulette."

"How ironic," said Dennis. "The holy water could kill us." Dennis didn't dump the blessed stuff, but hauled it back home. Jimmy bought a packet of sea monkeys, brine shrimp, from a comic book order form and grew them in a small aquarium filled with the holy water. He called them Our Sea Monkeys of Guadalupe and made a tiny bathtub grotto at the bottom of the tank, of a statue of the Virgin Mary and half a plastic Easter egg, for the sea monkeys to swim through.

Dennis remembered this after eating a third oyster and he said, "Do you still have the sea monkeys?"

"No, they died while I was in Minnesota on that one trip. A friend was house sitting and changed their water, but he used tap water without the salination solutions."

Isabelle ran her fingers over the salted ice tray on

which the shucked oysters were displayed. "You must be very sad," she said.

"They weren't pets," said Jimmy. "They didn't have names. They're cold blooded, you know. Fish. I never feel bad about eating fish. They don't seem capable of feelings. You can see feelings in a dog. I could never eat a dog." He looked over at Dennis while he said this. Dennis thought, does he think I have no feelings?

Isabelle's face fell. She said, "We had to make Jana go to sleep last summer."

"You did?" For some reason, Dennis was incredulous. "I had no idea she was old."

"She was not old, but nobody would play with her. She was mostly alone."

"No love," said Jimmy.

"Do you know what is love?" asked Isabelle, since she couldn't get an answer out of Dennis earlier, when she'd picked up the Portland gardener.

Jimmy leaned back in his chair, filled with raw oysters, pure protein. They said oysters were an aphrodisiac. "Love is dangerous. Everybody starts off being safety-conscious, but sooner or later, you throw caution to the wind. Every time you don't wash your hands after you touch a doorknob and you still don't catch a cold, you care less and less. It's not unsafe sex or festering sores. The dangerous stuff is love, stuff like that. You think it's like candy, you think little fairies come to bring it. It looks like a honeymoon, but it ties a chunk of lead around your ankle and throws you overboard."

He took another oyster and sucked it down. "I suppose if you kept love moving, boy to boy to boy, you could escape the ruination." He stopped to think. The waiter put the check next to him because he looked like the founder of the feast, the way he was talking, swaggering back on two chair legs, and when Dennis reached for it, Jimmy pulled it away: he was indeed paying. "But no, I always thought fairy love would never damage me, that it was the last thing that could affect me in a world of bad digestion and poisoned blood. But love screws you up, even when you think it's just a little damage, even if you see the ending before the start. Even if you are the lover. It affects you. It cuts your life short. It lops off your limbs and it ruins your liver."

They'd gotten the check without the option of dessert. That's when Dennis noticed that they were the last ones in the restaurant and the waiters were putting chairs on top of the other tables so they could mop up. They wanted to get rid of them.

He thought Jimmy was finished, but he suddenly started up again. "But love is best in life, worth dying for, don't you think? It's not sweet, like you would think, not anything like what they call a honeymoon. It's a ball of black thread you put in your trousseau." Dennis watched Isabelle recognize the French word. "The trousseau of your heart, and your head." Then Jimmy smiled like a bad boy. But he was finished.

⌒

238

On the last night on Whidby island, Dennis walked the road alone, judging the neighbors' gardens. These people grew everything, because they could in this climate: bushy blue spruce next to the thin spray of Japanese maple, weedy daisies, lush poppies, sunflower and cactus; none of it was harmonious. Anything could grow here, but did it have to?

Since the road was straight and there was no traffic, Dennis could see Isabelle approach from a long distance on a bicycle she'd found in the garage. The island was so flat it almost looked downhill, and Isabelle made the task of cycling seem effortless. She drove directly, but the pebbly road made her figure blur and jar just a little, a can of paint in a hardware store mixer. It proved how young she was, for nothing jiggled, nothing sagged.

"*Bon jour,* Isabelle," he called to her. She didn't get off the bike but peddled slowly, sometimes circling him like a pesky fly to keep her momentum.

"*Bon jour,* Veekair oav Feeshweech. I will go to the store to buy groceries for the deenair," she said. "What would you like?"

"We don't have any more food?"

"No, you fat boys have eaten everything. And you will think we receive food from heaven just because you are a holy man?" But she said this while smiling. Then her face turned serious as an idea went through it. "Dennis, do you think that God is working at things in the world or sits in his heaven just watching?"

Dennis was going to answer, because he'd thought of God as presiding over some perpetual motion machine, and then he stopped himself. God, maybe he was some sort of deist and not a Catholic at all—but too late now.

She wasn't even looking for an answer. She said, "For I am so glad that you will live much longer. I do not know what the world would be like without you and Jeemmy in it. Surely it is God at work?"

"Then why can't he send us food from heaven so you don't have to shop?"

She waved to him, she could sense that he didn't feel like having a serious conversation. She put her weight into one of the bike's pedals, and her whole body straightened up. "I will surprise you!" she said, referring to the groceries. He realized that he had not thanked her for being happy that he was alive. And he forgot about it later.

Everything Fruits

Vancouver, September 1999

River Dream

Flat land, and after dreams
Of tropic streams in blue,
I dream one dusty brown:
Logs float in lines, a few
Rusty hooks hold the beams.

I'm trying to drive out.
Though roads are flat, the truck
I'm in is going down,
No brakes, the steering's stuck;
The water ends my route.

Two muddy rivers merge
And ride low to the bend.
Logs jam, the brown-in-brown
Where roads and rivers end,
Downwards, downstream, they surge.

241

> Few make it to this place,
> Just teenage boys who screw
> Or take road trips to town,
> Boat down the narrow slough
> Which ends some time, some place.

The seat was hard. Dennis, sulking, felt like a butterfly in a collection, pinned to the chair. No, a beetle. Jimmy kept calling him to look out his window, you're gonna miss it, you're gonna miss it, but they'd been walking around town all day and Dennis just sat there. It was the morning after the Quebecois incident at Hooters, and nobody was really interested in speaking to anybody else, but they were bodies in motion staying in motion. They were on a day excursion out of Vancouver, up to Squamish, on a big clangorous metal train.

Jimmy was sitting alone in a seat behind Isabelle and Dennis. Isabelle wasted a window seat by sleeping in it. She slouched, crumpled like a dropped marionette. Dennis glanced at her every time the train hit a bump, but nothing roused her. He didn't want to talk, so he watched the cars pass on the side of the tracks. An hour ago, they had passed a man, a businessman, driving alone. He was crying. Really bawling, tears streaming down his face, the whole thing. Did this guy really think he was private, just because he was in his car?

When they got off the train, they went to a lodge

242

and had hamburgers made out of moose meat, and big beers. They'd been eating fish for every dang meal since they got here, so Canadian cuisine was a welcome break.

"This just seems like more America," Isabelle said, holding another large Coke up to show them. She was trying to be sociable, but she was still upset about the Hooters incident, and her turtle eyes were downcast, a sullen child awakened too early from a map.

Jimmy said, "You think it's the same, but it's not. It's just like in *The Sheltering Sky*." They had had a long conversation about this book on Whidby Island during the rains, discussing Paul Bowles's novel about people being done in by their own lust for wandering, a lust the three of them shared. Eventually, they each admitted, they would, one by one, be led into the alien desert of a foreign country and destroyed in some way because, said Jimmy (and the two others nodded knowing and fondly), "No matter how much you think you've conquered a foreign country, it's ultimately savage and it intends, like Kali, to collect your head for her belt."

Now, Dennis spit out a caper. There were capers on his mooseburger! "This is what is going to kill me."

They laughed. Everybody had wanted to laugh. Everybody was tired of the strain and wanted to get along. It was at these times that Dennis warmed to Jimmy, became proud of his bull-headed, burr-headed yellow-journalist . . . friend—yes, friend, he'd live with that for a little while longer, especially if he was going to laugh at Dennis's jokes.

"I think this wish to die while traveling is terribly romantic," said Isabelle. "You do not think you boys are romantic, but you are terribly romantic. My vampire gayhomosexuals."

Dennis was not romantic, he protested, he was a man of the cloth. "And Jimmy isn't romantic either," he added. "When he goes to movies they call romantic comedies, Jimmy is the one who laughs the loudest when somebody is trying to make sweet love and it goes terribly wrong."

They walked along, talking like this. Along the paths, they saw impossible configurations of flowers, cattleya, lilies, saxifrage, chrysanthemums, and violets—planted, but so different from the confounded corporate garden outside the clinic in San Francisco. When they came into the big nutty bazaar of a market house, they wandered off in several directions. Jimmy photographed tile patterns on the floor. Isabelle flirted. And Dennis, alone, leaned over the gallery and marveled at the variety of produce in gigantic piles, filling bins and baskets and blankets. Isabelle sneaked up behind him and whispered, "Everything fruits."

It made Dennis quiet while he tried to figure out what she meant. She took his arm and they strolled through the market, not afraid to look carefully into every basket. They ran into Jimmy and he too seemed revitalized. There was a lot of competition among the market men, so they were very forward with the tourists. Isabelle had decided to stop and listen to whatever these guys had to say.

"Fala Portugues?" a man asked, thinking Isabelle, with her dark hair, was Portuguese. But she shook her head. *"Parlez-vous Français? Sprechen Sie Deutsch? Habla español?* Do you speak English?"

Jimmy said, "A polyglot like him, what a waste. He ought to be in New York translating for the United Nations."

"You are English then," he asked in a thick accent. English was not his first language.

"No, American," said Jimmy.

"The most powerful nation in the world!" the man exclaimed. "Do you like what you see?" He waved an upturned palm over his bins of exotic fruit like a sorcerer. He wore a T-shirt, many times washed, with the insignia Benfica, a soccer team of some sort. The hair on his arms was thick and untrained, unsightly like a layer of dog hair on a blanket. Dennis suspected him to be not Portuguese but something mixed in—Arab, Gypsy, something the locals considered unlocal.

"What are they all?" Isabelle asked, even though Dennis made hand motions, come on, get away from him, that's trouble you're getting into.

"This is the maracuja." It was a passion fruit, but Isabelle must have known that, too. What none of them knew was that there were three different kinds, eggplant purple, lemon yellow, pear green. There were four different kinds of bananas. Pomegranates. The man had a dagger, which he used to cut open samples for Isabelle to taste. "Here, go ahead." Behind him, two younger guys (assistants? apprentices? sons?) watched too. They seemed to be in training, how to sell, how to be a huckster, a polyglot jive talker. Even during the exchange between Isabelle and the man, Dennis could almost see the whole thing; it was as inevitable and instructive as a fable of Aesop, or a high school safety film.

"And have you ever seen this?" he pulled down a scaly green thing, the size and shape of a corncob. He inserted his dagger and pulled out what seemed a hexagonal kernel. On the inside it was dull yellow. "Some call it the cheese fruit, for at first, it tastes like cheeses and then it becomes sweet in your mouth."

Isabelle nodded at Dennis and said, "It's true!" Dennis leaned forward to try. It was mealy and milky like whey, but the more he kept it in his mouth, the better it tasted. He rolled it over his tongue, and the juices made it seem to have an infinite curve of tasting better. Still, it melted in his mouth before it ever got a chance to truly taste great.

Isabelle said, "What is this called?"

The man said something in his own language and shrugged. What could he say? "You weel take some. I'll fix you a bag with several different kinds."

Dennis thought, Isabelle, you want to be sold a bill of goods. You want to be taken for a ride, duped if need be, into something, just to see what it's like.

The guy was jamming produce into a plastic bag. He had a big mole on his face. Some dark lady or other probably thought it was sexy. Wasn't it funny how different people were attracted to different things? The guy was putting way too many fruits into the bag. "Sixteen dollars Canadian," he said, hanging the tied-up bag off the blunt side of his dagger.

Oh no. Dennis felt a tingle in his hands, which he got whenever something was going wrong. But Jimmy was the one who said, "That's too much." But that was too ambiguous—did he mean the price or the amount? And the market man took the bag and began to pull fruit out. He wanted to give the dumbass tourists the shaft, but he wasn't quite sure how to proceed now.

Isabelle offered, "Eight dollars."

But that was too much, too, Dennis thought. It would come out to a buck a fruit. The two men both looked embarrassed at the weirdness of the situation: the fruiterer and the tourist allying in a rip-off, and nobody backing down. The negotiation happened. The man took Isabelle's money and Isabelle took the fruit as if they'd exchanged hostages.

It wasn't until Isabelle caught up with Dennis and Jimmy that she got angry. If they hadn't watched, she could have pretended the whole thing never happened. She made them miserable the whole afternoon.

They sat on park benches with nothing to do but stare at some mountains and wait through the two hours before the ferry came to take them home. "Well, look, Isabelle, he was a jerk," Dennis said. "But it's not as if he's going to take your eight dollars and fly to vacations in America. He'll feed his poor family with it, or have a drink." It scattered them again, all the goodwill sucked out by Jimmy's keen sense of justice.

Jimmy was a know-it-all, Isabelle conceded to Dennis when Jimmy went to the restrooms. "And he's vain," said Dennis. "Did you see his shoe polishing stuff? God, half his luggage must be taken up with shoeshine crap." Dennis had always lived on these trips with Jimmy's shoeshine gear; it was no laughing matter.

⌒

The next morning, they met on the stone patio of their little hotel for breakfast. The garden here was English style, with sugar cane and pole beans as well as camel's foot trees, agapanthuses, cassavas, Norfolk pines, wood smoke, hibiscus trees—they'd never seen big hibiscus before in all of their collective travels. There was some flowering tree whose blooms looked like the deflated bladders of red balloons. Dennis loved the bread, but wished his coffee were stronger. He was discontent over little things: none of his clothes were ever drying out completely after a hand-wash, his toe fungus was acting up again, somebody screwed in the bathroom towel bar without anchoring it and it had fallen off.

But Isabelle had brought to breakfast her bag of overpriced fruits and she borrowed Dennis's sharp pocket knife. She would give them a presentation and they'd all get to sample the wares.

248

Jimmy came down, and as if he'd heard Isabelle and Dennis talking the day before, he wore shoes as shiny as the surface of the Pacific, but black as licorice. "Did everybody sleep well?"

Isabelle said, "Yes, I always do."

From the sack, Isabelle pulled a guidebook. She must have purchased it after the other two had turned in: *A Field Guide to Native Plants in British Columbia.* "This," she held out a small green apple, "is a custard apple." She passed it around, and passed a passion fruit, too, and another kind of passion fruit. When she cut them open they were like tiny soups, and she stirred them up with the knife point and let each of them take a slurp.

"I don't like the yellow passion fruit," said Jimmy. "Too mealy."

"Me either," said Dennis, waiting for the thing to be passed to him.

Isabelle pulled out the grand finale, the long banana-sized fruit of hexagonal nuggets.

"Isabelle!" said Jimmy with complete revulsion, "look at what you're feeding us!" He held a piece of the cheese fruit and pointed directly behind him at a wide-fronded houseplant-looking thing. Its fruit was identical. "That guy sold you the fruit of a philodendron," said Jimmy, grim, intimidating, haughty, imperious. "That's disgusting." And then he flung it across the garden.

249

"Jimmy is always the smartest one, Jimmy must always be superior," Isabelle lamented right in front of Jimmy. Somehow, they had gravitated to the market again. The front was gorgeous, full of flowers like a French tapestry. "You are not so smart, Jeemmy."

So many of Jimmy's bad habits were coming back to Dennis. He'd have to end this friendship soon, before he forgot again, or stopped noticing. When he was in the seminary, he'd have to work in the refectory on long shifts, peeling potatoes or washing silverware. After having his hands in warm water for hours, he once reached deep into the sink and accidentally grabbed the blade of a knife, so sharp against his soaked-soft skin that he had no idea he was slicing deep. He'd even continued washing for a while before the tub full of red water revealed the accident.

"Look, there's the rip-off artist," Jimmy pointed down the aisle.

"Oh, Jimmy."

Jimmy looked forward, a man unmistakably up for justice. "I want to do something."

"No, Jeemmy, come on."

Jimmy pulled away from her and walked up to the fruit grocer. He was wearing the same soccer T-shirt, had the same mole. The same two guys were loitering in the back, and when they saw Jimmy coming up, they slipped behind some baskets. It was as if no time had passed.

"Good day," he said with the courtesy of a stranger

in a strange land. "I'm searching for more of that delicious cheese fruit you sold to my friend here. Do you have any?"

The man was almost quaking. He squinted, apparently trying to clear things up. "*Sí, ya,* yes, I have more." He pointed to a basket by the (probably fixed) scales.

"I would like a big sack, please." Jimmy pointed to the large plastic bags on a spindle. "Fill 'er up."

Suspecting some kind of trick, the grocer watched Jimmy instead of the bag he was filling, and he kept missing the opening. He watched Isabelle, too, who was pretending to study wicker furniture in the far corner. Like two cons trying to out-con a shell game operator. It obviously threw the shyster, for she had no apparent part in this encounter.

"More please. That's not nearly enough."

The man said, "I have so little left, what will my other customers do?"

"The others? We have a saying in America," said Jimmy, and he told him the one about the early bird.

"Eight dollars," the guy muttered.

Jimmy screwed up his face theatrically. "Oh, that can't be correct. You gave Isabelle half this many for that price yesterday. You should pay attention or somebody may cheat you. At least sixteen dollars, don't you think? Eighteen. Here." He pulled a Canadian twenty-dollar bill from his wallet. "The rest is a tip. Do you tip in Canada? Certainly for good service. Thank you!

Have a nice day! President Clinton! Statue of Liberty!"
And Jimmy, ripped off, stepped over to the trash can
and dropped the whole bag of cheese fruit, the fruit of
a houseplant, in among apple cores and fish heads.
Then he stood smiling at the fruiterer.

The hairy man did not quite know what had happened, but he knew enough that a gauntlet had been
thrown down. He stepped up to Jimmy. He paused
enough to be thought deliberate, and then he spit. The
loogie was meant to hit Jimmy in the face, but it merely
landed just below the elbow on his forearm.

Jimmy laughed, turned on a heel, and strode off.

"What are you doing, you stupid boy?" Isabelle
wanted to know, trotting along to keep up.

"I'm having a secret moment. I'm very happy, so
leave me alone."

Dennis followed along, too. He started to grin, as if
he were the one who got spat on. Dennis knew about
those secret moments. It was what it all used to be
about for him, to be riven to nothingness by a faraway
culture that cared not one bit about what he did or
worried about, which made him feel humble and invisible, and then when it seemed he was his most belit-
tled, a woman would sing a folk song and smile, a man
would chant Ephesians into his ear while running a
hand down his leg, a soldier would show him an erection as a French girl without panties slumbered on his
shoulder, and suddenly, Dennis was feeling privileged,
marvelous.

252

Later, after several drinks and a lot of bewildered laughter in a small bar where none of them cared whether the locals thought them loutish tourists, Isabelle leaned forward and said, "You must tell me, and tell me true, how does it feel to have a man spit on you?"

Jimmy took a slug of his beer. "It felt like a wet kiss," Jimmy told both, "or wax when it drips on you from a candle. Hot mistaken for cold."

Dennis turned in right after the beers, but Isabelle and Jimmy played Yahtzee again. They had stolen it from the house on Whidby Island, and Dennis was probably supposed to have been angry about it, except that it was an old set of dice and a felt-lined Naugahyde cup; it didn't even have score sheets.

He dreamed. He dreamed because he always dreamed when he traveled, because he wasn't in a familiar bed, and dreams felt like something luxurious—he could have any sort of dream he wanted and still be celibate. This time, he dreamed he was the survivor of a shipwreck floating in the water while clinging onto an unlikely, even silly, buoyant object, like a balloon in the shape of a cow or a piece of oversized luggage. This he did in his dream all through the night. He liked dreams, because it was as if he got everything his own way.

Bore Tide

Alaska, September 1999

Horse Latitudes

The rain has stained these sails
A darker shade of white
But I can't turn about
I'm still in ocean's night
Without a living gale.

The other sailors sailed.
Yet here I float alone
No wish, no breeze, no route,
Without a force, not one,
As if in doldrums stilled.

No more the currents come
No roaring rapids ride—
Oh just to turn about
I'd settle for the tide
To carry me back home.

> The tide's a kind of Grace
> I'm not allowed to have:
> One foot in time, one out,
> It seems dead calm, yet moves,
> Horizons shift in place . . .

He had a stanza to go but no more to say. How to re-solve the song? He'd made a trap of his own rhymes, not as many words rhymed with "out" as he thought, and a song about the doldrums, how could he be ex-pected to make it move? And it had nothing to do with the Yukon or the Klondike, which is where he wished he weren't, but was.

It was early September, and the Alaskan fish nets were filled with ugly salmon they called dog fish, the bad kind, with their lower jaws thin, thorny on the end with teeth like sharp weapons. They tore the nets, and they were green and not worth cutting up, except to feed the packs of sled dogs that bayed all summer on the shore, tied on posts.

It was as if the three had brought the rain with them, a drizzle-mist, and an Athabaskan guy snuck up on them while they were staring at the river. His shirt was torn and his beard was sparse around his mouth, not very clean. He looked Mongolian, with sharp-cut eyes set wide in his face. "How ya doing," the guy said. His breath could be smelled, magnified in the chill. He had the accent of the native who learned English later, though well, and he carefully separated words, lingering over certain sounds that appealed to him, like "mice" and "bucks." Poets did that, Dennis thought; he did that when composing his water songs.

Isabelle said, "We are very fine."

That thrilled this guy, a pretty girl being nice to him. He put out his hand for Isabelle to shake, and Dennis noticed an open sore in his palm, a little grimy at the edges where the skin was torn, and it looked as if it might be trying to heal itself, secreting a balm the color of corn syrup. He went to shake hands with Dennis, too, and though Dennis did, he held his breath to avoid smelling him any more.

She pointed to a mountain peak and asked him, "What is the name of that?"

He shrugged. "It doesn't have a name."

Isabelle was in ecstasy. She repeated it. "It doesn't have a name!" Odd, untamed. Perhaps, Dennis thought, I'll name all the peaks after myself, and go to my grave thinking I've conquered the wilderness.

"I could use a cigarette," the guy said.

"We don't smoke," Dennis said, but Isabelle was already handing him one from her pocket. When had she started smoking?

"Thanks, girl. I'm Charlie," he said. He suddenly went on about how quiet it was now but it was usually busy with birds. "Ptarmigans and chickadees and bunches of ducks." He said the last three words as if they had flavor. He pooched out his lips, his lips were all over the place, surrounding Isabelle. My God, he's coming on to her, he's being lewd, getting away with it right in front of him.

As he was gathering the nerve to scare the stinking man away, he looked down into the river and there was a dying salmon, its mouth hooked down like a modern toothbrush, slowly dying, gasping, its gills opening and closing as it lay on its side, a broken wind-up toy. It was late summer and the leaves were already changing, nature breaking down once again. This is the land of the ends of things, Dennis thought.

⌒

Later that night, just before dinner, Isabelle said something directly to Dennis. This meant she wasn't as angry with him as she was before. Isabelle had been gabbing gaily with Charlie, and seemed entirely oblivious to the lecherous way he pitched himself at the sweet French girl. He told them all sorts of yarns and she took it all as gospel truth, until Dennis shooed the guy like the stray dog he was. "Just leave the girl alone," he said sternly, and it was the only time on this trip he had wished he'd been wearing a white collar.

Isabelle didn't thank him for the rescue because she didn't want to be rescued. Help came automatically, Dennis knew from the soup kitchen, and it went unthanked. After hours of sulking, she said, with a drink in her, "Can you believe what he said of the whales?"

"He was drunk and making it up," said Dennis. The man told them it was in weather like this that whales got lost and wiggled their way into freshwater rivers.

"Why don't you think he tells the truth?" asked Jimmy. "It could happen."

He'd been full of whoppers, like the man with the fruit in Squamish. Now they were staying at a lodge that was converted from a mining operation. It had a veranda and on it they drank cocktails and watched a glacier advance. Dennis the geography teacher marveled at the havoc this ice floe had spread before them, an apocalyptic wasteland where boulders had been ground up and left in piles of gravel where nothing could live. The glacier was as blue as his protease inhibitors, cornflower blue, so blue that when Jimmy got his photos back two weeks later, he said that they all had a prescient blue cadaverous pallor from the light reflecting off the ice.

"Oh, bluey blue," said Jimmy now, two drinks ahead of them. "Oh, icey's nicey twicey." Isabelle giggled. She'd laugh at just about anything, wouldn't she? She made a significant "shush" look at him, but couldn't help but laugh again at some private joke between them. Then Dennis heard it: "We love to dance we love to sing and make the flowers float, and then we laugh and laugh and laugh and fold a paper boat!"

Jimmy was striking a pose, his hand on his heart. And then the two of them, in their own little haw-haw world, pitched their heads back as if tornadoes would spout from their mouths, and instead came the laughter. Isabelle put the heel of her hand to her mouth trying to stifle the sound, but that just made the sound visible.

Dennis stood up, handed his drink glass to Jimmy. "Enjoy the glacier." He went off to his room, where he could hear some foreign people arguing through the paper-thin walls. He hoped Isabelle would come to fawn over him—why are you so mopey?—but she didn't, and he didn't see either of them again until morning.

Until then, he lay under netting, and mosquitoes swarmed it. They made a steady humming that first irritated him, but later settled him into sleep. He dreamed viciously of pouring used filthy motor oil into clean swimming pool water. After blackening the pool, he was part of a double suicide (who was the other figure that made it double? he asked himself when he recalled the dream the next day) when he set the thing in flames and plunged in. Yet somehow, he could only describe this as a good dream.

⁓

At the Alaska State Fair, they saw how midnight sun forced vegetables into unnatural sizes—eighty-eight-pound cabbages, thirty-nine-pound broccolis, ridiculous zuccinis. Isabelle bought snow pants. The 4-H kids raised reindeer as well as rabbits, pigs, and goats. They put signs over them that read, "Thanks, Safeway, for buying my pig!!!" Isabelle would talk to the knife sellers and the Republican Women's Club.

On the road, Dennis told them how glaciers left U-shaped valleys while rivers left a V-shape. He told them things from the guidebook, like when the purple flowers got taller than the fireweed, it would snow, and that the suffix -na meant "by the water," and was in practically every one of their words. They didn't listen to him, so he was left to ponder things, like the past.

They'd rented a heap, and the front passenger seat was held in place by a rope and the bottom was rusted out—in one corner, Dennis could see the road beneath blur by. Jimmy had set the radio to scan in order to pick up any stations, but it flipped noiselessly through the bands without stopping on even the weakest signal.

Jimmy drove and Isabelle sat in front to sightsee. Dennis sulked in the back with his notebook full of water songs. He opened it to the first empty page after his last composition and found instead several columns of Yahtzee scores: "Aces," "Twos," "Full House," "Large Straight," "Bonus Score," et cetera. Lists of numbers were headed *I* or *J*. Isabelle, apparently, was a very shrewd gambler.

From the guidebook, he tried again. "You see, Isabelle, the Japanese are obsessed with the northern lights. They come to Alaska for their honeymoons hoping to conceive their children under the aurora borealis. It's considered good luck. They have special hotels with skylights."

260

Now Isabelle said she wanted to see the aurora borealis, and Jimmy did nothing to disabuse her of the notion that she could.

"Isabelle," said Dennis, "it's summertime. The sun barely sets here this time of year. It won't be dark enough." Must I always be the spoilsport, he wanted to know. "What is wrong with you, Jimmy?"

"It can't hurt, what does it hurt?" Jimmy had said the same thing the very first day they had met, at Rigo's party. Just as they were saying good night at the door of that ghostly penthouse—the southern lawyer who rented it had died years ago, and left all his wigs to Rigo, who'd passed them on himself—Jimmy confided to the host, "I just interviewed a guy for the paper who had lymphoma in 1983 and he hasn't been sick again, since."

"Really," Rigo had said.

When they got on the street, Dennis had said to Jimmy, "That was bullshit about the guy who hadn't been sick since 1983, wasn't it?"

"It can't hurt, what does it hurt?"

Now, Isabelle said, "You two bicker, bicker, bicker, when you should love, love, love." Then she pointed and shouted, "Look, you must stop!" What was it now? Grazing reindeer? Foxes on the run? Stupid ptarmigan? She pointed to a sign next to a waterwheel. It said, MOOSE PASS IS A PEACEFUL LITTLE TOWN IF YOU HAVE AN AXE TO GRIND DO IT HERE.

Jimmy stopped, and Isabelle pulled out her camera. "Stand by the sign, you boys," she commanded. Jimmy tried to get chummy but Dennis got on the other side of the waterwheel.

Song to the Moon

I'm river, reaching end.
I seek slaking salt sea—
To evanesce, rest,
To cease to do, but be.
See? I ebb round this bend,

A current easing east;
I'm flowing, nearly calmed—
So why this lapping west?
There's tidal pull, dark charm
That sings me back from peace.

It is a bore! A moon!
That shows its face, then force;
Before, it waned, I'd guessed,
Its halving, quartering source
Like a fading lover's tune.

Waxed now, it sings, it calls,
It croons, it warbles love
Harangues its urgent quest
It sings—to me?—who moved
Alone in purple pall.

Oh moon! You want? You would!
Singer of bright borrowed light

Though I hear care chorused
You've no source constant bright
To change my course for good

Yet such a tugging song;
I'm pitching back. I heave
My riverbed against
That gravity of love
Desire for which I've longed.

I feel I can't ignore
I'm lapping out too soon—
Or late? Is this a test?
So what—I curse you moon,
You lover, even more.

But moon, could you save me
Each day? Hold back this change?
All moon song ends, at best,
And you cannot arrange
To halt the pull of sea.

See then: the moment's passed.
It's only silt that's moved;
Above, nothing attests
To any great beloved.
I'll ride to sea, at last.

If he kept crossing his arms like this, it was going to
look like the way he felt: This Had Better Be Good.

Jimmy and Isabelle were talking again at a place farther down the bank. Dennis stayed close to the car to prevent thefts, though God knows the only possible thief within miles was maybe a moose.

They'd come to the buggy mouth of this river to witness the bore tide, a phenomenon Dennis had unfortunately mentioned in one of his backseat lectures on geography, which the other two had latched onto. The river, emptying out to the sea and, like the Columbia, subject to the tides, was at the end of a cycle reduced to a trickle and would be met with the surging incoming tide so forceful that it would look like a surfer's wave, high seas on an inland river, tubular, killer, frothing.

After Dennis casually mentioned it, Isabelle had to see such a thing. You are our guest, Jimmy said. They got hold of a tide table and drove to a place along the riverbank to wait. Dennis was bored. There were islands of mud where the river had run dry at this low point. Isabelle walked out into it, picking her way over stones and strands, and she put her hand up over her eyes as a salute-shade. Spotting Dennis, his arms at his sides, she motioned for him to come join her. Jimmy stood at her side, looking for pretty stones. She might fall in, he thought. She shouldn't be out in the middle of what would soon be a mighty replenished river.

He slid down the embankment and scratched his ankle on brambles. It spooked two ptarmigans, stupid animals, and they spooked him. Isabelle stood and stared downriver, waiting for the water to return to her. She could have been some goddess of the waters, Gitche Gumee.

Without looking at him, she imitated his cross-armed defiant stance and said, "Your poems are okay-fine, Dennis. But they need some nice hallelujahs here and there, don't you think? Hallelujah! Hallelujah! The Lord is supairb!"

Dennis waited until the celebration she'd sent into the air had cleared, and then he said to her, "I am afraid this bore tide is going to disappoint you. I don't think it's going to be as dramatic as you imagine it. It's just water, switching direction."

She turned to Dennis. "The only reason he is being cruel to you is because you are cruel to him."

He knew she'd be frightened when his forehead snarled into those Vs of anger and frustration, but they came of their own. "I'm cruel to him? He's the one who wrote a nasty article. Did you know he wrote a nasty article?"

She nodded, and that surprised him. "He wrote it because he was hurt by you. You did not invite him on our journey. He is our friend, Dennis."

Dennis shook his head. He would tell her, she would at least know. "It's not true, Isabelle. I'm afraid we have no reason to be friends. We were planning to die and then we didn't, and now we're left with a friendship neither of us really wants. He doesn't want to be friends."

Now she looked confused. "But this is not true. He wants to be friends. He wants to be more than friends. Don't you understand? Jimmy loves you. Jimmy is in love with you. Why would a person write such an article if he did not love you?"

The sun did not come from behind a cloud, but there was a kind of brightening, perhaps from some other source, open water maybe. Loved him? How bewildering.

"That's something you've decided, Isabelle. That's something you think you see in your romantic brain."

"No! It is something he has told me many times, for many years." He heard that quizzical French question she left unspoken: "And he has not told you?"

How improbable and yet possible. He stared at Isabelle. "Thanks for the news, Flash," is all he said, and then just started walking alone farther into the muddy riverbed.

He thought of the nuns at the soup kitchen for a moment. They had not cared because if they cared, the endless hopeless neediness of the world would grind them to nothing. Dennis had so little knowledge of love, he was familiar only with lust—after all, he'd correctly recognized it in the Athabaskan guy and the gardener and the soldier on the train so long ago and he knew how to protect Isabelle from it. But both love and lust recognized beauty—Charlie and he were connected by that.

There was Jimmy, for example, barely visible except in a general way on the shore, and he was beautiful.

When a man was beautiful, Dennis felt two emotions at once, sorrow and pleasure—was that joy? He winced. It made his eyes sting.

Loved him? How could he be expected to recognize that? His foot caught in a soft bit of muck and it made an obscene sucking noise as he pulled it out. He kept walking. It was a minor grievance—how could he sink so when he felt suddenly light as a little sea foam?

Isabelle yelled to him and Jimmy yelled too, way over there, but he had to think, had to be alone to do it, and to get a better view, open space, untamed wilderness. He could see a long strand almost dead center in the river. He leaned forward: was this freshwater or brine? He scooped it and slurped it; it was brine, but that meant nothing, because it might be just a little spillover into what was mostly fresh. He thought, because his mind rushed away on its own currents without control, flash flood, how far back to this river's source would I have to go to find the true nature of the water, salt or fresh?

On the strand, he could see the ocean. It was magnificent, freeing and soothing and clear. And he could see everything—including the look on the faces of Isabelle and Jimmy, which were wide and fearful, a kind of blooming he probably had on his own face, because they were all hoping for a tidal wave.

The bore tide was coming, it would roar in. He could see it advancing far ahead, something better than he'd ever imagined. No wonder the ancient Greeks saw teams of white horses galloping in the waves, Poseidon or Neptune or whatever god of wrath or forgiveness dwelled in the depths, riding his chariots pulled by those splashy stallions. They would probably trample a man, but their glory was so wondrous that any thought of danger seemed mistaken. He watched them approach, his view was best. He would write a water song about the tidal bore, and it would be his best one yet.

Jimmy and Isabelle yelled, more urgently and more urgently. And then they stopped. It was for nothing: by the time the shifting river reached his bit of wet sand, it made the cuffs of his pants wet, and nothing else. He supposed, later, all the way back home, that he should be grateful for surviving it, but on the other hand, not even nature was powerful enough to sweep him away.

Boom Economy

San Francisco, November 1999

The city was in scaffolding. Every house was being bought up at huge prices, and with all the extra money, the houses were getting gay new paint jobs, roofs, updated plumbing. Every escalator into the subterranean Muni stations broke down, groaning under the weight of throngs. The mail came at 6:30 P.M., when it came at all, thrown onto the step by a haggard, hardly uniformed carrier. Gold rush apartment buildings were being thrown up as quickly as possible. Millions of square feet of office space were not enough, and the mayor had approved millions more. Where would everybody live? Every shop had a Help Wanted sign (no doubt, there were no escalator repairers), every person did the work of two; every apartment for one housed two.

Dennis didn't have a chance on his seminarian income to find a flat in San Francisco. He stayed in Santa Clara, near the university, and always took Caltrain up

269

to San Francisco. Today he was doing this in order to meet Jimmy, because they both had been called to the clinic where a few years back they had been part of the dosage study for the protease inhibitor. It wasn't so long ago, but the plans to meet the appointment had the gush of nostalgia, and austere Dennis felt self-indulgent.

Self-indulgence hid away; they said the HIV virus didn't completely go away even in a body whose blood counts, not unlike his own, looked normal, virus free. It hid away in the lymph nodes, biding its time, waiting for better weather, or mutating one day, perhaps masquerading as self-indulgence. "Conversion," he said out loud, and was suddenly aware of the people around him on the train.

All of them were twenty-seven years old and looked like frat boys or sorority girls. Practically all of them, and those who weren't looked haggard. Across the aisle, a balding man, who seemed as aware as Dennis of being out of place, scribbled madly on a legal pad. The words were big enough for Dennis to read. As far as Dennis could tell, it was an exercise assigned to him by a psychotherapist, or a creative writing teacher, or a minister, to explain why he felt guilty.

"I make over $75,000 a year, just to write a little Javascript, and I don't feel like I truly deserve it," he'd written.

It wasn't this guy's fault the city was being borified. In fact, it felt more the fault of Dennis's own generation, the selfishness of the golden-agers, who devoured the city with a weird nostalgia. He had heard that Italian matriarchs passed on their famous spaghetti recipes from generation to generation, but purposefully removed or mismeasured one key ingredient, ensuring that the great recipe was watered down through the years.

At the Caltrain station, he waited with six other people for the bus. It was late, or broken down, or about to skid by them. Gleaming black funereal SUVs buzzed his face, so new they hadn't received permanent license plates yet. Their drivers talked on cell phones about unfinished business. IPOs were only Pre-, everything started up, nothing completed. Their cars, where so much more time was spent these days, were the mode of discourse. So before license plates came little bootleg images of cartoon Calvin, pissing on whatever it was the driver didn't like—Ford truck logos, Oakland Raiders, the Jesus fish. Dennis also saw Jesus fishes a lot, and Darwin fishes, too. The Jesus fish was often shown eating the Darwin fish, survival of the fittest. He'd never seen so much religion in this pagan town.

Jimmy's flat was rent controlled, and the landlord already lived in one of the other four units, so Jimmy couldn't be evicted. Nevertheless, the landlord resented Jimmy's not paying the market rate for his one-bedroom place—Jimmy paid six hundred bucks a month when it could go for sixteen hundred—and he made it tough on Jimmy: the paint was peeling off the building while the rest of the Victorians in their row gleamed with fresh coats and gold leaf. He took Jimmy's parking space because he needed it for his own gleaming black funereal SUV.

Jimmy opened the door before Dennis could knock—once again, he was late. Jimmy stepped out, jacket on, and said, "I just sold my mother's dishware on eBay." They talked about their favorite television program, *Antiques Roadshow*. Now was a time of swapping fortunes, of finding the missing dish in that set of Fiestaware, the missing pawn to a chess set. All the lost would eventually be found in the new revolution.

The clinic had changed. It served not only HIV patients but all sorts of chronically ill people, outpatients, homeless, addicts; they conducted studies for sleep deprivation and smoking cessation. On the plus side, it didn't feel like a rest home anymore.

The first thing Dennis saw was Rigo's silhouette, hunched over two middle-aged ladies. His beefed-up arms were bulging out of his T-shirt, chest and abdominals defined beneath that tight fit, the showoff. The thing was: his face. It was drawn and caved and dried like poorly cared-for hide, as the drugs slowly rearranged his body fat and sucked up all its moisture. All the body's challenges over the years were there to see, the acne and warts and wasting and reinflating and dock and port and surgical scars. Scientists, it was reported, had just mapped out DNA. Dennis had a terrible thought: what if they all lived *forever?*

Rigo was telling jokes. "Tallulah Bankhead met a starving woman sitting in an alley behind the star's dressing room. The starving woman said, 'Help me, ma'am, I haven't been able to eat in a week.' And Tallulah said, 'Dahling, you must *force* yourself!'"

"I told him that joke," Dennis told Jimmy. "Funny, how certain people fit better into certain times. Tallulah was funny to say that back then, but she wouldn't be now, not with the loony street people out there." And then there was Rigo. Some species that was supposed to have gone extinct ten years ago, like the dodo or the coelacanth, still here, looking out of place.

That wasn't fair. It was just that Dennis and Rigo hadn't been hanging out as much as he expected they would when returning to the Bay Area. Dennis lived down the peninsula. More than that, though, it was the Jack-Spratt-and-Wife problem, because Rigo couldn't eat food with his protease inhibitors, and Dennis had to. Since eating was a social occasion and it was all they had time for anymore, they never quite managed to meet up for months at a time.

But how could Dennis miss Rigo if he wouldn't go away? Or Jimmy, or the whole mess of them? So it was an ugly secret: Dennis had stopped liking them, a proxy loss. He'd stopped liking a lot of things, the endless wait for a table at a decent restaurant, to get a dentist's appointment, to get on the list for a house-cleaner. To stop liking was to stop wanting, but then, that was not exactly generosity.

"Hey, Jimmy. Hello, Dennis. Tallulah Bankhead went to a high Episcopal wedding of an important friend, and the wedding was performed by the bishop himself, in full raiments, swinging his censer back and forth, the whole ball of wax. She was all groggy from a long night's drinking, and wasn't familiar with church things, don'tcha know. So as the bishop strode by, she tugged on his cassock and said, 'Darling, your dress is *divine*, but your purse is *on fire*.'" Rigo enjoyed Jimmy's laughter.

Dennis said, "I told you that one, too."

"Oh, I'm sorry, Dennis honey. I forgot you were a religious man."

"You're looking great," Dennis said.

"Don't lie, if you're going to get all religious on me. God thinks liars are poop-heads."

Jimmy said, "Do you know why Sue has called us here?"

Rigo smiled. "You don't know? Oh, you're gonna *love* this one." As if it were another of his clean, corny jokes.

~

"Show me what you're taking," said Sue. She'd had Jimmy and Dennis strip down to their underwear, and Dennis thought suddenly to himself, hey, does she have a right to do that? All those years ago, she'd said she wasn't into sadomasochistic scenes. What, then, was all this? He got up to get his pillbox. His legs stuck to the roll of butcher paper that covered her examination table, and made a peeling sound when he stood up.

No doubt about it: Sue had gotten cranky in the last couple of years. He'd heard her say out loud, "Let them wait," when Rigo, the receptionist again, reminded Sue that Dennis and Jimmy were still in the waiting room. When Rigo looked up and it became apparent that Dennis had heard her, Sue made a brittle little joke, *sotto voce,* to soften the snarl in an unlikely way: "We've got issues of *Highlights for Children* that go back to the days when they were actually dying."

Now in skivvies, humiliated, he took the pillbox out of his trouser pocket, hanging from a peg. The pillbox was a testament to the Problem with Generosity. All these years, he'd tried his best to relinquish and give and donate and shed. The response was: gifts in kind, including this—a silver pillbox with his initials engraved into the lid so that he couldn't donate it to anybody else, something he could take to his tomb. If that were not enough, the pillbox was too small to carry his daily regimen of pharmaceuticals. He showed the contents to Sue, however, smashed into pieces so that they would fit.

He kept expecting that the pills would become, he didn't know, more . . . developed, flashier, packaged. But since the day he sat in the clinic with a dock in his arm wondering what was more poisonous to the world, that homeless guy's meat packages or Dennis's own curdled blood, waiting to see what the protease inhibitors would do, they had made just one color change, from pink to blue—a sex change, as it were, but still they seemed, otherwise, generic. As did this life transition that seemed to turn and turn, unshaped, no permanent license plate yet.

"And how are you doing on these?" Sue asked. She used to smile.

Well, maybe Sue was sour because no one had respect for her. People used to have respect. But what was she? A nurse practitioner, more than a nurse and less than a doctor. They'd done a television segment about her and a handful of other nurse practitioners back in 1994, and she was hailed as a hero. She'd been loved by her patients but now they were mostly gone, so what good was all that love? Was somebody generous if it was impossible to take generosity's measure? She was as useless as most of her lab equipment now, that centrifuge over there that nearly killed her. She'd had to take the handfuls of AZT for the time after that accident, and it staved off the infection, but the AZT gave her an ulcer that flared up now and then. Maybe it was flaring up now.

"Viral load undetectable," said Dennis. Jimmy agreed.

She paced. "There's something we want you to do for us." She asked this breathlessly, as if she were trying to keep her nose from smelling a bad odor. He had heard the same exhaling over the phone when she had called him for this appointment, and couldn't tell whether she'd been sighing, weeping, or chain smoking. What she was doing, though, was holding her breath—as in, don't hold your breath.

"Another wonder drug?" Jimmy asked.

"Not really," she said. "We'd like you to stop taking these pills."

Dennis felt the soaring feeling in his body, the weightless zooming that accompanied both delight and terror. Were they suddenly discovering the side effects? A cancer, a mutation?

Jimmy said, "Is there something wrong with them?"

"We hope not," she said, but she didn't want to say more than she had to.

Jimmy nodded. "A drug holiday." He understood something Dennis did not: "You want to see how powerful the drugs are. You want to see if the virus will mutate around the drugs if they aren't constantly taken. Given."

She didn't shake her head no. Instead, she pulled out a manila folder and handed to each of them an original signed release, the one they both filled out five years before, three apartments ago, one of any dozen forms Dennis had signed during those lost years of the 1990s, holding drug companies and scientists and Sue herself harmless, the Declaration of Educated Guesses. At some point, Dennis had stopped reading those things, the fine print, the clauses and warnings, mostly because it was generic, utterly abstract, as anything conciliatory tended to be. He was an old warehouse back then, ready to reuse.

"In 1994, you agreed to participate in this study and adhere to the stipulations set forth by the company," explained Sue, pointing to a tiny tiny paragraph. She'd obviously rehearsed this moment. "We haven't taken any blood draws or monitored you, but the study never ended."

"You're joking, right?" said Jimmy, who was much better at being an activist. He could do the right thing in the heat of the moment, while Dennis needed time, the contemplative life. "You want us to honor a five-year-old photocopied waiver?"

"It's a legal and binding document."

Jimmy said, "If that's the case, then . . ." he said, studying it, racking his brains. Dennis watched him. His life suddenly depended on Jimmy racking his brains. Jimmy had his hand to his forehead. Dennis wondered how people knew that the brain was the source of intelligence. Did they cudgel themselves to get an idea in ancient Mesopotamia? The stomach, instead, seemed more the wellspring of deep thought.

While Jimmy read and read the document, Sue said, "You know this isn't necessarily life threatening. There are other protease inhibitors, a whole new line of drugs, it's just this one. We'll watch you closely. The minute we see a sign of danger, I'll be there to catch you."

Then Jimmy looked up with triumph's trump card. "Then how come the drug company hasn't honored this clause here?" And it was his turn to point to a tiny tiny paragraph.

"What clause?" asked Sue.

"The one where the company promises to supply the drug to us free of charge for the rest of our lives."

They had? It said that? He'd been throwing a thirty-buck copayment each month at this stuff. They stopped supplying the protease inhibitor three years ago.

Sue had grabbed the sheet from his hand. She puzzled it out, its meaning. And then she became defiant. Her face drew back. Dennis studied that face, her skin a soft white Nordic kind that had a down over it, pulled across fine bones. It made her strong without seeming harsh, unless she spiked up her hair, the way she did so many years ago at Rigo's party—but also it made her look ageless, the way people certainly quite old look ageless. The skin betrayed her every now and then when it bunched into a frown or now, this defiance. "What about your promise to dedicate your bodies to science? What about your vow of generosity? Do you think I don't remember that? How we were all in on it together, how we promised to help each other out? You promised," she hissed that, the second time.

Dennis said timidly, "Why would you want me to throw something like this away?"

She stared at him. He remembered her beating the centrifuge, hugging him with his positive purple slip, inserting the dock in his arm, listening to Rigo's clean jokes.

Jimmy said, "I'll do it."

They both looked at him. "You will?" said Dennis. "There was a promise," Jimmy reminded him.

Now both of them looked at Dennis. Jimmy was supposed to have rescued him by racking his brains. He had no such hidden clause to pull out of a legal document. All he had was . . . what? He'd given everything away in the age of generosity. Contracts were being dishonored left and right—an eviction, his trust, these pills—why should he honor them? "I wish you could see how pretty things are to me now," he squeaked, and was he being insincere? "Even ugly things, obscene things." He'd always wanted to make Rigo swear.

Sue sighed again, which sounded like a sardonic drag on a cigarette, and said, "What has happened to kindness?" and it should have been a sentence for Dennis to say, but he couldn't bear it.

Dennis could only shake his head, and put his pants on as quickly as he could. Half-heartedly, he lifted his eyebrows at Jimmy, which meant, do you want me to wait in the reception area until you're done here? His coat slipped right on.

"I'll make my own way," said Jimmy, smiling, really without any malice at all. He *would* feel that—sure, it was easier, to give away everything when you had nothing.

And Dennis fled. Outside, it was a weekday, so a lot of people were at work, and it didn't seem so crowded. November light slanted against tough surfaces, and glared, sucking oxygen, again, out of the city. It looked pretty and merry, like a popular amusement park, in the off-season. People stood in long snaky lines for hours for an overpriced dinner and surfed on couches for months waiting for a decent apartment in San Francisco. It was a resort, a pleasure dome, full of fine restaurants and sunny avenues. You came to a resort, and everybody smiled at you, as long as you paid. Dennis lived in the outskirts, away from this town for over a year. He didn't count on anybody recognizing him on the street, already it was full of strangers, new vacationers, new funmakers.

Dennis was different; he'd rejected fun. He'd just turned down a drug *holiday*. Resorts were indifferent, an effulgent surf that washed over the sand castle you built. You left no mark on it. He'd lived here for fifteen years, and it might as well have been fifteen minutes; he'd made no impression upon it. No matter how we linger in the sun or shade, Dennis thought, there is no lesson learned from either, no redemption for the soul. It teaches no message. Isabelle's voice said it in Dennis's head: We are out*raged*.

And look how young they were—discovering pleasure and sex as if they'd invented it, but clean, so very clean cut, boys with video games and girls in skirts waiting for a boy to ask them out. It was *that* sort of clean cut—but rude, too, because true wealth meant not having to depend on others. But just as he was about to pass judgment on them all, Dennis spotted him—a defiant goth gay boy riding by on a girl's bicycle, tassels from the handlebars, which he gripped with fingernails painted black. He had a pink fur handbag slung off his shoulder with curly glitter letters stenciled over it: "I'm taken." He peddled with legs in black leggings that announced: I know all about eros and thanatos. Dennis, growing unexpectedly old, knew far less of death now than he had ten years ago.

There was something youthful about enjoying the feeling of the world ending, something romantic, a feeling that those goth kids with their black fingernails and lace felt. Of a falling, a heartache or emptiness that was enough to fill a million pop songs. How could Dennis, or anyone, or Sue, ever let go of such a delicious wretchedness? "Hallelujah, hallelujah," he said out loud.

Back in reception, Rigo had asked him why he was in such a rush, knowing full well what Sue had asked him to do, knowing full well what Dennis had decided. Dennis thought Rigo wanted to make fun of him, after making such a big deal about being selfless all these years, but Rigo confided: "She's pissed off at me, too. I keep calling her Zoe, for one thing, but that's her own dang fault. Plus, they've named this guy at USC to receive this year's Rodrigo Dominguez Award, and I get final approval, and I don't want him to win, and she just wishes they'd named a memorial award after somebody who was actually dead." They made plans to have coffee next time Dennis came to the city.

When he had stepped out of the clinic office, leaving Jimmy alone with his decision, Sue had run out into what was once the corporate garden and was now a Japanese stone arrangement with a Starbucks cart. She grabbed him by the shoulder and made one last attempt. "How could you be so ungrateful?" she asked, and what Dennis thought was that she asked not only because of his refusal to participate in the new apocalyptic study, but because he perhaps found the name—an obscene one, a swear word—for longing's opposite, which was survival.